Praise for NINETY DAYS IN THE 90s: A Rock N Roll Time Travel Story

❝ How did Andy Frye write perhaps my favorite piece of fiction about my least favorite decade? Beats me, man, but more of this mystery and magic, please.

~ **Kevin Smokler**, author of *Brat Pack America: A Love Letter to 80s Teen Movies*

❝ This book transported me to a ten-year stretch in which I spent most of my summer days hanging out at a record store, watching Bulls games, playing music, and playing games of I'm-more-punk-than-you with my frenemies.

Spacey was such a painfully believable character that I feel I must have known her in a 90s parallel universe. Anyone who lived in this decade needs to brace themselves before reading *NINETY DAYS*. You're about to go back.

~ **Jeff Winkowski**, author of *Time of Your Life: Hardcore, Punk, Indie, Rock and a Life Well Begun in Milwaukee*

❝ Andy Frye's *NINETY DAYS IN THE 90s* is an intelligently written, pop culture-filled blast from the past. A great read to ease one's aching nostalgia. Or to some, a journey back to discover why the 90s will forever remain an obsession.

~ **Stephanie Wilson**, author of *Big Waves & Wooden Benches*

❝ This book gets right what is serious and what is funny, without contradiction. And it's entertaining! But it's more, too.

It's as Matt Sorum (of Guns N Roses) said: Rock 'n' roll is about the celebration of life, the celebration of being an individual. Freedom. The freedom to be exactly who you are, whenever you want. Whenever.

~ **Doug Milam**, author of *Still the Confusion*

66 I f***ing love this book. It takes all the angsty, music-loving elements of *High Fidelity* and mashes it up with the fast-paced humor of *Hot Tub Time Machine*.

Grab a flannel, dust off your Doc Martens, and prepare to be transported on a wild ride through the best decade of the 20th century.

~ **Steve Lemig**, author of *Just Act Natural, A Memoir* and
Camping Anatomy Activities for Kids: Fun, Hands-On Learning

66 They say you can't go back... But Pearl Jam named their greatest hits album *Rearviewmirror*, so let's humor Andy's premise. In *NINETY DAYS*, Andy Frye paints a picture of a time and a place, taking you, dear reader, back to a bygone era: a simpler time called the 90s. Chicago is as much a character as it is a setting, and Frye rivals Nick Hornby in his ability to use musical references as a storytelling device, navigating relationship highs and lows. Sometimes you can go back. Sometimes it's great.

~ **Jim Ryan**, writer at *Forbes*, *Daily Herald* +
broadcast contributor to *WGN Radio*

66 I enjoyed ripping through *NINETY DAYS'* rock history, punctuated by booze, bands and dreamy Chicago landmarks. Frye's written a fun time trip that feels like an everlasting punk tour where the van goes around in circles in Schuba's parking lot.

~ **Bill Davis**, guitarist and lead singer of Dash Rip Rock

NINETY DAYS IN THE 90s

A ROCK N ROLL
TIME TRAVEL STORY

ANDY FRYE

atmosphere press

A portion of the proceeds from every sold copy of *Ninety Days In The 90s* is donated to **KT's Kids**, a Chicago-based nonprofit organization that plans and provides recreational events, field trips, and outings for Chicago children and teenagers with physical disabilities.

Check out the organization at **KTsKids.com**

A person often meets his destiny on the road he took to avoid it.

~ Jean de La Fontaine

SELL OUT

THE PRESENT

Everybody said it was going to happen in the summer. Live music was coming back. Rock 'n' roll was back. And 1990s music was finally, thankfully coming back. New concerts and small club shows were being announced daily, and bands long on hiatus would soon pack cramped, historic little venues like they once did in their heyday. Thanks to the COVID nightmare receding, nightlife was coming back too. So, Darby got her tickets to a big, big show.

Where? Wrigley Field. When? Just a month away. She couldn't wait.

Dreaded Letters was the first all-woman punk band inducted into the Rock and Roll Hall of Fame and they finally announced their long-awaited comeback tour. Soon enough was their first Chicago date since Darby last lived in town. Back when they were both nobodies.

But for now, a mundane Tuesday morning, Darby looked out toward the aisles in Martin's old record store. She killed off her third coffee and flicked on the lights to watch each fluorescent beam brighten the quiet space, row by row. Once their buzz faded, she unlocked both deadbolts, knowing that the usual vintage record shoppers would begin rushing in by noon.

Nothing mattered now but starting over, and she was taking that and this new record store thing day by day. Only ninety days ago she became Revolver Records' second owner, just after everything came crashing down. Back in New York, Alan had left her, and the last few trades that killed her Wall Street career had also wiped the floor with her emotionally. Why she'd ever done that last crypto trade left her scratching her head from Manhattan all the way back to the Midwest.

Spacey then arrived at eleven, the same as every morning. She pushed aside the long, purple-blue streak hanging in the front of her otherwise blond hair, and took off big shaking headphones, with something pressing and immediate to share. An episode the day before.

"Morning, Darby. Hey—so, something weird happened! Right after you left."

"Hi, Spacey," Darby replied, happy to see her. "Something, like what?"

Smart, moody, and unintentionally hilarious, Spacey was the most dependable of the three employees Darby inherited. Darby figured her 23-ish, maybe 24, and pegged her more Gen Z than Millennial, because of the way Spacey hated social media, swore often and began most days talking about the perils of pop and the goodness of old, vintage things.

"So, check it out," Spacey started. "Some old guy bought all those CDs you dumped into the 'Bargain Buys' bin."

"OK. Which ones?"

"*You know*. The bubblegum music."

Top 40 was one sub-genre Spacey would *not* do. A week earlier, when Darby had unpacked more boxes of moving junk, she poked at her, "You like Macklemore?" (Darby didn't.) Predictably, Spacey just eye-rolled.

"So, yeah," Spacey went on. "He traded in some hair metal. Poison, Dio, Twisted Sister type stuff. But he took *all* the BTS and Jonas Brothers. We sold out our teeny-pop!"

Darby's last box of junk from the move unveiled the *worst music* she'd ever owned. She hadn't made the decision to purchase such lousy radio pop music herself but had taken custody of it nonetheless. It was Alan, her ex, who had the bad tastes—real bad. *Basic bitch bad.* Thanks to the store, Darby now could shed the crappy CDs she'd inherited. Ever since she'd taken over Revolver for Martin, her inner music snob had begun rearing its head, and was alive and kicking again.

"Just so you know, I never ever listened to that stuff," Darby told Spacey.

"*Riiight,*" she said, kind of not believing her. "How'd you end up with that shiz anyway?"

"When you're with someone who likes passing fads and one-hit wonders"—Darby felt elderly just saying that—"their stuff just ends up in yours. Especially after a breakup."

Darby barely tolerated her uptight ex's Maroon 5 "adult contemporary" stage. She hid her loathing for his Nicki Minaj fetish. And she hated his Nickelback, goddammit.

"That time he brought home Smash Mouth—I should have told him it was over." Dumping it all in the $1 bin meant expunging her recent past and its musical shortcomings. "The 2000s were rough on me, OK?"

Spacey couldn't waver on that point. "No shit, man."

Revolver Records sat in Bucktown, just northwest of downtown, in a district that tried and mostly succeeded in maintaining its rep as a nonconformist's paradise. This edgy enclave was a block stocked with by-the-slice pizzerias, resale shops, and brownstones, wedged between tree-lined boulevards and busy train stops. But ever since the late '90s, Bucktown had let its guard down, so the corporate world snuck in a Game Stop, a sprinkle of mall-grade chain restaurants, and a now-closed Williams Sonoma. There were too many coffeehouses, easily six or eight, but just one record store, Darby's place. The neighborhood felt like one big twenty-something hangout and doubled as a Gen-X wildlife refuge, where failed forty-somethings like her could flee from life's judgments.

Spacey, the store's best worker, bestowed other gifts upon Revolver besides her knowledge of music history. She could keep her two elder coworkers Mark and Conrad busy and in line with her bossy ways. Her quips and barbs kept the two self-proclaimed music experts attentive to the store's demanding and inquisitive customers.

At one o'clock Mark and Conrad stood out front, now babbling ahead of their shifts. The girls could hear their histrionics through the storefront windows.

Conrad: "You know The Clash is *not* really a punk band."

Mark, angrily: "Dude. How can you say that?"

"Proto-punk, not actual punk rock. Punk looks, but not punk sound."

"Wrong, *wrong*... wrong! The Clash—they were 'band zero' for punk!"

Mark was vaping and came to work clad in a wide copper brown tie expertly mismatched against a wrinkled teal button-down. In that outfit and his Nickelodeon curls, Mark looked like a short Ron Burgundy knockoff or a 1970s game show host. Conrad, old school and looking cool, finished a hand-rolled cigarette, standing in battered jeans and mirrored sunglasses that made him look, all svelte and handsome, like a taller version of Lenny Kravitz. Conrad also had on one of the twelve Iron Maiden shirts that defined his daily wardrobe.

After nicotine fixes, their debate was swept inside. Mark still wasn't having it.

"The Clash were inventors and visionaries! You metal-heads don't get punk rock."

But Conrad had sharp opinions and sharper goals. Like getting under Mark's skin.

"They just recycled Elvis. The Clash is the favorite punk band of posers; the favorite punk band of people who don't really even like punk rock!"

"What? What! How can you say that?" Mark begged for a lifeline. All three of them looked at Darby. But she didn't know why it was on her to deliver a verdict. Just because she was old didn't mean anything.

"Music is music, boys. To each their own," she said.

"Lame!" Conrad declared.

Spacey, chewing her gum, blew a big, obnoxious bubble and then popped it loud. Like every day, she'd break the tension with snark aimed at the boys.

"You guys should work at the mall. I bet Hot Topic's hiring."

It felt perverse now to think that Martin's death had come, strangely, at the right time. He'd lived a long and good life, and Revolver Records had grown into a unique music institution beloved by the locals. Surrounded by hordes of youngsters eager to part with so much cash, the business basically ran itself. Above the shop, there was also a cozy two-bedroom apartment that let Darby dwell at no cost. But inheriting it all felt like a petty, terrible consolation for losing her favorite uncle. She already felt a little like an imposter, taking ownership of an indie rock Mecca she had no part in building.

On top of that, the upcoming Labor Day marked the anniversary of her first exodus from Chicago. Her last departure came after Darby's longtime best friend Alex Spiro deserted town, and after a hot-and-cold, failed relationship with Lina. Darby began to remember the past fun.

When the store closed that evening, she went upstairs and picked at the last of her unpacked moving boxes. So far she'd avoided it, knowing it held sentimental things.

In the box Darby found pictures. She and Lina both grinned in a photo booth strip from one night out. There too were wrinkled group photos of friends and party highlights, along with a house key, a long-expired Illinois driver's license, papers in envelopes that included her acceptance letter from the Manhattan School of Management. Plus a concert ticket stub.

Darby tossed the letter, but the ticket she'd have to show Spacey.

Back since June, Darby now pictured her New York life behind her. All that she once had there—stability, a reputation, and a little bit of wealth—it mattered no more. Almost marrying a New York socialite also counted for nothing.

Her old plans to conquer the world had come and gone, and it made her still, in a way, feel stupid and a little inauthentic. Maybe those last few bad trades and Twitt Coin's ticker symbol—TWIT—should have been a clue.

DIG ME OUT

"Holy... frickin'... mother of the music gods! What is THIS?" Spacey said, excited as hell. Darby had it mish-mashed in a pile of things she'd brought downstairs to work.

"It's a ticket stub."

"Um, yeah," said Spacey, still dumbfounded. "I know."

"I was there. January 9, 1996," Darby told her. "Dreaded Letters' first show."

Dreaded Letters. The last of the great '90s Chicago bands to go from tiny clubs and street festivals to the United Center, Giant Stadium, Red Rocks, Wembley; bona fide rock stardom. Twenty-five years on, the band was now mega-famous, beloved, and exalted as innovators. Darby saw them at a now-defunct spot called Lounge Ax one chilly Tuesday night out.

"Just the band, me and a friend. Maybe a dozen people."

"I'm really super fucking jealous," Spacey said, without jest.

Everyone knew that the 1990s spawned hundreds of great bands, but only a handful of artists really defined that decade. Nirvana was its standard-bearer, just like the Beatles brought rock 'n' roll to the '60s. But other bands left their imprints too.

Green Day was the first world-famous commercial punk band. Oasis brought back the British sound. Nine Inch Nails took industrial out from the dark, secluded dance clubs to the top of the charts. Pearl Jam, Soundgarden, and L7 mainstreamed grunge, and Alanis Morissette showed that a woman's voice wasn't just for singing sweet love ballads.

Then there was Dreaded Letters: a guitar-drum-bass power trio that was the 1990s' answer to The Police and the Jimi Hendrix Experience.

"*Velvet Mourning*—goddammit. I love that album as much as I love my cat," Spacey said passionately. "I have all their records. Some on vinyl." She held the ticket stub up to the store's lighting for a better view. "Wow."

But Darby asked for the ticket stub back, and Spacey frowned a split second.

"It's OK, Space, I have something better for you." And she did.

Darby fished out a big yellow envelope, one beat up enough that the metal clasp was long gone, its outsides looking like a bag of cigarette stains. Out of it came a wrinkled blue paper that looked like it was spit from an ancient Xerox machine and then stepped on a dozen times. The 18x24-inch poster bore the band's name and the dates—"*Dreaded Letters. Two shows ... Jan 9 & 10 only*"—in scratchy black print. It was a concert bill from the show.

Spacey regained her excitement. "Whoa. No way. Holy shit!"

"I managed to pull this off a wall on the way out," Darby told her. "Had it here, stuffed here in an old box for years."

"Decades."

"Yes, decades. Anyhow, now it's yours." Darby then idly complained about a Lollapalooza shirt she swore she'd packed away. "Wish I knew where *that* went."

But the poster itself was Smithsonian-worthy to Spacey.

She sat at the cashier counter, holding it fingernails-o
trying not to stain it further with her touch.

Yet Darby had one condition: "Don't go sell it on eBay or
anything."

"Dude—I'm not fucking selling this! Might frame it,"
Spacey said. "I collect two things—concert posters and weird
jewelry. You might be the best boss ever."

Darby put *Velvet Mourning* on in the store so that they could
listen to it front to back. There was ample time before Mark
and Conrad would arrive for their afternoon quarrels, and
enjoying a landmark '90s record in full before the rabble
seemed a perfect way to start the day. The album's sedated
tones dug out the nostalgia for Darby and commentary from
Spacey.

"Such a great record," Spacey said. "Weird that it came out
just after I was born."

"You were born when?" Darby asked.

"In 1996. So was the album, you could say."

Darby remembered that year now. "Huh, 1996—that was
the last time I lived here. Before I moved back in June—to take
over for Martin."

"He was a nice man. A great guy." Spacey's compliment
prompted silence before she reopened the 1996 topic. "So,
what was it like to be alive then—the 1990s in general?"

"*Well.*" The question made Darby smile. She didn't know
whether to begin with her own story or the state of the world
under Bill Clinton and Jerry Seinfeld. But their favorite
subject, music, was an easy place to start. "Seems weird now,
but music really was *everywhere*. But I wasn't in a band. I

didn't wear flannel or do the whole '90s ragtag grunge look. And I wasn't, like, dating with Liz Phair or anything."

"Hot. Yeah, *you wish*. So, what then?"

"I don't know. I was a twenty-something like you. Maybe not as cool."

"*True.*"

"I was young, clueless, just trying to get by."

But Spacey knew more about 1996 than any Gen-Xer like Darby could ever hope to recall. She rattled off favorite bands formed in 1996—Nashville Pussy, Split Lip, Butter 08, and the Drive-By Truckers. Plus bands borne of '96 she hated—Linkin Park, Good Charlotte, Mudvayne, Coldplay. Spacey knew the year's concert circuit inside out too.

"You know Ozzy's so-called 'last' tour was in 1996? The *Retirement Sucks* tour."

"*No.* Maybe I forgot."

"Plus, Nine Inch Nails did the *Self Destruct Tour*. Ooh, and that Sex Pistols reunion. And Metallica headlined Lolla!"

"You know the '90s like the back of your hand."

"Yeah, I should be a historian."

Darby summed it up: "1996, a great year in music. Spacey was born." Then she exposed a more personal note. "Back then I was, very briefly, a music writer of sorts, you know."

"No way! Where? How, what, when?"

"*City Scene*," as Darby described it, was "a hip, twice-weekly free paper founded eons ago. Anyway," she went on, "I was just penning concert announcements, mostly."

Spacey immediately pushed: "You see free shows? Meet any bands?"

"A little."

"How come you never said anything? Dream job!"

Bragging wasn't Darby's style, and she described the work there as "fun, but nothing revolutionary." Then, catching a spell of Spacey's enthusiasm, she listed a few Chicago bands she had seen. "Veruca Salt, Local H, Material Issue, and, yes, I saw the Pumpkins early on. Guestlist. All for free." Darby needed to catch her breath. "I guess it *was* pretty great."

"Must've been. So, Dreaded Letters. You kinda discovered them, right?"

"Did I discover them? No. Not technically."

"January 1996? Twelve people at the show? I think you discovered them!"

Darby remembered vividly that young women weren't exactly taken seriously as music critics then. *Maybe Sarah Vowell, over at Spin—the exception,* she thought. Plus, there was Ellen Willis, Jaan Uhelszki, Terri Sutton, and Jessica Hopper, too. *OK, anyhow*—that's how Darby felt back then, and it's why she hadn't spoken up about the new band.

"I was just—*at* that show. No one special. I wasn't someone that anyone else would've listened to," Darby relented. "Especially an editor."

Perhaps a generational tick, Spacey seemed disappointed at Darby's unwillingness to speak up and lay claim on such a groundbreaking find.

"That's too bad. But at least you got to see 'em. Must have been legendary."

Thanks to Spacey's probing, Darby thought about *discovering*—using Spacey's words—one of the biggest bands of all time. She could have introduced Dreaded Letters to the world. But it wasn't the only reason the show was special. Lina had gone with.

Later, the shop was ready to close and Darby had her feet up at the counter. Spacey was long gone and off to skate practice, and Conrad was out for his thrash band's rehearsal session. Only she and Mark remained, him tidying up. Darby put on Dreaded Letters' second album, *Bus Station Hangover,* and watched Mark strumming his air guitar, mouthing every lyric.

Pen in hand and a yellow pad on her lap, she had started jotting things down. It was the start of a list of wants or goals or something potentially meaningful but incomplete:

I. WRITE... ABOUT MUSIC AGAIN

In a snap, she decided that she needed an opinion, and Mark's point of view would do. He was a legitimate, proper, full-fledged music snob.

"Hey Mark, how old are you?"

"Thirty-one. Why?"

"Nothing. You look younger. In a good way." Darby didn't want self-conscious Mark to get even more neurotic. "Anyway, question: What's your all-time favorite year in music?"

Mark warmed up to the query instantly. If anyone had thoughts, he did.

"Wow. Don't know. There are so many good ones," Mark replied.

"OK, shoot."

"So... maybe 1978. Punk's first big year! The Ramones' *Road To Ruin*, the Pistols' tour in America. Talking Heads. And, of course, The Clash had their first run too."

"OK, good." Darby went back to her yellow pad, but Mark had more.

"Then again, maybe 1991. They called it, you know, *the year punk broke*. Great albums: *Nevermind. Gish, Blue Lines, Trompe le Monde*. Real breakout of indie rock."

"Great."

Mark kept rolling.

"Or 1975, when *Physical Graffiti* came out. But, actually, hold on." Mark became momentarily flustered. "Really, every Led Zeppelin album—and *every year* they put out an album—was good. So maybe then, 1971, for Zeppelin IV. Or 1969, for the first two."

"Sounds good—"

Still more from Mark.

"But, what about 1985? Live Aid! Or 1984? The Smiths' first album, and *Purple Rain* too. So, I, I—I don't know if I can choose just one."

Mark's rambling ended feebly, like a car sputtering out of gas. Risking he might go on for hours, Darby asked about one more year.

"What about 1996? I was just wondering—"

"Nah. Worst music year of the '90s! Tupac dead. Bradley Nowell, dead. The Spice Girls? Nu Metal! Celine Dion? And that super long Prince triple-album? 1996? Awful."

At least *that* settled it. Mark put on his ugly gold corduroy sport coat to leave for the evening. Halfway out the door, he turned back to Darby with a final thought.

"Whatever the year, I'd try to discover its music that I missed."

Darby said goodnight, and then updated her list:

1. WRITE... ABOUT MUSIC AGAIN
2. DISCOVER DREADED LETTERS. AGAIN.

An hour later Darby was by herself, doing paperwork in the store's back office. Her pen ran out, so she trifled through Martin's desk to find another one. The middle drawer had only pencils, but she wanted a pen. She checked the right drawer—nothing but crumpled scrap paper. The left drawer had no pens but a peculiar-looking electronic device with a rubber wristband.

It looked like one of those new smartwatches everyone was wearing, with a sleek rectangular top. The battery looked dead or needed a charge, as its face indicated no power, no flickering icons. Just a darkened ruby crystal face. Darby put it around her wrist, thinking she could hit the Apple Store the next day and let them have a look.

After closing up shop, Darby went upstairs and grabbed a pen from her own stash. Still sitting on the table was that last sentimental moving box. From inside it, she picked up the photo booth strip again. Looking closer, she felt the emotions within each frame:

Top photo: Darby and Lina, looking upward, smiling wildly.

Second photo: Darby saying something into Lina's ear, causing her to laugh.

Third photo: Lina looking to the right, at Darby's face.

Bottom photo: Lina's hand half blocking the view, the two of them kissing.

Maybe it was listening to *Velvet Mourning* that did it, or maybe it was all that talk about the 1990s. But Darby was stuck in a hole, a rut of past feelings she couldn't dig herself out of.

Looking at Lina's face in black and white made it either worse or more enjoyable, she wasn't sure which. And each time Darby looked closer at the photo booth strip a void was filled, even if only for a split second.

Just like the sounds of a long-lost favorite song, the void kept coming back, running its notes over and over in her head.

MALADJUSTED

Sunday afternoon Mark and Conrad held down the store. Darby ventured out to do something she hadn't done since moving back. She met up for a drink with an old friend.

A server brought tequila and laid down two shot glasses hard like death sentences.

"I'm glad you haven't changed," Tam said. "But can you still hack it?"

"Old habits die hard. And, yes I can hack it," Darby replied. "I love tequila."

"OK, big shot. Wall Street, and now your uncle's record store?" Tam said. "What else you been doing for the last quarter-century?"

"Nothing special. Made some money, lost some money. Got engaged to someone—a guy—that I had nothing in common with. Then we broke up. Then my career caved in! But I've never been one for self-pity!" Darby tried to joke.

Her old work pal Tam was still single too after all these years and had little responsibility other than herself. Yet Tam always got what she wanted in a way that Darby wished she could. Now Darby needed to hear something uplifting from at least one of the two of them.

"Now tell me about *your* adventures, Professor Tamczak."

"Well, ya know," Tam said, as she took a big surly breath, "I did school forever, and a research paper no one read. That's how Ph.D.s go. Met a girl, broke up. Then, a yearlong fellowship in London. Met a fine lass over there too, broke up, and came back. Then got a normal job, teaching uppity college kids here in Chicago." Tam poured the last tequila drip into her beer, took a gulp, crossed her arms, and smiled. "So, how you like that shit?"

Tam's for real, Darby thought. *Someone who's figured life out.* A bon vivant. She was now also an esteemed lecturer and media talking head on local PBS shows. But Tam declared that she hadn't changed that much, and it hit Darby that friends like Tam probably brought out the best in anyone. Darby was having a blast just being there.

"You shouldn't have left. Maybe back in the '90s I shoulda convinced you to stay." Tam continued: "Important part is, you're back."

Darby agreed. "Yes. This is fun. Don't know why I left either."

Darby and Tam consumed more drinks at their old spot, Nisei Lounge, which was a 1950s era refuge for heavy drinkers nearby Wrigley Field, known more for pushing the local favorite, Jeppson's Malört, more than any of its tequilas. There, the two women recounted past life: Working for the big city paper, before Tam went off to "study hell" as she called it, and Darby went off to the hip semi-weekly. Over their conversations, they recaptured the first half of the 1990s in fewer than three drinks. All the parties, small indie rock shows and big concerts, workdays and late-night rewrites, plus the drinking binges they'd been on together long but not really that long ago. Maybe neither of them had really grown up.

After a while, Tam let on that she was sorry she couldn't

stay out longer this time.

"Gotta head back and pack. I have a little trip planned."

"Aw, good for you," Darby said, happy to hear but slightly jealous. "Where to?"

"Somewhere super, *super-secret*," Tam joked. Tam got up out of her chair, slung her jacket on, and smiled. "Just off-grid for a while."

"Ah, to see a girl?"

"You never know." Still coy, Tam gave Darby a hug. "It was great to see you, girlie."

Darby was elated to see her friend but slumped emotionally in the moments after Tam left. Darby didn't want to stay there and be alone at such a buzzing place. And she hoped Tam wouldn't be one of those friends who were *too busy*. Like she once was.

After she left Nisei, Darby wasn't drunk but didn't feel like turning in so soon. It was still early in the evening, and she knew the Cubs were on TV. Before heading out to see Tam, Darby had slung on her decades-old Cubs cap backward, and just the sight of other people in the area with blue caps on made her wish she'd been back earlier for the whole World Series thing.

A few doors down was a dumpier bar, one with no establishment name visible, only a Heileman's Old Style sign above the outside door. She could see it had TVs on inside, and as a bonus, it looked to have a comfortably short supply of other people. Darby walked over, settled into a vacant barstool, and saw that the Reds were up by three in the fourth inning. One other person sat at the bar, an older man watching the game.

Over her tall cheap beer and a few bad plays, Darby dialed in. She became animated enough to yell a "C'mon!" at the TVs above, after a Reds double-play. Maybe she *was* drunk.

"Like the Cubs of old," a voice said. "Put 'em on base, leave 'em stranded."

Darby glanced left at the other bar patron, a guy easily in his seventies. He looked nothing like the typical barfly you'd see at places like these. Instead, the man was tall and strapping, sitting upright with arms folded. He had a weathered shine, beaming from what was left of his white hair.

"Definitely not like the Cubs of '16," Darby said.

"Nope, Maddon's team was special. He had a way with them."

Just like her dad, Darby was always a pretty deep-cut baseball fan. The Yankees never grabbed her interest during her Manhattan years. And she liked that this guy was one of those old-school Cubs fans. He mentioned another game from that championship season.

"That no-no Jake Arrieta threw against these guys, 16-zip. Game was beautiful."

"Yeah, sick," Darby concurred. "Nice game for a road trip."

"Watched it twice," the man said. "Beautiful each time."

To Darby, this guy seemed like a real diehard, one who made her wish she had recorded the 2016 World Series. Then again, her DVR had been flashing I2:00 for at least a decade.

"You saw that Reds' no-hitter, away in Cinci?" Darby asked him. "Or just on TV?"

"Both. Three times, actually," the old man said. "Second and third time, I made the trip out to Cincinnati. They call it the Great American Ball Park."

"Yeah, I know," Darby said to him while thinking something else: *Three times? What the fuck is this guy talking about?*

Maybe this old timer had lost his marbles during the championship parade. Cubs fans were and always have been a delusional sort, but this man didn't seem senile or daft, rather sharp as a tack, at least on the topic of baseball. After another swig of beer, Darby wanted to clarify: "So, you saw three Cubs-Reds games in 2016?"

"*No,*" the man said, smiling devilishly. "I saw Jake's no-hitter. The 16-0 game. A few times. But only two times at the park."

"Is that right?" Darby said politely, thinking, *Shut up, man.* Darby hoped he wasn't hitting on her. If that was his plan, such weird assertions were not impressive. But Darby didn't want to be rude to a fellow Cubs devotee. Just for fun, she asked, "So, what other big games have you seen, sir?"

"Don't call me sir," the man said abruptly. "Name's Del."

"Hi Del, I'm Darby."

Del said he stuck mostly to home games. Burt Hooton's legendary 1972 no-hitter was one, and Del said he saw Milt Pappas's almost-perfect game that same season. "Umpire stole that one," he told Darby. The last game Del said he "went back in time to see" as a spectator was Kerry Wood's 20-strikeout game in 1998, the player's rookie year.

"Time travel was just sports for me. Just baseball. Nothin' else."

"Time travel? For baseball? Of course." Darby played along. If you *could* even time travel, Darby figured she'd have her own much better uses for it. Like doing things over and undoing big mistakes. *Un-fucking up your life.* Baseball seemed an innocent thing to do if that was your thing. Just hop in a phone booth or ski lodge hot tub, right? Darby got jokey.

"So, how 'bout the 1908 team? The original World Champs! Ever see them?"

"Well, you can't go back that far," Del said. "Grey Line only goes back to about 1947, but there's plenty of great games after that."

There were always urban legends bouncing around the 1990s about everything. Some people said the advent of the internet made it so. But at most, Darby only half-paid attention to stuff like that, even the local rumor about "The Grey Line," a time-travel subway train somewhere underground. Like other great American myths—Bigfoot, the Mothman, and the New Jersey Devil—of course, it wasn't true.

"So, this legendary train," Darby said suspiciously. "Anyone besides you use it?"

"Oh, yes." Del claimed that Jake Arrieta, the Cubs pitcher himself, went back to "find his stuff" and watch other greats pitch right before he won the 2015 Cy Young Award. Jumping off baseball, Del said Rahm Emanuel went back after he was elected mayor to talk with the first Mayor Daley. Del said, "But you know them guys, I bet those two didn't get along."

Darby eagerly listened and Del elaborated on more Grey Line traveler folklore.

"Chicago Candy Lady," Del said of the famous missing person, "she used it. And Jimmy Hoffa, too." Del insisted Hoffa was not murdered but slipped aboard to shake off some heat. "I was in the union then. Some said he escaped just in time. No pun intended."

The evening's tipsy spell of bar fables started to make Darby feel like a local again, even if it was just beer-swilling nonsense. That felt important to her. When the game broke for the 7th inning stretch, the Cubs were blowing it, 11-0, just like old times. *Time to go.* She felt like she'd made a new friend.

"It was nice to hear your stories," she said, as she felt compelled to shake Del's hand. "Maybe see ya at Don Cardwell's big one," she said, of the famous 1960 game.

"Saw that one too. Only cost two bucks to get in," Del smiled. As Darby neared the tavern's door, Del raised his voice. "But be careful. Even back then, those visiting Cardinals fans were a little bit mean and nasty."

Darby smiled. "Thanks—I'll watch out."

KERPLUNK

Besides the battery-dead faux Apple Watch, there was another special relic that Darby found in Revolver's back office the next day. The Chicago Rock Catalog was a music lover's bounty and a choice piece of memorabilia. In tiny print, it listed every concert that befell Chicago since 1978. Every music fan loved books like these.

"You gonna let me see that thing or what?" Spacey said. "Like once... ever?"

"Give me a minute—like five minutes."

"*Fuck*, man. You said five minutes twenty minutes ago!"

"OK, OK. One minute, Space."

The "Rock Log" was a bible-sized book, compiled by an unknown guru who went only by Johnny Concerts. Whoever he was, he was a distant cousin of every music nerd alive.

Spacey kept on her. "Lemme see. You know, I like music too," causing Derby to relent and hand it over. Spacey nearly ripped it open. Darby said she also had a condition about the use of the Rock Log.

"So, Spacey—I'd like it if you didn't let Mark and Conrad know we have this."

"Sure," Spacey responded, not looking up. "But why?"

"I'm just afraid it will get over-read, overused, abused, beat to hell, that's all."

Darby had once owned a copy of the Rock Log and lost it. Since it had just gone out of print, she fawned over this final edition now like a rare gem. Good rock 'n' roll books were hard to come by, and it was bad enough Mark lost Darby's copy of *High Fidelity*.

"Imagine one day it gets borrowed by our own bickering musical Siskel & Ebert here. Either Mark or Conrad will definitely lose it. Poof! Gone. We'll never see it again."

"OK, good point," Spacey said. "Who are Siskel and Ebert?"

Spacey flipped more through the book and spent the next 20 minutes rambling off notable show dates. "Did you know— Naked Raygun played six years ago? My nineteenth birthday! I was there, ya know."

"Nice."

"Ex-boyfriend took me. Know who else played that day? Bon Jovi!"

"You see them too?"

Spacey responded only with a vile puking sound.

"C'mon! Bet you'd love you some Jovi if you gave 'em a chance," Darby joked.

But Spacey hinted the mere suggestion was crazy.

"No way, man. Can't believe they're in the Rock and Roll Hall of Fame. Seriously."

Spacey was all punk from head to heart, and for her, music was about good tunes and DIY ethic, not mohawks and safety pins. But she had the look to go with her life philosophy. Most days she wore the same weathered jean jacket over a black concert T-shirt, usually something '80s psycho-billy, like X or The Cramps. The purple-blue streak dyed into her blond hair seemed to punctuate her outspoken, "fuck everything" nature. And each day, she rolled in like a rock star, wearing both Lizzo's lion heart and the freckle-faced youth of Billie Eilish.

"I could read this all day," Spacey blurted out, finally looking up from the Rock Log. "Digest this book, Darby, and you might be cool again someday, just like me."

"Don't you have a roller derby practice, Spacey Musgraves?"

"Not 'til 6 P.M. Wanna come skate and hit people?"

"Kill me now," Darby said.

Darby then regained her turn with the Rock Log and like Spacey spouted her own trivia.

"Check it out: The Ramones and Runaways played Aragon here, in 1978. And Billy Idol played his first solo gig here in 1982."

"I'd go just to see pre-facelift Billy Idol!" Spacey asserted. "Too bad we don't have a time machine. Woo-hoo!"

After the day was over and everyone was gone, Darby spent a few hours doing busy work, paying bills, logging inventory. She was still getting the hang of small business ownership and the record store's retail drudgery. Closer to midnight, she was tired enough to head up to bed, but the Rock Log stared at her, wanting to be reopened. The day's conversations made her wonder what she'd missed after leaving town on Labor Day 1996.

She flipped through the Rock Log's pages, scratched notes, and made more yellow pad lists. She marked down band names and show dates, creating sub-lists of shows she'd seen and others she'd wished she'd seen. Artists like The Roots, Pharcyde, Ani DiFranco, Shelter, Ned's Atomic Dustbin. Plus, she'd missed two J. Davis Trio shows, and dates of the Pistols' *Filthy Lucre* and Bad Brains' *Black Dots* tours. A Woodstock worth of music. She imagined being with her best pal Spiro at each live show, had they both stayed in town.

Darby caught herself almost on the floor, sliding out of her chair. The Rock Log tumbled from her lap and hit the floor with a loud thud, and she opened her eyes to a clock searing ꒡:꒢꒢ ꒜꒟ from its prehistoric lime green readout. This was the first time she dozed off and fell asleep in the store, and she'd conked out hard while fantasizing about music and the past. A minute later a loud shriek railed from somewhere behind or below.

"Fuck!" she said out loud.

Following that noise was a rumble that swelled down to nothing. Darby stood up quickly, back aching and weary from yet another night of low-quality sleep already in progress. Out the tiny back window she looked, but the alley had no garbage trucks grumbling outside.

She was now too tired to head upstairs, and just rolled onto the back room's leather couch. But after more rumbles, she couldn't rest through it. Frustrated—pissed off, frankly—she kicked a blanket onto the floor, got up in a huff, popped in a Keurig cup. Now she was *up*.

Behind Darby, metal shelf racks moved and squeaked at the joints. Next to it, a pile of cardboard boxes stacked tall, filled with ancient cleaning supplies, stood in front of an overpainted door. She'd never messed with the door and figured it led to a basement below. But now she moved the boxes and put her ear against it, hearing shrieks and rumbles.

It would take a hard pull or two, maybe a crowbar to get it open.

With pokes and prods, Darby broke a sweat. Maybe work was being done on sewers. *Maybe it's trolls or rats,* she thought. Darby joked in her mind that her ex had moved in and was squatting downstairs. Eventually, with some elbow grease the door popped open. Now in a mix of caffeine, adrenaline, and sweat, she felt confrontational over her loss of sleep, and her inner tough girl was ready to take a look—maybe have a word with someone. She pulled the stubborn door open, peered downward, and saw steps and a faint grayish light. She brought the crowbar along—just in case—down into the space.

Several steps further the grayish light got brighter and she walked down a lit hall. More sweat broke and her heart pounded as a train sound rumbled. And after no more than another ten steps, she paused at an arched opening and two access doors flung open.

The device on her wrist—*apparently not an Apple Watch*—now woke up and vibrated, and its face lit up brightly and almost flared in illuminated red.

Darby wasn't feeling comfortable enough to pass fully through, but she popped her head through under the arch. Lights flashed in her face and a subway train rolled forward and slowed down to a stop. Darby backed up quickly and looked up at a sign above the archway.

In chipped and shriveled old paint, it read: "Welcome to the Grey Line."

EITHER/OR

By 6 A.M. Darby was on her third cup of coffee and customarily wired, albeit hours earlier than normal. Long after she closed up the dusty door and moved the boxes back in place, she sat, rocking in Martin's office chair. She hadn't changed out of her jeans and shirt from the day before, and fiddled with the thing on her wrist, looking over its flat, glowing face of red.

None of her employees would be in for a while, so she fired up a fourth Keurig and decided to jump onto her Mac. She could easily kill hours searching up this Grey Line myth.

Darby hit Google and first typed "time machines"—*too generic*—then changed it to "subway time travel."

That just sounded dumb, so she backspaced and typed "Chicago gray line," to see what came up. Search results led to a bus company called *Gray Line*, with an "a" in its name and a website with text about group rates and corporate discounts.

"Fuck it," Darby said, as she threw the kitchen sink at her browser.

"Chicago GREY LINE rumors secret train subway time travel portal urban legend."

That brain dump brought up an onslaught of random links. Darby scrolled to the bottom, to tap the blogosphere and web pages with weird names.

Chicago Mysteriez

One blog aptly titled *Chicago Mysteriez* was cheerful and disorganized, looking like a free Geocities stub put up by a tween for a 6th-grade project. Its brown background and yellow text reminded Darby of the dreadful outfits Mark wore to the store. The page had a spinning globe logo and a misspelled tagline: "dis cover chicagos mysterie'z!"

"Seriously?" The whole thing looked like a fucking joke. She begrudgingly scrolled on.

But Darby found that 'Mysteriez' read better than it looked, at least for entertainment's sake. Its detailed intro stated that the Grey Line was designed in 1947 as a prototype after which the rest of Chicago transit was built. It elaborated on the system being "abandoned by the City," which led to its "unauthorized use by secret rogue scientists" who piloted "time-space experiments to other realms!" In keeping with its hodgepodge diction and wacky color scheme, the blog listed an array of convenient if misspelled bullet points.

Even better, they were in Comic Sans:

- Grey line runs from 1947 to present
- Time-traveler's can only travel present date (meaning today!)
- So if today is Jan 18, 2005 you can travel to Jan 18 any year:
- Grey Line travelers can stay in the past as long as they want
- Date you leave is the date you travel

Gleefully, the blog author also crafted an example:

> Sugesstion for time travelers:
> - You leave Jan 18 and stay five weeks till Feb 23rd. You can come back Feb 23 or wait
> - On Feb 23 You can also grab train to different decades. Any year from 1947-present
> - No fare required but must wear time-pass

Chicago Mysteriez had one heavy final point for such a playful font:

> Will I run into my "old" self" back in time? (like Bill & Ted, Marty McFly)
> - Rule: You only exist once in all time continuums, won't runn into yourself
> - If you prefer to maintain current time-age (your age today) use paradox control

Darby clicked back to search for something more serious-looking.

The ULTIMATE Time Train RESOURCE

The next web page had the look of an ersatz military dossier, constructed by some secret agent wannabe or X-Files geek. Crafted in a sober black-and-white typewriter font, the "Resource" served up a conspiratorial tone, written by an author codenamed "Anonymous."

> The Grey Line was a secret U.S. Government project, later abandoned by the now-defunct War Department.

Objective: Preparedness for national security, serve as a means to transport munitions to defend against invasion by Nazi Germany, Japan, and other belligerents, present, future, or past.

After the intro, its author corroborated some points and introduced others in its FAQ:

Grey Line FAQ:
Where does the Grey Line run?
Known boarding locally in Chicago, Ill. various secret stops.
What time period does the Grey Line run?
Current service runs from 1 Jan 1947 to present.
When can I travel?
Travelers with a time-pass may board present date and travel to that precise date in another time-year.
So, how does it work?
For example, travelers leaving at 16:00 20 June 2010 traveling to 1986 will arrive same place/time/date, thus 16:00 20 June 1986.
How long can I stay/travel?
Travelers can stay as long as 90 days as time-pass permits.

The last thing the "Resource" provided was a "Map of the System." Darby clicked to see a sketchy map, detailing stops clustered by decades in different city areas.

Both websites mentioned a time-pass device. One made it sound like a transit card and the second hinted it was a 90-day timer. Darby's third search, "time pass watch bracelet," returned photos of jogging trackers and "fight cancer" wristbands. But something else too:

CHICAGO 2 THE PAST.COM

Darby's last find read like a slick QVC ad with a color diagram. No mention of trains.

> *Time Pass Watches present incomparable versatility. Each watch offers time travel access and a battery life of 90 days. Features: 100% crystal table, 90-day time battery, adjustable band, paradox control. Limited supply.*

The item pictured matched Darby's wrist device. Below the photo were two links. One link read "product details" and there was a "Buy Now" button. She clicked the button, and seconds later the web page blanked out to a dead link.

What Darby saw that morning below her record shop's basement was either some off-map train line or indeed the time transport the old man talked about. Either the websites were the work of schizoid sci-fi dweebs with too much time on their hands, or they served as real documentation of a revolutionary phenomenon. And either the Grey Line legend was true, or Darby wanted it to be true. She wasn't sure which.

Spacey arrived at work on time at eleven again. When she walked in, Darby was visibly tired and jacked up on coffee. And she was frustrated that the TV and remote wouldn't work.

"Spacey, how do you get this damn thing to work?"

"Here," she said. "Good morning, by the way."

"Hi. Good morning. Sorry, didn't sleep much."

"Yeah, I can tell." With one button click Spacey put the TV straight, and set it to MTV Classic. Seeing '90s music videos put Darby at ease. "See—not hard. User manual's in your office. Might wanna read the instructions."

Spacey then began talking music again, on the same exact mental plane as the prior day. She chatter-boxed about concerts, which was music to Darby's exhausted ears.

"So, my skate coach—he's old, like you—told me he saw Wu-Tang and the Pharcyde at The Congress here in '95. So, add that to my wish list."

Spacey grabbed the Rock Log, flipped it open, and continued talking music.

Darby interrupted her. "You know, Spacey, you really do have great taste."

"I know, but thanks," Spacey told her.

GREAT ESCAPE

Later that day Spacey commented on the newest addition to Darby's wardrobe.

"Cool gadget. Did you get an iWatch? Fancy."

"Huh?"

She asked again: "On your wrist—*duh*. Is that an Apple Watch or whatever it's called?" Spacey was even more of a tech Luddite than Darby was, and barely used her own janky flip phone. So anyone could believe Spacey wouldn't know an Apple Watch from an apple pie. Yet, Darby felt the need to conceal her morning adventures.

"This? Oh, no. Just a bracelet of sorts."

"You wear bracelets now, Darby? So *cute!*"

"No. Yes." Darby anxiously invented a story. "I got it... back in New York."

Darby took the device off and shoved it in her back pocket. From the same back pocket, she pulled out the yellow pad sheet folded over, from the day before. She unfolded it to find the list she had been working on. It now read differently:

1. WRITE ABOUT MUSIC AGAIN
2. DISCOVER DREADED LETTERS. ~~AGAIN~~
3. FIND LINA

Spacey pried once more: "What's that?"

"Nothing. A list of stuff to do."

Spacey had a knack for being nosy and getting away with it. She also had a knack for changing subjects mid-conversation and getting away with that too. Now both.

"*So*, Darby—Why *did* you move away to New York anyway? Like, why'd you stop being a music writer, to go wear dress clothes to buy and sell stocks and bonds and bullshit like that? Seriously, why would you do such a thing?"

"It's complicated."

"I'd kill for that job. Get paid to see bands and write about 'em? Uh, yeah!"

"It wasn't because I didn't like it," Darby explained. "It was fun, but not going anywhere. And I needed to get my shit together." She conjured the face of Lina, the last girl she loved. "And, something happened. I broke up with someone here."

"OK. That'll do it."

Darby's radical departure from Chicago seemed inevitable then. And just now she realized that each time she had a bad breakup she ended up moving across different states. Off to New York, after Lina. Then back to Chicago, after Alan and her career meltdown, but really because of a whole bunch of things. Like a need for a new, real, authentic beginning.

"I needed a change. But my time in New York got old. So I'm back."

"Good thing," Spacey said. "The world needs less Wall Street, more record stores."

Darby liked owning a record store and she knew she was carrying on Martin's legacy. That felt honorable. But the whole gig was something she liked, not *loved*. Sure, it was cool to be surrounded all day by music lovers, even Mark and Conrad, with their overbearing, male expert opinions. But after her soft landing and a few months owning Revolver, Darby knew that it was not paradise for her, but a job. The panache that came with selling vinyl and underground "super DJ" mixtapes to passionate music aficionados also came with retail tedium. Maybe running a record store, like being a rock star or spy, was really a young person's game. Martin was always younger at heart, much more so than Darby ever was.

After all those long, high-stress years of chasing money, prestige, and the next big thing, and after putting up with Wall Street machismo and corporate bullshit, the idea of going off-grid and playing hooky from grownup life for a while, Darby decided, just might do the trick. Plus, the situation rumbling below the record store tickled her mind. What if she really could time travel? Fix a few things. Maybe even start over, reboot life? Do things over with Lina.

Late afternoon Spacey was about done with her shift. Darby called her back for a chat.

"Got practice soon," Spacey said softly. "What up, boss?"

"Say, Spacey—if I took a trip out of town, think you could handle things here? At least a couple of days. Maybe longer."

"Sure. Where are you going?"

"Not sure. Maybe off-grid somewhere."

"Off-grid? *Ooh, sounds adventurous!* Are you going camping? Hiking? Rappelling?"

"Nothing outdoors. I fucking hate camping." Darby told Spacey that if she could open each day and keep the boys productive she could pay her extra and give her a little cash up front. "You like mornings, right?"

"For sure. No problem," she told Darby. "Bring me back a souvenir, 'K?"

Darby knew Spacey could hold down the store but imparted a last-second thought.

"So, Spacey—if I don't return in, let's say... ninety days."

"What—ninety days? *Where the fuck* are you going?"

That didn't sound like it made sense.

"No, OK, let's just say, like, if something were ever to happen to me—crazy, I know."

"Ha! OK. Is the mob after you now?"

"Just listen. I'm serious."

"What? Dude, I gotta get going."

"Hold up. Stay for just a minute or two—"

"I can't, I have derby."

Darby had to speed the conversation up.

"OK, but, just—if something ever happens to me, if I got—OK, whacked by the mob, or abducted by aliens or whatever, doesn't matter," Darby said, playing along. "If I didn't return—just sayin'—I'd want you to take over. I mean, the store is yours."

"Wow, the mob really *must* be after you." Spacey made it like she was in on a big joke, but placated Darby's worry, even if taking her half-seriously. "I got things here. It'll be fine. Don't worry. Have a good trip."

At ten in the morning the next day, Darby left an envelope with $500 cash and the bookkeeper's info, sealed tight and marked "SPACEY" on Martin's old desk. And inside it, Darby also left her Dreaded Letters tickets. In case she didn't make it back for the Wrigley gig.

For herself, she'd packed a bag of things for her trip: more cash and a few spare garments, a long-expired ID, an old key, and other randoms she might or might not need. Darby wasn't sure how long this excursion would go. At least a few days. Maybe longer.

She came downstairs dressed in jeans, a button-down, and a leather jacket; all comfortable travel wear. She then jumped back onto her Mac to print the "Resource" blog's Grey Line map. Just like the TV, the printer wouldn't work right, so Darby hit "print" a few times. In the same vein, she knew her iPhone wouldn't work where she was going, so she'd leave it.

Down in the Grey Line train cavern, peacefully alone, Darby stood nervous but excited. Her wrist device glowed, stoked for the trip too, and she saw a feature on it she hadn't observed before. The display was populated with two bits of information.

It read DAYS LEFT: 90. Like the urban legend said, she had ninety days to travel into the 1990s or anywhere else she wanted to go. At the bottom in text almost too small to read it said, PARADOX CONTROL: OFF.

Darby played with the button on the side, popping it in and out, and with each on-and-off flick, the setting went "On" and "Off" and "On" and "Off" again.

Lights flashed Darby in the face and a minute later a roaring train pulled up and rolled by her before stopping. It was clean, shiny, apparently empty, and opened its sliding doors. "Caution, doors closing," said a Stephen Hawking voice. A sign above the middle window, just like on normal Chicago Transit trains, corroborated its next general destination: *1970s.*

All she had to do was wait for another train to pass, so she could grab the *1990s* train.

THE 1990s, A SECOND TIME

DEFINITELY, MAYBE

SEPTEMBER 2, 1996. BACK IN TIME.

The rush was quick and before Darby knew it, she was at an underground stop with signs bolted onto the walls, reading **1996.** The doors slid open peacefully and she got off the train car quick, fearing she might somehow miss her stop. A dash up more dim concrete stairs and a push through a metal door put her outside. And as that door slammed behind her, Darby looked at the surroundings. An abandoned lot covered in weeds, encircled by a bent-up fence. She recognized the block; it was a half-mile from home.

Through the old neighborhood, Darby smelled truck diesel and beer stench from the bars. In the streets of 1996, young people looked more casual than the kids of the uptight 21st century. Their clothes were baggier, and no annoying Bluetooth earpieces hung off their ears. No one stared down at smartphones. She was elated to see one kid walk by with living room stereo-sized headphones, like the ones Spacey wore as a part of her vintage fetish.

A short walk and minutes later, Darby stood in front of her old apartment door. She looked at the time-pass watch on her wrist, which now read 2 SEP 1996 up in the corner. Still, she worried for a second that if she somehow wasn't really *here* then she was very, very lost.

But her apartment building looked the same and inside the atrium, it smelled the same. Darby walked upstairs and the steps creaked. When she reached her old apartment door, the same cruddy old doormat sat in front of the door, and seeing it again made her feel less of a trespasser. Its tawdry jute stared up, stating happily, ***Welcome Home!***

Darby then bent over and slipped her fingers under the mat just to see if the old spare key was there, and it was. When she stood upright again, her back wasn't stiff anymore. Strangely she felt younger, though she didn't get exactly how.

Darby had once lived with three guys, her best mates, back in '96. They always called the apartment "the loft" for no other reason than the fact that Simon, who was from London, England, called it that, and the name stuck. Like a loft in the New York art district sense, the old apartment had gigantic windows and high ceilings that commanded the lion's share of light from Chicago's overcast skies. Just looking at the front door flashed memories of these friends she hadn't seen in forever:

Roommate #1, Simon, was the apartment jester. About six feet, with a melon-shaped head covered in batches of premature grey hair, Simon spoke almost exclusively in jokes and pop culture references, and when not joking or babbling about soccer ("football" he called it), he'd often break into song. Darby always thought him hilarious, yet hard to get to know. The Limey, they sometimes called Simon, came over for his work with an international trading firm.

Roommate #2, Rod: Short, business-like, opinionated, Darby's second cohabitant had a taste in finer things. His scotch, cigars, and shiny accessories seemed to match Rod's obsession with James Bond and the movie spy's glamorous style. Like Bond, Rod had a practice of carousing with gorgeous, high-maintenance women—all of whom were taller than him. Darby always figured that Rod liked the implied adventure of their elegance, which made up for their missing personalities. By day, Rod worked for an ad firm, but his main expertise was film noir and action movies. If there were ever a sequel to the film *Swingers*, he'd be in it. Just wait 'til he'd find out about the *Ocean's 11* reboots.

Roommate #3, Deighv: Dave, David Coopersmith or "Deighv," as he preferred to write his name, for the sake of quirkiness, was one of Darby's friends from college. When Darby and Deighv first moved up to the North Side they got a tiny two-bedroom in Lincoln Park, an area rife with super-jocks and women in Monica and Rachel haircuts. Deighv worked as a "digital editor"—a new world term then—at a hip firm called GigaWire that produced "online news," crafted for the first generation of humans who could read stuff on a computer screen. Once the four of them moved into the loft, Deighv got a steady girlfriend, and they didn't see him much.

"You guys better be here," Darby said to no one but herself. Her key turned, the door popped, and like a stranger, Darby whimpered a feebly voiced, *"Hello?"*

Three heads above the back of the couch turned slowly, as apartment sounds stopped and the silence ended in a theatrical, English accent.

"Well, hello!" Simon yelled. "Whooooo goooooooooes the-rrrrrre?"

Darby didn't remember anyone getting up off the couch. Or anyone offering a hug. So, it was weird to find her arms around Simon, hugging him, as a normal person might do after suddenly escaping death or being rescued from a deserted island. (Or after 25 years.)

"Good to see you too," Simon joked. "Miss us already, yeah?"

"Sorry," Darby said, letting go of Simon. "Yeah."

"You're a sentimental one, aren't you?" His jokey tone deflated the awkwardness.

So did Rod's words. "Don't hug me. I'm not missing you yet," Rod said, unenthused. "Aren't you supposed to be off to New York right now?"

Darby improvised: "Well—I'm not going."

"You owe me, mate!" Simon said over to Rod, now irritated. "It was 20 we bet!"

"Limey asshole." Rod became irritated and mouthy with Simon, which wasn't that unusual. "Well, welcome back, D," Rod added sardonically.

Then Deighv confirmed the instant suspicion.

"They had a bet. Simon thought you'd back out and not move to New York. Rod thought you were gone for good. So did I, but I didn't make a bet."

"Back out?"

"Not that you were lying," Deighv explained, "but I thought you'd change your mind. Besides, your mountain bike is still in the basement."

Darby didn't remember leaving behind a bike, but that clue made her departure a contentious point of debate, so much so that Simon and Rod wagered on it.

"I know you got it," Simon said to Rod. "So pay up, sharp-dressed man!"

Simon badgered Rod for his cash, mainly for the fun of irritating him. Rod responded feistily, saying, in his familiar Chicago accent, "*hang on*" and "*chill out*," repeating both a few times. Twenty bucks was nothing for Rod, but the loss demoralized the Vegas hotshot in him.

"Darby, you got your haircut, all fancy," Rod said. "What are you gonna do now?"

"Stay for a while. Maybe get my old job back."

But Simon said he knew all along that she'd be back.

"I didn't see you going through with it. I knew you'd change your mind about New York. Definitely. No maybe. Now I'm $20 richer. You're a lousy bet, Roddy Clark *ha-ha-ha*."

Simon had won this round, but Rod's pride argued it. Like old times, her old goofy guy roommates were into their comic routine. Darby took off her jacket and slung it over a chair.

"So, yeah. I'm back, I guess."

"Good thing," said Deighv. "Now, no need to look for new roommates."

"We'd get some freak from the personals of that beatnik paper you write for," Rod said. "So Darby, I hope you weren't in on this bet—as a side deal with Simon."

She didn't get Rod's angle. "What?" she said.

Rod went on. "I mean, if you need ten bucks from your half of the swindle," he said, "I could just spot you. Might be handy, now that you've just fucked your future."

IRRESISTIBLE
BLISS

SEPTEMBER 10, 1996

Alex Spiro sat happily at his favorite hip, grungy coffeehouse, nose stuffed into an old book that he found deep in the stacks at the college library. Harriet E. Wilson's novel was required reading for his graduate American Lit course, or maybe it wasn't; he couldn't remember.

Cafe Urbanite was known for its bold coffee and three-dollar bottomless cup, and both were benefits of hanging out there all day. The other draw was that this coffeehouse, urban legends had it, was the haunt of rockstars. On any given day, people said you might see Iggy Pop, Prince, maybe Lou Reed or Sheryl Crow walk in for a cup to-go. And if not bona fide legends, then local indie heroes like the guys from Material Issue, Ministry, or the Smoking Popes might make appearances. Spiro never saw any of them, but he liked Urbanite because the place was beautifully rustic, with high walls and pillars that suggested a past life as a morgue or city jail. The place had weathered the first waves of Chicago's *Great Gentrification*, keeping its elegant, tattered grandeur in place, without flinching at the new Starbucks up the road.

Darby stood in front of Spiro, silent at first, watching him burn off several seconds to complete whatever passage he was reading. Finally, he paused to acknowledge her.

"Well."

"Well, what, Mr. *Spee*-row?" Darby said.

"Well, hello again. You never explained this New York trip of yours, by the way."

"I decided not to go, so we can forget it now." Darby thought it settled. Not so.

"Not surprised. No go, yo," Spiro rhymed. "Knew you'd never go anywhere."

"Thanks, Spiro. You make me sound like a bum."

"Hey, I didn't mean it that way." Spiro wasn't mean enough to tell his best friend she was selling out. But typical Spiro would see her ideas about business school or anything enterprising as a waste of time. "Probably the right thing. Better a bum than a business person. You'd be working ninety hours, dating hyper-competitive lawyers with Prada brief-cases."

"Maybe."

"You'd be sitting in a pantsuit, in a cubicle. And—you got your hair cut. Looks nice."

She ran her fingers through her side-swept undercut. "Thanks."

But what did Spiro really know about New York anyway? Not much more than what he'd seen in Scorsese films or NBC crime shows.

"The business world: just like proctology!" Spiro said. "Too many assholes."

"Good job," Darby said back. "You saving that one up?"

"Yep."

The short diatribe reminded Darby of her friend's quirks and how she missed them. Spiro then continued on, and picked up the day-old copy of the *New York Times* in front of him, recounting his usual shtick of peremptory statements about corporate everything.

"Look at this ad—DKNY has bottled water now!" he proclaimed.

"Interesting." It was *not* interesting, but Spiro's anti-consumer mania was amusing.

"And the Olive Garden! I can't believe Americans eat this fake Italian food! Know why I come here and not Starbucks, with their medium-heat, extra-foam lattes?"

"To read the *New York Times* for free?"

"Well—yes. But even the coffee I drink is all about integrity. Down with corporate coffee!" he said, nearly shouting. "DOWN WITH CORPORATE AMERICA!"

"OK—OK, Spiro." *God.* "I agree with you, sorta."

She'd never let her friend know that she'd once actively traded the stocks of these enterprises. *Down with Corporate America*, indeed.

Spiro tossed the news broadsheet back onto the table and broached another topic.

"We should see a show. Some live tunes. Tonight!" He named a band he wanted to see called The Enlightenment. "They're a bunch of legit Buddhist guys, bald and badass."

For the first time in a while, Darby really had nothing to do. No after-hours trading, no quarterly earnings calls. No crushing failure to sort out over tequila. And no record store employees to manage. Nothing to do but hang with a great old friend—and she needed that.

"So, what's this band like?"

"They're good. They play this sort of glam metal that's awesome, and a little hilarious."

She remembered it wasn't until she came to the Midwest

for college that she found out things could be "a little hilarious." People said that in Chicago, placing forth the nuanced idea that things can be hilarious in smaller measure, not stifling in their hilarity, just a *little hilarious.*

But there was one other old ritual besides live music that Darby had forgotten.

"On top of that," Spiro added, "it's one-dollar Malört shots!"

"Please no," she said to him. "I hate Malört."

Tonight's band, she thought, might be either the next Foo Fighters or total garbage. It didn't matter, and Darby was happy to let loose, experience some bliss—and even, maybe, do a shot of that awful yellow potion.

Repeater

Every bit of Spiro's chatter gave Darby a nagging *long-time-no-see* hankering to ask her friend how the hell he'd been. But she bit her tongue, knowing that to make this all work she would have to stop being a living, breathing anachronism for a minute.

Spiro moved over to the big sofa next to them and knocked his coffee onto the floor.

"Holy coffee foul," he said, as hot brew splashed all over the left leg of his jeans and the floor, with some seeping into a grated floor vent. Good thing it was free refills.

"I see things haven't changed." Darby smiled, the spill triggering more memories: not just that Spiro was eccentric and clumsy, but that he had a star-aligned, perhaps star-crossed relationship with luck. Good luck, bad luck, sometimes just dumb luck.

As a penny-pinching grad student, Spiro was a patron of thrift shops and yet had developed a knack for picking out clothing items with money abandoned by previous owners. Once it was a cowboy shirt with $20 in the pocket, another time it was $50 of tens rolled tight like a cocaine straw in a

pair of dress pants. Darby never understood this phenomenon. But Spiro's bad luck was equally uncanny. He also had a
consistent habit of being splashed by passing cars, crapped on
by birds, and stepping in dog excrement. This dovetailed with
today's coffee accident, which now summoned an exasperated
cafe employee with a mop. Clearly, Spiro's oddities weren't
extinguished during this blip back in time.

Spiro then rolled out questions. "So, what happened with
that girl?"

"What girl?" Darby said, knowing full well whom he asked
about.

"Come on, you know. The babe with the dark hair."

"Lina? We broke up. For real, last time."

After an awkward pause, Darby looked down at Spiro's
jeans, soaked in coffee and covered in remnants of wet napkin
shrapnel. It spurred a sense of immediacy.

"I should probably go home and change."

Darby followed her friend out of Urbanite into the streets
of Bucktown, and they were off toward Spiro's new apartment, where he'd been living for a short time with a weird guy
he met through the classifieds. Darby wasn't the kind to trust
newspaper personals—they just felt creepy. But for Spiro, it
worked, and it got him a quality apartment in a nicer part of
town that he could not normally otherwise afford. This fun,
artsy part of Bucktown had an appeal and creative spirit that
was essential for Spiro but wasted on his tacky roommate.

"So, yesterday," Spiro chuckled, "my roommate peed out
the window—for no reason!"

No one needed a reason to pee out a second-floor window,
but Pete's mere existence was a reason he would. Darby met
Pete once and regarded Spiro's roommate as a cartoonish
nuisance. Spiro then described him with a ten-dollar word he
didn't deserve.

"He's so uncouth."

"Uncouth is one way to describe him." Other ways to describe him? Unkempt. Irritating. Loud and sweaty. Chauvinistic. A real-life rendition of Booger from *Revenge of the Nerds.*

Pete Sorenson's resume would be impressive to any bigwig in the haughty circles of the Fortune 500. Despite his prestigious job title and business suits, Pete always looked at best disheveled and duct-taped together, and not in a sprezzatura kind of way. Like a lot of guys in their twenties, Pete lacked the subtleties you'd expect of someone employed in downtown skyscrapers. In addition to being windblown and messy, he also had a somewhat troubling personal avocation: Pete was a self-proclaimed aficionado of notable strippers and porn stars. As such, their apartment was littered with Playboys and Hustlers. Pete even had signed glossy photos of Debbie Dallas or whoever from the latest Adult Expo.

Spiro seemed unbothered by his roommate's weird ways. But to Darby, Pete seemed like little more than a standard-issue beer-swilling, straight male idiot, a past-its-prime archetype; hopefully the last of a 20th-century dying breed.

Right when Spiro unlocked the apartment's front door, the first crack showed that Pete was home. Under her breath, Darby said the first thing that came to her mind.

"Fuuuuuuuuuuck."

Spiro, amused, looked back at Darby with a pantomimed laugh.

Pete saw them and said, "Yo there!" At the same time, he was trifling with a TV remote, trying to find something seedy on cable, possibly The Spice Channel. Pete's briefcase sat there, carelessly dumped on the floor with papers sliding out of it, while Pete stood there barefoot in suit pants and a ratty undershirt, manhandling the TV remote. Up at the top of Pete's shirt, Darby saw his chain and gold arrowhead dangling, helplessly ensnared, drowning, sinking, dying—falling into the plume of chest hair atop Pete's white V-neck. She suppressed her gag reflexes.

Pete looked at Darby, seeming disinterested in her. But since she was a female in his apartment—likely one of very, very few... ever—he gave Darby a mighty look up and down, and eventually stopped visually at her denim-wrapped thighs.

"What you guys up to tonight?" he said.

"Live music," Spiro responded. "We're gonna see some bands."

Pete fired back: "Who's playing? Grunge?"

Pete's question made it sound like he thought that 'Grunge' was the name of a band. This wouldn't be surprising to either Darby or Spiro, and it triggered their old favorite old hobby of messing with the musically oblivious. Now with a target in the crosshairs, Spiro looked over at Darby, crafting an answer.

"Well—it's a new band, totally brand new. They're called The Bee Gees," Spiro said. "GG Allin & The Bee Gees!"

Darby's inner music snob arose, wanting in too.

"Yeah," Darby added, "GG rocks, man. He's crazy." Darby said this knowing that GG Allin, the extreme rocker best known for fighting fans and defecating on stage, had been dead for at least three years.

Spiro kept on.

"The opening band's supposed to be great too. I forget their name," Spiro said. "Didn't you buy their record, Darby? What are they called, Darby?"

Spiro expected a howling answer to further goad Pete. Flustered, Darby couldn't conjure one and settled for the first thing she could squeeze out of her 21st-century brain.

"Uh—Yeah! ... Kim—Kim and the Kardashians," Darby uttered.

"Coolness! I think I've seen 'em on MTV!" Pete responded passively.

Technology then came to the rescue, as Pete's newish cellular phone issued from work buzzed. It rang erratically, in a chirpy stream of beeps and shudders that sounded like a frantic bird trying to flee the room. Darby didn't remember mobile phones ever sounding like that, and Pete's chunky, plastic Motorola piece looked like ancient history, with its pull-up antenna and downward-folding jaw he had to yank open just to answer it. Yet, before Pete could reach his phone it convulsed and hopped all over the coffee table, surfing on a lagoon of loose change and pocket lint that had probably been there for weeks. Eventually, Pete was able to grasp it.

"Hello!" Pete yelled proudly to the caller.

Darby nodded at Spiro. *Time to go.*

Spiro looked into a mirror, puffing up his maple-red hair, and left briefly to change his jeans. He returned a split second later in new pants and a work jacket with someone else's name, *Ralph*. They said bye and left Pete to his important call, which got louder each second.

Outside Spiro's stony building, Darby looked up at the trees creating a canopy over the streets, marveling at the beauty of the Chicago boulevards.

Spiro looked at her incredulously, almost offended.

"Who the hell... are Kim and The Kardashians?"

"No one," Darby said, nervously. "I don't know—I just made it up."

ACE OF CLUBS

They hopped a cab and arrived at Lounge Ax, on Lincoln Avenue. Darby was immediately taken by the fact that she was in front of the old music venue that captured her nostalgia-soaked daydreams in the days before she hopped the Grey Line. Seeing it open—now, in the '90s, again—gave her tremors of joy. But before passing its door, a bouncer stopped them cold.

"You twenty-one?"

Probably baby-faced Spiro he's talking about, she thought.

"Well?"

Darby answered for the two of them: "Yes."

"Oh, yeah? ID, please."

Darby looked the bouncer in the face. "*Who?* Me?"

"YES! YOU. Who'd you think I'm talking to, missy? I'm gonna need to see ID or you're *not* coming in tonight!" The mean-looking doorman wasn't bothered by Spiro's young mug or the way his ginger soul patch made him look like a bearded baby. The bouncer then cross-checked Darby's face and her Illinois license a few times, as if she were some runaway child. After another close look, the big guy eased up.

"OK, you're good."

"How old are you?" Spiro asked her.

"Twenty-five? Just like you."

It was now true.

"You don't look a day over nineteen, kiddo!"

Fucking smartass.

They waited in a short line to get inside, and Darby's mind trickled away. *If I go back further—to that 1978 Runaways show—do I look like a little girl?* She couldn't venture a guess. Her 21st-century brain was on again, and she got an enterprising idea, like a TV commercial:

> *Do you want to go back in time?*
> *To see Nirvana... Led Zeppelin... The Beatles?*
> *LIVE in concert! Before they were famous!*
> *Book your ticket now... back into rock 'n' roll history!*

Darby's *Rock 'N' Roll Time Travel Inc.* could sell all-inclusive packages to starry-eyed rock aficionados just like her. (She could make millions!) Only thing needed was more time-pass watches for the clientele. Finding those would be hard.

Spiro snapped her out of it.

"I think you're gonna dig these guys. They're just these Buddhist guys who wail."

The whole thing sounded right up Spiro's alley. Something different rolled up with a little bit of madness. Maybe tonight's adventure would become another great story these best friends could gleefully rehash someday.

Lounge Ax was hallowed ground to anyone who loved cutting-edge alternative music and indie rock. It wasn't just Darby who thought that. Like other legendary venues such as CBGB in New York, L.A.'s Whisky A Go Go, or Washington D.C.'s 9:30 Club, Lounge Ax had its own rich history. Although lesser known than those venues, the place was revered by musicians and the people who came to see them just the same. One step inside would spark a special feeling.

Looking left, a Plexiglas picture case was mounted by the bar's front door, and in it, Darby saw a series of black-and-white photo booth strips from the machine inside the bar, the same one where Darby took her kissy pics with Lina. Many of the bands who played there from 1987 until its closure in early 2000 had stepped into that photo booth to mark their visits. Artists like The Breeders, Band of Susans, and one-off photos of Elliott Smith and Mojo Nixon were encased with hometown favorites Ministry, Tortoise, U.S. Maple, a very young Smashing Pumpkins, and Spacey's favorite, Naked Raygun. Plus one unsigned band few knew, called Dreaded Letters. Scores of musicians captured in their most natural state; a hit parade of the underground.

Moments later, the short line began to move forward, and Darby saw it all in place. The long bar, purple sofas, and memorabilia-clad walls ensconced together like a big, rock 'n' roll living room. On stage sat shiny instruments and chrome microphones, tinseled up like a Christmas morning.

"Grab some seats," Spiro said, pointing halfway down the bar, as Darby looked for a bartender to call on. Spiro then yelled to someone Darby couldn't see at first, and a woman approached, and then it was pretty clear why they were really there.

"Darby, do you remember Michael?" Spiro's face was flush with excitement.

"Hi, Michael-Leslie, actually," she said, nodding semi-formally. "Pleased to meet you."

Michael-Leslie, Darby remembered now, was someone Spiro once dreamily described as *that girl* he liked, and also his "inspiration," a woman who stoked his inner Shakespeare or Henry Miller, as it were. Darby remembered now that she'd even met this Michael-Leslie.

"Not sure if you remember me," she said, as Michael-Leslie shook her head, *no*. "Anyhow, I'm Darby."

Spiro's muse looked like a Bettie Page motif, replete with black hair, black boots, black clothes, and a little attitude. This young woman Spiro had his designs upon was a little punk rock but more glamorous than punk, with a studied affect. She didn't smile, but smirked; she made eye contact, but wouldn't truly acknowledge you. And when Spiro spoke, Darby couldn't tell if Michael-Leslie was appreciative of his attention or amused by his gushing.

A moment later, another woman in black joined them. Michael-Leslie balked at introducing her friend, who introduced herself.

"Hey, I'm Rachel." Her forward ease contrasted Michael-Leslie's poker face, but the two friends complemented each other like a dynamic rocker duo. Rachel's long, red hair illuminated the freckles that exploded across her face, and her black leather jacket looked every bit bravado as her Mötley Crüe T-shirt. "Cool club. Never been here."

Darby was instantly smitten and spoke.

"Hi! You're decked out for some metal tonight," Darby nodded to Rachel's shirt.

"Yeah. I like all kinds of music. Rock 'n' roll, man!" Rachel made a heavy metal fist, poking fun at herself, before aiming at Spiro. "So, you're—*Ralph*? Hi, Ralph!"

"Huh?"

"Right there." Rachel pointed out the elliptical patch on Spiro's thrift store gas station attendant jacket. Evidently, he'd never paid any mind to it.

"Oh, no, that's not my name."

"Ya sure? I know a Ralph when I see one! You the real-life Ralph the Mouth?"

"He does have a mouth on him," Darby said.

Then a firm hand and a foreign accent grabbed Darby's shoulder.

"I see we keep the same hours!" said Simon, as Rachel smiled at the intruding weirdo. Simon then elbowed Darby. "Sorry, didn't mean to interrupt your date! Is this a double date?"

"No it isn't, Simon," she said. "But, thanks for checking in on me." Darby noticed Rod, Deighv, and a few other friends also in tow. "Rachel, these are my roommates. Simon, here, with the suspect accent, Rod, and Dave. *You're a stalker*, Simon."

"Stalker? *STAW*-Ker!" Simon repeated this word with Alfred Hitchcock film eeriness. "Maybe you're the stalker, ole friend. Nice to meet you—Rachel—right?"

"Yes."

"Watch out for this one," Simon said, meaning Darby. "She's a bit of a toe rag."

"You got it!" Rachel smiled.

Seconds later, the fuzz of amps climbed to full blast and the bar's crowd was thicker than minutes before. Rod stepped to the bar, raising himself on its footrest to hail a bartender.

"Might as well get a groove on. This one's on me. Malört, please, for—hold up—one, two..." Rod counted heads of all four roommates, Deighv's girlfriend Jenna, plus Spiro, Michael-Leslie, Rachel, and Rod's supermodel date behind him. "Seven, eight, nine, looks like."

"No, no thank you," Simon protested. "I'll have Cuervo instead."

"Nope, I'm buying, so you're drinking Malört. Don't be a

wuss." Rod got militant and declared that all were compelled into this classic Chicago ritual. "It's a rite of passage."

"Rite? More like shite," Simon said, as Darby silently agreed.

"What's Ma-lord?" Rachel asked.

"It's shite!" Simon said again.

"No really, I'm not up on Chicago traditions. I'm from Minnesota. Minny-*sohda*," Rachel said it again in a comical thousand-lakes cadence. "Is it a gin or brandy kinda thing?"

Darby jumped in and described it, wanting to keep Rachel's attention. "It's not sweet, and doesn't taste like hairspray as gin does," she said, not being of any help. "I mean, it's *not* good. Like schnapps, but bad."

Rachel said it couldn't be *that bad*. "OK, so, Darby, right?"

"Yes."

"How's this goin' down?" She touched Darby's wrist softly. "Why should I drink this 'shite' with you?"

"I don't know. To me it tastes like gasoline and dandelions," Darby said, again not being of help. "But after a Malört shot, everything else tastes like ice cream."

"OK, sold." Rachel was in.

The bartender, a tough-looking, tall woman in a tank top with arms covered in tattoos appeared. She pulled up a bottle of the infamous yellow liquid, and with each pour, Simon lodged a mock protest, irritating the barkeep with his antics.

"Noooooooooooooo!"

"You'll be fine, Simon," Darby said. "Tough it out. If I can, you can."

The bartender poured another shot.

Simon again: "NO! Noooooooooooooo!"

And another.

"Noooooooooooooooooooooooooo!"

Eventually, the bartender broke a smile. Simon's protests made it like they were throwing him down a well, a well full of Jeppson's Malört, liquid mania.

The friends gathered round, and once everyone got their shots, Rod called a toast: "To Ch'cawgo traditions."

Spiro joined in. "Bumping into friends," he said, mostly to Michael-Leslie.

"To Darby, and her massive return," Simon added.

"And hard-rockin' bands!" Rachel proclaimed.

Darby, even more taken with her new bar crush, followed Rachel.

"To Minnesota and Malört firsts. And getting this over with!"

"Nice knowin' ya," Simon said.

Cheers.

All nine swallowed down the bitter potion. Rod beamed, Spiro pretended to love it, Rachel winced while Michael-Leslie remained fashionably indifferent. The rest of them convulsed with muffled grunts. Despite its awful flavor, Darby was soaring.

Rachel rebounded first. "Wow. I'm awake now."

Simon yelled to the crowd: "I've drunk death and lived to tell!"

A round of beers later, Rod Clark still hadn't introduced Sarah, the lanky, elegant blond in a sleek silver dress, whom he brought along. Darby remembered Sarah now as Rod's "hot mom from Hinsdale," and noticed that her pumps accentuated the fact that she was easily 5' 9" without them, and possibly a foot taller than Rod with them on. Besides Malört, Rod was drinking his requisite Scotch, Glenlivet 15. Both overdressed and now possibly over-served, Rod and Sarah suited each other's tipsy glamor and style like a lounge act.

"So, the little guy," Rachel said softly to Darby, nodding at Rod, "What's his deal?"

"Yeah, can't explain it. He has some magic ability to attract supermodels and would-be movie stars." Darby joked. "Clearly, it's not his exquisite *Ch'cawgo* accent."

"You from *Ch'cawgo* too? You're definitely not a comedian, so don't quit your day job, dream girl."

"I'm from New Jersey, originally," she told Rachel.

So it became Rachel's reason to pick on Darby. "Jersey, huh? Bet you love Bon Jovi!"

Just like Spacey, Darby hated any suggestion that she'd ever listen to that '80s pop hair disaster. But she loved Rachel's sass. Even if the question was a joke, she had to reply.

"Bon Jovi? Hell no! Can't even believe they made the Rock Hall of Fame."

"What—Since when is Bon Jovi in the Hall of Fame?" Rachel asked, puzzled.

Darby's brain was, alas, still in the 21st century. Again.

"Never mind. Brain fart."

Then Rachel pulled out a serious question. "So—your English friend sounded like he was saying, with his double date smart ass comment that—maybe—you date girls?"

Darby had never ever officially declared herself a dater of girls or women; nor had she ever asserted herself *gay,* formerly or occasionally straight or officially *bisexual.* She never called herself *fluid* or whatever the label was back in the 21st century now. She always just went with what felt right. And what felt right was that she'd better answer that question, quick.

"Yes, I date girls. *Women.* Mostly, yes." Darby was awkwardly satisfied with her answer. "And what about you?"

"Kind of a new thing for me. But yes. Glad we have *that* in common."

The club's lights dimmed suddenly and people turned and cheered.

"Take it they don't have Buddhist metal bands in Minnesota?"

"Nope," Rachel said.

During their gripping conversation, Rachel and Darby missed that the others had gone toward the stage. They got up to follow and Rachel led the way, grasping Darby's sleeve first and then her index finger between her knuckles, pulling her along. Rachel looked over her shoulder. "C'mon," she said slyly. If this *was* an impromptu first date, Darby was acing it.

Stage lights went up and four men in billowy orange robes tromped out on stage, their demeanor serious as soldiers. One grabbed his six-string and gave it a strum that raged like a chainsaw. The singer grabbed his microphone with a chokehold and spoke: "Greetings, earthlings. We are The Enlightenment, and we're here to blow your minds."

Guitars rang hard and the band jumped right into it. Roaring, The Enlightenment energized the crowd, who woo-hooed more. Rachel pulled Darby close enough to the stage that she could feel the drummer's cymbals rippling vibrations into her face.

Spiro turned around, yelling nothing but noise: "Ahhhhh!"

"You're right, this rocks," Darby yelled back.

"What?!"

"GOOD CALL!"

"I KNOW!" Spiro said, as far as anyone could make out.

Darby looked to the right and saw some kid in bottle-blond dreads climb the corner of the stage and jump off, into a cluster of people who caught and passed him around. Darby then felt some hands grip her and pick her up too. She couldn't tell if it was Simon or Rod instigating, but an instant later she was also atop a row of people who passed her around.

Like a champ, Darby, the former Wall Street stiff and

ornery record store owner, didn't fight the fact that she was crowd surfing. Instead, she let loose and stretched out, riding along like a 1990s poster child.

Darby knew she hadn't crowd surfed since the first Lollapalooza, but she was now riding atop hands that passed her along, in front of Rod and his date, and then Simon and Spiro, Michael-Leslie, Deighv and his girlfriend Jenna, Rachel, everyone.

Then everything went dark.

Answer The Phone, Dummy

SEPTEMBER 11, 1996

The next morning Darby still had her boots on, fully laced up and double-knotted below her jeans. Her jacket was on the floor, mostly, except its right sleeve, which was inside-out, twisted, and wrapped around her forearm, hanging off her wrist like a tourniquet. She had made it to bed in one piece. This was no small accomplishment.

Her eyes opened wearily, one blinker at a time. She didn't know where she was but then recognized the uncomfortable futon under her. She sat up and felt—not drunk, but boggy.

The phone in the apartment rang authoritatively, but it stopped before she could stand up. Then it rang again, and she let it go, but the answering machine wouldn't pick up. It rang a third time, so Darby, clearly home alone, got up to trudge down the hall and get it.

Hello, goddammit.

"Yo!" It was Spiro, much too chipper for such an hour.

"What time is it? I'm not hungover, but I don't feel right."

"Oh, about eleven. Say, you rocked out a little too hard last night." Spiro laid it out with enthusiasm: "Shit got crazy. You got up on stage."

"Don't recall that," she insisted.

"Yeah, dude."

"I don't think so."

"You were riding the crowd! Did you jump off the stage?"

"No." Darby rubbed her eyes, head splitting. "That doesn't sound like me."

"OK, but you *were* crowd surfing." Spiro went on about how "awesome" it was, but Darby wanted to know straight, what happened. She didn't remember leaving the bar.

"How much did we drink?"

"Not that much, but—"

"—and I have a lump on my head," Darby told him, touching it. *Ouch.*

Spiro then replayed the whole thing like a sportscaster.

"There we were at Lounge Ax, for the big show. We bumped into Michael-Leslie. You know, that girl I like?"

"Yeah."

"We talked to her and her super hot friend with the red hair. Then your roommates showed up and started buying shots. We drank 'em, and the music started, and The Enlightenment starting tearing it up! Then people in front of the stage got rowdy and—anyway—you were, like, floating, and people were handing you around. Then the crowd just, you know, *ended*, I guess you could say. After that, me and Simon took you home."

Spiro informed Darby that she had fallen head-first onto the floor of the bar, and after that, Simon pulled her out from under a crowd of people. Once she stood up, a bouncer checked her out with a penlight, and she seemed all right, but was told to call it a night.

Leave it to Darby to go acting like a dummy her first night out in 1996.

"So, yeah. Just, you know, *down you went*," Spiro explained. "You OK?"

"Yeah. I'm fine. I'm gonna go lie down now."

Spiro said, "OK, cool," before adding something Ohio people always said when they hung up the phone: "Bye, now."

Darby put the phone back into its wall cradle and bent down to touch her toes. She immediately contemplated large amounts of coffee versus more sleep. The phone rang again, and she assumed Spiro had something else "awesome" he wanted to share.

"What?"

"Darby Derrex?"

This time it was not Spiro saying her name.

Darby reiterated her greeting, "Yes, hello?" more politely, almost professionally. It sounded important, like her father or the police calling. She faintly recognized the voice.

"Sorry to ring you at home. This is Hammond. At City Scene. How are you?"

It was Mr. John Hammond, from Darby's last Chicago job. Her boss's boss, the publisher and big cheese of the little semi-weekly paper where she worked. Darby didn't remember them being on a phone-me-at-home basis. But, *holy shit*, he sounded the same. Hammond's stony lilt, like that of an old-school newsman, a Walter Cronkite, was polite but straight-forward.

"I know you're on vacation, but we are a little short-staffed as it would turn out. Some events to cover. Local entertainment and such."

Did they not know I quit? she thought. *I did quit, didn't I?* Darby didn't know what Hammond was on about. But the man talked about workload, and then was curt, asking Darby straight off when she might be back in the office again.

"Could you come in tomorrow?" he said. "Tackle some write-ups and editing?"

Still in a woozy state, Darby said yes.

"Good. See you then." Hammond didn't fail to wish Darby, very firmly, a nice day.

Suddenly, inadvertently, it seemed Darby had her old job back.

Hammond's call made Darby wonder if her old editor/boss and friend, Terry Mills, was another casualty of the paper's acquisition. Earlier that year, a bigger media company bought City Scene and its sister publications from Hammond's family. Or maybe HR screwed up, and somehow, Hammond never got the news Darby quit.

But now she pictured it: being back in her old role, the last job she *really* loved. Doing things she liked to do. Tasks that weren't really work. Like listening to music. Tracking what bands were in town. Doing nothing a so-called responsible adult would do with their life while getting paid at least a little money for it.

Music writing, despite the so-so pay, was way more interesting than the minutiae of earnings ratios, market volatility, and the other esoteric Wall Street stuff she'd reluctantly mastered. And unlike owning a record store, it involved no inventory or other people to manage.

Instead of going back to bed, Darby made coffee. And in her foggy mind, she conjured the gist of her last conversation with Terry, maybe two weeks earlier on the 1996 calendar.

"Jordan's on his way out," Terry said. "Bulls too."

"Doubt that. Jordan's back and they're going for six, maybe seven or eight."

Their after-6 P.M. office ritual was shooting buckets in the Nerf basketball set Terry brought in. Terry Mills was City Scene's resident New Yorker in Chicago and came on board after five years with the New York Post. The Nerf set's backboard had the old all-caps KNICKS logo over a collage of players that had lost the 1994 Finals to Houston. Darby figured out that if you lobbed the ball and hit Patrick Ewing's face near the hoop, it went in every time.

"Boosh!"

"Lucky," Terry proclaimed.

"Not really. *Jordan-esque.*"

Darby had been a Bulls fan since college. And she always hated New York teams, the Knicks and Mets especially, ever since her mother ran away with that biker guy from Queens.

During office hoops, Terry would expound upon the historical virtues of the Knicks, before Chicago's dominance allegedly "ruined basketball" and how the Knicks, he said, "will grab the trophy this year."

"I doubt that highly," Darby said.

But she liked Terry and had to give it to him that he had New York's back in everything. His schoolyard hoops hubris came with that stern college player look: six feet and slim, short blond hair, looking nothing like a New Yorker, but instead like one of those cocky little point guards from Kansas or Nebraska. Their last shoot-around that one day also covered that other subject, that Darby was quitting City Scene and moving on.

"You're a good writer, Darby," Terry said congratulations with a smile and then sunk a long shot from his desk. "New York is great, but sure you wanna do this?"

"It's time. I will always write." Darby remembered saying that, unconvincingly.

Since that chat, Darby hadn't written much more than a few investment newsletters to her cranky high net worth clients before her time at Warner Klein investments came to an abrupt halt. And she hadn't kept in touch with Terry either, since shoving off to New York.

But perhaps today's phone call was time's way of telling Darby she might have more music stories to write, maybe more hoops and Bulls-Knicks trash talk to share with Terry Mills.

GENERATION TERRORISTS

By 1:30 P.M. Darby was showered up and more clear-headed. She left the loft and walked around the block, under beautiful fall weather. When she turned the corner, she saw it sitting there, and it became clear that friendships, bands, and Lounge Ax weren't the only things intact in 1996. She looked up, and remembered the last thing she did before leaving town.

Darby had rented a car.

"Fuuuuuuuuuuuuuuuuuuck!"

The little Subaru shined in its outdoorsy hunter green paint, looking cozy and rugged, like the automotive version of an L.L. Bean sweater. The sight of the car and an itch on her chest made Darby reach into the breast pocket of her jacket, and there she found a wiry key ring looped through two plastic-top car keys. Stepping closer, she recognized things in the car: a suitcase, a tire pump but no bike, an Adidas shoebox full of CDs.

There were also things she didn't put there.

Adorning the windshield were six Chicago parking tickets in orange envelopes. Bright orange. Traffic cone orange. *Fuck you, pay me* orange. Even worse, she'd left it parked there over a street cleaning day.

"Bullshit!" she said, mostly to herself, resolving not to pay. The idea of returning the car made her contemplate driving it into Lake Michigan, Thelma & Louise-style. But she felt a sense of responsibility and cooled off to open the driver-side door. At a minimum, she now had more outfits to wear. Plus, there were things she didn't want to leave behind any longer:

- *The Runaways*, a debut album from Joan Jett's all-woman band that, besides Dreaded Letters, was Darby's all-time favorite band. Their eponymous record sat face-up, with the band's blond-winged singer, Cherie Currie, looking slyly at her.
- *Legend*, the Bob Marley "hits" disc that Island Records issued posthumously to get Generation X hooked on the reggae icon. Thanks to Columbia House everyone in the '90s had it.
- A baseball signed by veteran Cubs players, and a plastic helmet signed by Mark Grace.

The backseat held an assortment of business school prep books she knew she'd discard. There were also Stephen King novels and a 1995 edition of the Rock Log that Uncle Martin gave her. Still no Lolla shirt. Her favorite old University of Chicago sweatshirt was also missing, very possibly lost somewhere in the '90s too.

Just then, roommate Deighv appeared.

"Unpacking? Nice set of books! You read *Cujo* and *Carrie*?" Of course, Deighv would get excited about the books.

"Want them?" Darby said. "They're yours if you help me move back in."

"You bought this car?"

"Nooooo. Rented it for the trip. But now I have to return it."

"I love those Subarus. Jenna wants one."

Darby wished she could just give him the car too.

Later, over at the car rental place on Western Avenue, some kid who looked barely old enough to be in the workforce, much less drive or rent someone a car, was at the front counter.

He said, "Hello again," acting as though he recognized Darby. He smiled at her, with a subtle dose of flirtation. And as Darby tried not to roll her eyes at him, the young guy got down to business. "Is the car—not OK?"

"No, it's fine. I canceled my trip. Change of plans, that's all."

"Looks like you got a haircut too."

"Yup, I did. Thanks for noticing." She fluffed up her hair again, looking at him with an unimpressed smirk. "So... how do I return this thing?"

All smiles behind his Leonardo DiCaprio bangs, the young man whose name tag read "Chip," was helpful. "I can refund you for unused days."

Chip handed Darby more paperwork than she remembered signing for anything ever just to un-rent the car. He then took her keys and a clipboard to search for dents and scratches, and came back two minutes later to give her the A-OK.

"You paid in cash," Chip said, "but we hold your card number in case of undetected damage 'n stuff. But I'm sure it's good." He handed her $93, and the refund seemed like a bonus for her hassle. "Thanks for renting with Reynolds!" chipper Chip said, as a send-off.

"No, thank you." The extra cash made her day.

Darby walked out and reached for an iPhone in her pocket, but there was none—so, neither Lyft nor Uber would be an option for the ride home. She thought about a cab, but once she started walking, a voice inside her head said *get on the bus,* right as it pulled up.

On the Chicago Transit bus, she saw a hodgepodge of Midwestern city folk inside. Professionals in office attire, old people in nappy sweaters, and a tubby guy in a Bears jacket with a Mike Ditka mustache as big as his face, all scattered around multicolored vinyl seats. The driver had in her hands what looked like a romance novel, sneaking a page at each bus stop. In back, there was a smattering of teens who'd probably just left school. Darby ambled down the aisle for the perfect seat, but when the driver gunned it during a yellow light, she fell into a seat.

At first, it was quiet among the passengers. One woman knitted silently. The Bears jacket guy seemed to be dissociating between his dark sunglasses and his blaring black headphones. Two teens a few seats ahead of Darby looked sinister and carried a lot of attitude for teenage girls. They were dressed darkly—goth or death metal—depending on your take, and they stood out with their black fingernails and band T-shirts, shielded under dyed tresses of long hair. The duo spoke to each other like they were hiding something.

The bus first stopped about halfway back to Darby's place and the knitting woman got off and was replaced by a few other older people in nappy sweaters and Chicago sportswear. And then a punky teenage girl got on, shouldering a school bag that read "Addison Prep" in big orange block letters. Also dressed in black with blue dyed hair and yellow-stitched boots, she strolled a catwalk toward the back, took a seat by the rear door, acknowledging no one, and then stretched her legs across two seats with her back to the window, pulling out a cell phone. The goth girls pelted her with looks of disapproval before she responded.

"What?"

"Nice telephone," one said. "Is that to call your mommy?"

Addison Prep responded to them: "What do you care, poser?"

A meaner half of the goth duo shot back, "You're the poser, poser bitch!"

"Yeah, that walkie-talkie doesn't fit your outfit," said the other. "Get that at the mall?"

But the prep/punk girl deflected their taunts. "What's it to you, trailer park ho?"

Darby didn't remember any time in history when cell phones weren't part of life, much less when owning one ever was by definition not punk or constituted a "sell-out" move. But the girls amped it up, oblivious of the boring grownups on the bus. Darby had seen public tussles before, mostly drunk idiots at sports bars. Yet the mean girl arguments rivaled all that and made some of the other passengers squirm. It sparked an action movie in her head:

> The mean duo yells "c'mon bitch!" and both take swings at the prep school punk girl. Nunchucks are drawn, throwing stars cut the air. Passengers try to flee but are trapped, some screaming and furrowing under their seats.

> Out of the corner of her eye, Darby sees Addison Prep cartwheel down the aisle, kicking both goth girls in the face. The portly driver slams on the brakes, puts down her book, and rushes to intervene, only to get cold-cocked in the mouth.
> Bus doors are ripped open. An onslaught of high

school girls pour in. They kick and punch for their side. Punk versus Goth. Cell Phone versus No Cell Phone. Some shoot lightning from their hands, like in Mortal Kombat.

But instead of punches, the three girls only threw auditory sticks and stones. The other passengers now had become amused by the creativity of every insult.

"Where's your cotton Dockers, you freakin' square? You make me sick."

"Can't afford a mobile phone? OK, fried hair. Whatever!"

For sure, one day these girls would end up fine members of society. But for now, they were edgy kids making bus passengers captive to their theater.

Darby's stop, or one close enough, came up.

"Excuse me, ladies," she said, passing a nervous grin. The girls hit back with glares and WTF facial retorts. Steps later, Darby had made it off the drama bus unscathed.

As the bus pulled away, Darby took register of the day's mundane accomplishments. She got her old job back, reacquired cherished belongings, returned a rental car, and came up with more pocket cash. And without planning it, Darby got schooled on a little social perspective about what *was* and what *was not* cool with Generation Y's toughest youth.

Different Class

Darby stood outside the auditorium, staring at an event poster that read like a concert bill:

Casper Blandon Bixby
A Q&A with the elusive and brilliant author of
'Encyclopedia of a Depressive'
Tonight only!

Instead of kids in concert T-shirts, it was grey-haired grownups in scarves lining up outside the venue this Thursday night. This guy Bixby didn't even have a second book out, but he was being hyped like the new Puff Daddy. Hip, new authors as rockstars were a very 1990s thing, and it made Darby seethe, just like every time a Phil Collins solo album topped the charts. Bixby's novel went bestseller two years earlier, with the buzz ongoing. Everyone hailed this book and its grueling prose nothing less than the decade's paperback zeitgeist. Some even saw Bixby's 372,000-word sob story as literature's answer to Nirvana's great album *Nevermind*.

But in Darby's mind, that was all bullshit.

She couldn't see why drug-addicted, middle-aged white men writing depressing fiction was special or trendy. Darby at least knew what did and didn't make for good pop culture. *Encyclopedia of a Depressive* just like a Nirvana album? What an idiotic comparison.

Yet here she was, standing in line with book nerd elites and the local literary Illuminati. Seeing an author, even an overrated and possibly a terrible one, did tug a little at Darby's inner intellectual-wannabe side. But the real reason she was here was that Lina was the host of the Washington Foundation's lecture series, and she was interviewing the famed author.

Darby first met Alina Heintze-Colero among friends, during some social thing that involved partying and drinking, that under no other circumstance would warrant any meaningful remembrance other than that Darby had met her. From the outset, once Darby got what her name was—A-LEE-na HENT-say Coe-LAIR-O—she loved its magnificent sound.

Lina had a strong personality to match her spectacular name, with intellectual stripes that were noticeable but not intimidating. Her looks, her perfect posture, and her very straight, dark, geometrical yet choppy, longish bob aptly demonstrated who she was, how she thought, the way she conducted her business. And within relationships, Lina also had a sense of independence, like that of a house cat, in the way that they're cozily friendly, but never reliant.

Darby stood in the slowly moving line and got almost misty-eyed remembering times they had. Seeing Lina first at a distance seemed safer now. Darby figured it better to see Lina query and deconstruct this world-renowned author before Lina might deconstruct her.

Still a tad early, Darby grabbed a seat alone in about the fifth row, tucked into the shadows away from center stage. She watched smartly dressed people file in, wearing wool jackets in brown and ash grey, donning horn-rimmed glasses that made it look like they'd all been fitted by the same posh optometrist. As the last hundred or so people came in and their noise tempered down, the lights dimmed, and the host, Lina, appeared.

"Hello, literary Chicago! Are you excited for tonight's author?"

The crowd thundered... *Yes!*

Lina smiled at the attendees and held an index card with intel on her guest. Darby's eyes widened at her past love, just yards away, standing on stage in a stylish red dress and high leather boots. Lina read the author's bio and a summary of his bestseller and short stories, before plugging the lecture series and the Foundation's benefactors. Lina then introduced the author formally, "Everyone: the great Casper Blandon Bixby."

People stood from their chairs, clapping. Darby didn't cheer but stood politely.

The author peeked from the curtains at stage left, which made the crowd roar more. Lina encouraged him like a shy child, *please come out*, as he foot-clumped out on stage in his long hair and glasses, tweed jacket and jeans, waving slightly to the crowd while looking down. Lina shook Bixby's limp hand, directing him toward the two armchairs that half-faced each other at center stage. Softer spotlights fixed on them, the audience quieted, and Lina began.

"Welcome!" Lina's voice sounded passionate and warm.

"Thank—thank-you," Bixby stuttered, mostly looking at her shoes.

Darby could tell from the start that Bixby was an extreme

introvert and a perplexed and tormented one at that. Lina, skilled and brilliant, handled him with kid gloves, like a little league coach coaxing a frightened batter at the plate. She asked about his characters and his creative methods, and the author talked about youth experiences.

"Drinking and drugs, sessions with my shrink. *That* made me bury myself in books," he said. Bixby talked about writing as an alternative to "getting a real job," and people laughed.

"Tell us," she said, "about the protagonist of your masterpiece, *Encyclopedia*."

Masterpiece? Ugh. Darby would never get it.

The author loosened up. "He's not me, nothing like me," Bixby said curiously, if unconvincingly. "He's symbolic of a postmodern world that devalues the meaning of everything."

That comment made Darby's eyes want to roll even more, out of their sockets and onto the floor and down the hall. Luckily, 30 minutes flew by, and soon the main presentation was over. But then it was question time.

Darby was restless, hoping the gushing would soon end. She just wanted to talk to Lina. But people raised hands, excited to ask their questions while ushers invited them to take a microphone to query their author king.

"What is the process of starting a new novel?" one asked.

"This is more a comment than a question," said a few guests, followed by neither.

"How do you guard against writer's block?" asked another.

Bixby's responses were unrehearsed but incomplete, rambling answers to what every writer has probably been asked thousands of times. After the Q&A session, Lina thanked everyone and gathered huge applause. Bixby would be present for the next 30 minutes at a table with piles of his books that guests could buy before getting to him to sign them.

Afterward, Lina stood off to the left below center stage as people gathered around her too, since she was really the star of the show. Friends, professors, and foundation people congratulated and hugged her. Then came students dressed in hoodies and parkas, some hitting up Lina for jobs and internships. But Lina spoke to the students the same way she addressed famous authors and millionaire benefactors. Instead of shooing them away, Lina listened to them with grace and a different class of elegance and kindness. She then looked over their heads and saw Darby. With that, Lina looked down and smiled slightly, looking up again while talking to a youngster, smirking.

Darby walked closer. "Hello, Lina," she said. Not sure what else to say, she blurted out, "Good job," as if Lina had hit a homer at a beer league softball game.

Lina said hello back, and offered Darby a polite but reserved hug.

"Hey there, stranger. I thought you'd have moved off to New York by now. And I see you got your hair cut. Looks pretty."

"Thanks," Darby said to Lina. "I decided to stay in town. For good, I think."

"Did you? Well, I'm glad. I mean, *good for you.*"

After a brief pause, Darby offered compliments.

"This is great, what you've done here. I like how you got this guy to lighten up."

"Yes, thanks. I just try to talk to them like regular people." Talking about writers and work let Lina be disarmed, if just for the moment, before Darby pounced.

"Well, you look beautiful, Lina."

"Ha. Thanks," she smiled. "Thought the dress would work. Let me walk you out."

Darby wasn't done and was not nearly the last person there. A line of book-buying fans was long and getting longer, but Darby was either worthy of a custom-tailored moment of Alina Heintze-Colero's time along with a quality goodbye, or

Lina was cleaning up the loose ends of a busy night and politely sweeping Darby out. She took Darby arm-in-arm up a ramped aisle and out of the auditorium, marching her out like a soldier toward the bright solitude of an empty, glassed-in concourse.

"OK, you get the host's tour of the lobby. I appreciate your coming. Should've told me."

"Call it a surprise."

"Indeed."

Lina looked to Darby with hesitant flirtation, yet the firmness to hint *time to go*. Darby searched for a reason to prolong the exit.

"Should we... grab a drink?"

"That sounds nice. But, I'll be here a while," she said. "I have people to catch up with, unfortunately, so—." Lina offered another diplomatic hug, digging her chin softly into Darby's shoulder. "It's really great to see you."

After their slight embrace, Darby reluctantly moved on toward the revolving glass door. Just when she passed the night guard and turned around to speak one last thought, Lina spoke first.

"*I'll* call *you*."

SET YOUR GOALS

SEPTEMBER 13, 1996

Darby hadn't remembered it at first, but 1996 was a pivotal year in music. So Mark, of course, was dead wrong about it being the decade's "worst" year. But maybe her record store underling was at least half right about his sentiment. Over the next year, Darby remembered now that the party fizzled. Shit got real, and it became the days in which, as Don McLean sang in "American Pie," the music died. At least good music.

Alternative music's great influence—from grunge to Britpop, from fem folk to West Coast hip hop—began to wane in a characteristically anticlimactic fashion. Indie music and people that made it, promoted it, and wholeheartedly loved it—would soon desert the scene.

By 1997, important bands like Soundgarden and Bikini Kill had disbanded. Smashing Pumpkins nearly fell apart on tour after their drummer overdosed on heroin and their keyboard player died from it. Sublime's Bradley Nowell overdosed and died on tour too. INXS frontman Michael Hutchence hanged himself on the back of a hotel room door. Tupac got shot. Band splits came almost daily. It looked like another swan song of rock 'n' roll's fate.

The pattern continued on into the next year, as John Denver, folk's ever-present spirit, would die in a plane crash. Outside rock music, Princess Diana's death was coming. Even Americans who didn't care about British Royalty would be saddened and thunderstruck, while her friend Elton John, newly minted as Sir Elton John, re-recorded "Candle In The Wind" in Lady Di's honor. That single alone would sell 35 million copies.

That tragedy would also provide radio pop with its rear-mament. Barbarians were nearing the gate, but they would not be true barbarians. Instead, boy band balladeers led by Britney Spears and her bottle-blond imitators would invade the nation and ransack the established order and what was left of good taste. The march toward inoffensive, dull culture was on again.

Thinking about the shifts in music and all the great records that came out in the '90s made her think about Martin, and that she needed to set aside time to stop into his store soon.

But for now, Darby was back at her old job. The first day back, and there was plenty to write about, boy band pillagers notwithstanding. At City Scene, two new things were afoot.

The first was a new crop of super-excited interns starting work. Each summer, the paper's management interviewed college students from DePaul, Northwestern, and the city colleges, to hire new little workhorses at the lowest possible wage on part-time schedules. Interns originally assisted in grunt work, but by 1996 they were being deployed as battle-field rangers in the new tech world that included tasks such as web page work and reposting digital articles that first appeared in print. They were energetic and diligent, lived and breathed technology, and knew a lot, or everything, so they believed. Moreover, the kids had a read on culture and the hottest spots around town. They planned for careers at Netscape, the Clinton White House, or directing music videos at MTV.

The other new thing abuzz at City Scene was its new space-age identity. Network names, email addresses, and everyone getting their own custom internet credentials. Two years prior, the office had shoddy IBM clones and its only digital footprint was the paper's general email address. But then savvier ownership put Apple Power Macs on every desk. Real-time communication became a priority. Soon enough, readers would respond just as fast, firing off emails accusing City Scene of being too harsh in its theater reviews, or condemning the paper's failure to grasp the lyrical subtexts spun forth by Ol' Dirty Bastard on *Wu-Tang Forever.*

Darby sat and turned on her desktop. Her computer was brand new, but to her, a bulky desktop with 64 MB of RAM wasn't impressive. Once she logged in, her email inbox had all of the makings of digital 1996. Way-too-long emails about conference room use and timesheets. Urban legends that were of course real. (None about trains, though.)

One email notified Darby that Microsoft was conducting "a usage test" and it said that if she passed the email along she would get a big fat check from Bill Gates himself. There were email pleas of mercy too. *Forward this email* and miracles happen! Wars end. A village of orphans gets a swing set. An exiled prince deposits $470 million to your bank account. Such emails are believed by people who mistake the CD-ROM drive for a cup holder.

But Darby's inbox did have one important message. It read "MEETING @ 11 AM, CONFERENCE ROOM - MUST ATTEND" from Hammond himself. The meeting was 90 minutes away, and Darby was curious what the 1996 internet looked like. So she took a spin.

By instinct, she jumped straight to Google but realized within seconds that Google did not yet exist, and a *404 Page Not Found* notice kicked back. Darby fished around more, looking up random things, to find that Internet 1996 was mostly static pages with logos and phone numbers. Which meant City Scene's new site was cutting edge by comparison.

The night before, Spiro mentioned a new spot called "Hot House" or "The Hothouse" he wanted to visit for its poetry slams. Darby didn't remember the place, but *Double-U Double-U Double-U dot hot house dot com* sounded funny to tap in. Nothing happened at first.

Then her screen went black and a cacophony of images popped up. Colorful and flashy, each was more suggestive than the next:

Welcome to THE HOT-HOUSE! *Get Laid!* read one popup.

HOT, HORNY COEDS want to meet YOU! proclaimed another.

One more, flashing yellow, boasted ***Submissive Russian Brides***!

"Shit! What the fuck?" Darby said out loud, as the images multiplied like digital cockroaches. The last thing she needed was people thinking she was the office perv on her first day back. Darby didn't remember the mid-90s internet being so seedy and misogynistic. And thanks to her swearing, a coworker looked over.

"Hey—You OK?"

"Yes. Fine!" Darby responded. "Just—a computer malfunction."

"Bet I can help."

"No!" Darby said. "No, I'm good."

Then the girl offering help got up. *Shit.*

Darby hit the power button hard. *Bam.* "That should do it." The screen went dark.

"You're not supposed to do that," the girl said. "You should never shut it off like that!"

Darby hit *POWER* again and the Mac beeped disapprovingly. Ashley "Ash" Holbrook—Darby saw her name dangling on the key card around her neck—sat back down.

"Sorry. You're right," Darby said to her.

Ash shrugged her shoulders at Darby the digital idiot. "Fine. It's cool."

A moment later a phone rang and she grabbed it. "Hello, Darby's desk, here."

"Ms. Derrex?" Hammond found her. "Good morning," he said, in his usual starched way. "Let's talk now that you're back."

This is a first, she thought.

Hammond then said that a new editor had been hired. And once she began to ask about it, Hammond said they should have a conversation. There were awkward and confusing silences before Hammond spoke again.

"Come down to my office, please."

"Yes. Sorry. Gimme a sec."

Hammond's little executive office was encased in glass like a square fishbowl, the only place on the floor fitted as such, and it robbed him a view of the workspace's homey exposed brick. His air was a few degrees colder and fresher, thanks to an air purifier in the corner.

"Well, let me start with some news," he said. "Your supervisor, the Editor in Chief, Terry Mills, hasn't been in the office a while, you could say."

"He get fired or something?"

"Well, no, not yet. It's more like he's just been absent."

Hammond's assertion made him sound this time like Robert Stack narrating an episode of *Unsolved Mysteries*. "Terry's not been heard from in at least a week. He isn't returning our calls. And you could say that he and the new ownership team didn't see eye to eye." Hammond added that Terry stormed out of a weekly management powwow almost two weeks earlier.

Terry was a bit of a rebel and the kind to let everyone know it. Darby could totally see it happen: that he'd get fed up with the management stiffs upstairs and quit outright, no formal goodbyes. Terry would be the guy who would say "screw you," jump on his motorcycle, and then spend a month or two riding around out west or back to New York.

"Between you, me, and the walls," Hammond said, actually pointing to the wall, "this is being sorted out. I know you two worked well, but I'd appreciate no gossip."

"Sure."

Darby remembered again that day she gave Terry notice over Nerf office hoops. Today a paycheck with her name was sitting at her desk, dated the prior Friday. Terry must have left, stormed out, whatever, without passing on to HR that Darby was quitting City Scene.

"New editor will have her agenda," Hammond said. "You can talk to her today."

"Who is she?" Darby asked.

Hammond said, "Someone we grabbed from a competitor." Hammond's phone then rang loudly, and as he picked it up, he signaled to her *thanks*, and that they were done.

Darby walked back to her desk, and one of those interns that she liked from the previous year had apparently gotten rehired. Jake Weinstein sat in the desk behind Darby's, their chairs back-to-back, and the two of them, she recalled now, had a very jokey work relationship. Upon returning from Hammond's glass box, Darby saw Jake facing his monitor, in front of a dozen Kansas City Royals knickknacks and doodads all over his desk. She smiled upon viewing Jake's stumpy presence, knowing that his insult comic personality would kick in as soon as he noticed she was back. A second later, Jake greeted Darby in the same way he always did.

"What's up, dump ranger?"

"Dump ranger?" Darby said.

"Yes, today your name is dump ranger," Jake said back.

"I'm fine. What's up, Rerun?" The fact that he'd gotten rehired as an intern wasn't usual.

"What did you call me, dung-faced dump ranger?"

"Rerun. As in the TV character. Didn't graduate? Still here?"

"Didn't graduate yet, but I will, Rodge Thomas." Jake mumbled something about a fifth year and his double major, and then called Darby the same thing again, "Dump ranger!"

"You know, you'll never ever get a girlfriend talking to women like that," Darby told him.

Sometime over the prior year, Jake developed a routine: Every day he would greet Darby with a new insult, and Darby would play along. It was on again.

"So what did you do this summer?"

"Ya know, usual summertime stuff," Jake said. "Hammond's mom."

While talking, Jake pushed his mouse, not working, but instead drawing what looked like a fire-breathing dragon with a basic desktop application.

"And now you're back," Darby poked, "ready to work very hard, I see."

"Ready and motivated," he said. "Settin' goals and smokin'

bowls." Evidently, today's goals were drawing pixeled monsters and avoiding work until the big meeting.

Darby never knew much more than the basics about Jake—just that he was a college kid, and a short, funny, prematurely balding Jewish guy from suburban Kansas. He joked about drugs and other taboo subjects at work, though she doubted Jake's life outside City Scene was anything to rave about. Jake mentioned the meeting's unknown purpose.

"Finally—they're letting you go today," he said. "I hope they make you stand before everyone in the company. I brought some food to throw at you."

"You wish. That's what interns are for. Careful. You're super expendable."

"You'd die without us," Jake blurted back. "Someone has to keep up the website."

Five-'til-11 rolled around, and soon enough.

"C'mon, skippy." Darby slapped inattentive Jake on the shoulder. "Let's go."

The conference room had entrances on three sides, two in the back and one to the right from the hall upfront. Most seats in the front were filled by about 20 people, so Jake and Dump Ranger slipped into the back and stood against the wall. Attendees also came from ad sales and other departments upstairs. Darby got "welcome back" high-fives.

The room got quiet when people heard Hammond outside the door. He tucked his tall head in the doorway and following him were Hammond's assistant Doris, and, to Darby, another person with a familiar face.

"Hello, hello everyone," Hammond said, as the three of them stood upfront. The new face scanned the room and looked straight at Darby. Hammond thanked everyone for coming, "not that any of you had a choice," a joke that fell flat, before summoning obligatory laughs. Without mentioning Terry's disappearance, he thanked everyone again for good work and segued to an introduction. "Everyone, I want to introduce Debra Tamczak. She'll be our new editor-at-large." Hammond then touted her qualifications and experience.

"Thanks, everybody. I'm Debra, or Deb—or Tam, some call me." Darby saw a reddish time-pass around her wrist. "Whatever you want to call me, it's great to be working with you."

Darby hadn't seen Tam since that day they drank beers and tequila at the Nisei Lounge. After the meeting, the staff all went back to their desks and Darby approached Tam.

"Off-grid, huh?"

"Surprised to see me? I'm a little surprised to see you."

"Are you?" Darby lowered her voice. "You'll have to tell me *what you're doing* here."

"I work here now."

"You *know* that's not what I mean."

"Let's grab some drinks soon and we'll talk. 'Til then, I've got assignments for you."

BLUR

SEPTEMBER 21, 1996

Autumn Saturdays mean buffalo wings and college football for most Midwestern twenty-somethings. But for Rod and Simon, it meant fighting sports, specifically verbal sparring.

Barely 10 A.M., Darby had just got up after their night out drinking. Spiro was slumped over, slowly awakening on their couch. Rod and Simon were already desecrating the morning quiet. But instead of quarreling over Iowa versus Ohio State, it was something else. Rod began by picking on Simon's shimmery red shirt.

"That's a shiny top you have on," Rod said. "Going bowling? Get a job parking cars?"

Simon had an explanation why he was dressed so brightly.

"You men have your Chicago Bulls. We have our Manchester United, beloved across the nation, right across the world."

Wearing his team's shirt for the big game, Simon would soon be off to the expatriates' pub to watch live English football. As he popped up the white collar on his acrylic scarlet shirt with the number 7 on his back, his subtle collar-up bravado made him look like a postmodern Redcoat or an English dandy, and flamboyant enough to be the target of Rod's barbs.

"But why are you wearing a—Manchester shirt? Aren't you from London?"

"Oh ho ho. Silly question, silly boy. Silly question," Simon laughed it off. "Manchester United are England's team!"

"So, they're like what?" Darby said, "The Dallas Cowboys of England? Well, that sucks."

Simon ignored Darby but leaned down closely to Rod, who was sitting and sipping his steaming coffee. Simon began cheering at close range, both to celebrate and be annoying.

"U- *NI* -TED!" Clap clap clap. "U- NI -TED!" Clap clap clap.

Rod pulled a cigarette out from his shiny metal box and looked at Simon acidly.

"But you're not even *really* from London, are you? You're, like, from the suburbs. Suburban Simon Lincoln. From-out-by-the-airport Simon Lincoln."

"Born in Whitechapel, London; raised in Ealing and Stanwell," Simon proclaimed. "Manchester United transcend one city! There's quite a lot of us, you know, us Cockney Reds."

Rod's rebuttal followed very predictably: "More like cock-ass reds."

Darby found their nothing dissensions amusing, even if it was way too early. One more reason to come back in time.

Off to his bar, Simon yelled "Laters!" and the volume of it made Spiro sit up now.

The evening before, Rod hadn't joined Darby, Simon, and Spiro at the booze cruiser. Instead, he opted for a movie with his cousins at The Esquire, his favorite downtown movie theater. Rod liked its name and glamorous Oak Street address, but it also had to do with the fact that he'd once seen John Cusack walking out of the lobby. The new film *2 Days In The Valley* was exactly Rod's sort of thing: part '90s period piece, part rom-com, part film noir. Rod described it as "film noir for *Pulp Fiction* fans, who don't get the genre." Besides the fact that *2 Days* was in early release, it had his favorite new blond goddess Charlize Theron as the main attraction. Rod wanted to see it again.

"One thing I hate," Rod said, searing, "is that my cousins talk and talk during movies. I'm never gonna see films with them again. So I need a second look."

Spiro got up feebly, eventually on both feet. "I need to go home to bed," he said, as he stumbled toward the door. "Thanks for the coffee."

Rod dusted off his Burberry check shirt, to head outside for a smoke. "So—Darby! I'm gonna go see *2 Days* again. Over at Three Penny, noon show. Wanna go?"

"No thanks," Darby told him. "Think I'm gonna loaf today." A look at Charlize Theron sounded great but she needed a day to do absolutely nothing. "I'm brain dead, anyway."

"Suit yourself."

Darby wasn't much into film noir, even "pop noir," or whatever Rod called it. When Rod left to smoke, Darby went to her room to try on some of those clothes she'd fetched from the Subaru. Thumbing through the suitcase that Deighv helped her haul up, she still wondered where her Lollapalooza shirt went and her U of C sweatshirt too. She knew that back in the 21st century other original Lolla shirts were fetching nearly $300. As a consolation today, she had a fitting collection of regular '90s outfits.

Unpacking that suitcase full of her contemporary clothes finds went mostly like this:

1) Trying on shirts and pants in the mirror.
2) Figuring out what was '90s enough but not ridiculous.
3) Repeating it, struggling with simple decisions.
What to wear?

After a few go-arounds, Darby settled on an old black zip-up retro-cool shirt, a long-sleeve thing with a grey vertical stripe on each side of a shiny chrome zipper. It was feminine and cute and bragged a hint of California greaser. It made her hips stand out in a good way, and she matched it with a pair of slim, black jeans she couldn't believe fit her body.

Dressed and ready, it was now time to experience a Saturday with nothing to do. Outside, the September sun was bright, as joggers negotiated paths between window-shopping city pedestrians. Football fans waited single file to get into Big Ten bars. Turning the corner, Darby approached her favorite old bookstore, the perfect place to do nothing on a Saturday.

Like Spiro's Urbanite cafe and Rod's beloved Esquire, the big Logan Bookstore had its own draw of recognizable people. Visiting musicians stopped in because the hotel up the street served as a place to stay when playing gigs at Metro or Aragon. Not U2 or Madonna fame, but good musicians nonetheless came in, to thumb through newspapers and CD stacks.

Once Darby got inside, she beelined it to the magazine section and sensed that it was really time to grasp 1996 in-motion. A look at periodicals might illustrate what was happening *now*.

Newsweek's cover read "New Menace," picturing Osama Bin Laden, a future household name, while another mag's headline read, "Tragedy In Vegas," with a photo of Tupac

Shakur, shot and killed just a week before. Besides weekly news and gossip rags, the music section sat *Rolling Stone* next to deep-cut selections like *Melody Maker,* which boasted "London's Swinging again!" over images from *Trainspotting* and the hyped Mike Myers flick, *Austin Powers.* Like everybody from the future, Darby had seen those films. She grabbed both magazines, along with a copy of *Gramophone* with Yo-Yo Ma's face on it. Then she heard a familiar voice.

"Hey there! Hey!" said the raspy tone. It was Rachel, the snarky redhead from Lounge Ax. "You remember me?" she said, dipping her gaze eye to eye with Darby, who looked up.

"Oh. Hi. Of course I do." Darby stood up straighter at the sight of this knockout wanting to talk to her. The last time they saw each other Darby was in the middle of a bar's floor.

"So—you OK? Your head, I mean. You look all right," Rachel said. Rachel saw the copy of *Classical Music* in Darby's hand and made a joke. "Next time let's go to the symphony. No crowd surfing there!"

"Oh, right. This isn't mine," Darby said, putting down the classical magazines and then touching the back of her healed head. "I made it home fine, thanks to the guys."

"Well, you *looked* like you were having fun."

"Yeah—I don't normally do stuff like that. Kinda dumb."

Rachel looked great. Her long hair sloped down over a worn-in leather jacket and black L.A. Guns T-shirt, atop broken-in Levi's. Memories of conversations came back.

"So," Darby said. "You must be here to pick up Minnesota Weekly."

"Haha. *Minny-sohda*'s not newsy enough for its own magazine. Make fun if you want." Rachel stated her own reason for being there, one that rang loud. "I'm not into football. And bookstores are like fun libraries. Great for browsing, without all the rules." She went on to say that simple things like people-watching and thumbing through magazines she had no intention of buying made it fun. "And you?"

"Same thing. Just loafing. Looking to see if they have *Stage Diving for Dummies,*" she joked, prompting Rachel to laugh.

Darby was captivated by the sunlight peering into the bookstore's windows, and how it played with the sparkle of Rachel's red hair as Rachel kept talking.

"Yeah, so sometimes I just browse. Most weekends I like to do nothing. Weekends should be one big blur. Grabbing a beer with someone, like an impromptu date, is nice too."

After a silent, uneasy moment in which Darby failed to respond, Rachel looked at her with long eyes and another smirk, pecking her with a hint. Then Darby caught on.

"So—you want to get a drink? Like, with *me*? Now?"

"Duh. *Uhhh*, like *right now?*" Rachel said, mocking her. "Yup. Let's go somewhere."

When Darby stepped on the Grey Line train almost three weeks earlier, the idea of going out on a date with someone like Rachel wouldn't have crossed her mind. But Rachel grabbed her jacket sleeve with her slight, freckled fingers, just like that night at Lounge Ax.

"C'mon," Rachel insisted. "It's a beautiful day. Waste it over a beer with me."

FANMAIL

OCTOBER 7, 1996

Tam walked over to Darby in a little bit of a huff and dropped a pile of letters on her desk. Darby had her headphones on, but the thud was loud enough to startle her.

"Happy Monday," Tam said. "Might want to make acquaintance with the mailroom."

"Mailroom?" Darby turned her music off and looked up at Tam, then at the paper mess.

"Yup. Mailroom. You know we have one, right?"

"Sure—I mean, I never got mail here before."

There were white envelopes and promo CDs from indie labels like Matador, Mammoth, Sub Pop, Dischord, Delicious Vinyl. Plus flyers from promoters and artist management firms, and also press packets for bands with weird names and gaudy logos. At least two weeks' worth of junk, addressed to some "Music Editor" at the publication.

"Either way, make it a new habit," Tam said. "Obviously, I won't have time to handle the music piece of things. But you will. You're the music editor now."

"I am?"

"Hey, attention everyone," Tam said, yelling around Darby's side of the office. "Just a little news, everyone! Darby Derrex is now our music editor."

A smattering of cheers and half-enthusiastic claps sounded. Jake the intern turned around from his desk and slapped Darby on the back.

"Congrats," he said. "Don't worry, you can still be the janitor too."

"Thanks, thanks, everyone." Darby looked up at Tam again from her desk and smiled. "Music Editor, wow. So—do I get a raise, or what?"

"Yes. Let's discuss later," Tam said. "But for now, I need a list of your features for the next two weeks. End of day." Tam pushed her glasses back up her nose, then stopped. "What do you have going? New music? Concert reviews?"

"Both."

Darby hadn't been to a live show since The Enlightenment's gig and reviewing it wouldn't make sense. Who'd want to read about the two songs she heard before blacking out on Lounge Ax's floor?

"I had this idea," Darby told Tam, now lowering her voice. "Vintage concert reviews."

"Vintage?"

"Yeah. Vintage, meaning like reviews of the great old concerts from days gone by. Nirvana, maybe the Pumpkins, before they got famous. You know," she sat up excitedly, hinting in a hush-hush way. "Pretend like if I one day I just went *back* to 1991 by train or something. To see Nirvana's first show."

"Go for it." Tam said. "Just—keep on top of your snail mail."

After Tam went away, Darby pulled up her sleeve to look at her time-pass. Its red glow had dimmed somewhat and when she looked closer it read DAYS LEFT: 59. Immediately she felt rushed, and pulled out the crumpled "Wish List" from the night she fell asleep in the shop. Smudged but still legible, it listed show dates. A few were coming up soon, and if she hopped to the right year, she could see a show or two and then pound out written reviews.

> NIRVANA... 10-12-91
> OASIS... 10-15-94
> PUMPKINS... 10-23-1995

Some were a ways off, unfortunately. One in just a few weeks would require no train ride:

> GREEN DAY... 11-18-94
> DREADED LETTERS... 11-29-96
> L 7... 2-28-97

Boarding the Grey Line again next week for the October shows would constitute another little adventure and she could review these historic small gigs of now-famous bands. But 59 days wasn't a ton of time to fix the other things Darby wanted to fix. Or to decide if she might even stay for good. So far she'd burned through 32 days. Yet, a month of fun, friendships, and a newish girlfriend wasn't so bad either.

Darby sat at her desk, sifting through her new music mail, and saw a press pack for one of Spiro's favorite bands, Hill Billy & The Podunks. The band's bio called them "Three Texas cousins who sing and drink like outlaws," and it was accompanied by a glossy photo that showed them in long hair and beards, dressed in Jimi Hendrix-type regal military jackets. Darby threw her earphones on again, but then her phone rang.

"Hey—What are you doing?" The wonderful, smoky voice was Rachel.

"Hey, babe. Working."

"I thought you'd be listening to music."

"I am. That is *working.*"

"Well, well, what a nice employment situation you have."

It was the third or fourth time Rachel had called Darby at work, and she usually called for no reason other than to make jokes and flirt over the phone. Rachel was a master at all of it, and having someone check in on Darby made her feel unusually special.

"What's going on for us tonight?" Rachel asked.

"Well, I *was* supposed to join Rod, Spiro, and Simon for pool at Lakeview Links. But Spiro's being flaky. Some poetry slam thing. Maybe he's chasing Michael-Leslie again."

"Good luck with that," Rachel said. "I can sub. I love pool."

On top of the "feeling special" thing, Darby liked the idea of Rachel wanting to hang out more with her and was a big fan of the fact that Rachel liked to do things and not just stay in and watch *Must See TV.*

The previous week, they had gone out a few times. First, Rachel wanted a tour of Chicago-style pizza spots and other decadent foods. They ended their "food crawl," as Rachel called it, just before midnight, at the Wieners Circle. Sunday before that, they swung golf clubs at the East Lake driving range, when Rachel shanked one left and high enough over the netting to land on a parked car's window.

"So, you any good at pool, dream girl?"

"I'm kinda terrible," Darby had to admit. "Are you?"

"Yeah, I'm good, actually," Rachel told her.

"Better than at golf?"

"Yes, smart ass. Don't believe me? I'll take all three of you."

"I believe you," Darby said to her. "See you there at eight."

Later, Rachel was standing there with a pool stick in her hand, looking rock 'n' roll as always. She had on jeans and an Ozzy T-shirt, her red hair knotted separately in tempting long braids. Simon wore his other Man United shirt, and Rod, cigarette in hand, had on a peacoat that made him look like a short Inspector Gadget. In customary fashion, Darby arrived last—and late—to the back table at Lakeview Links.

The first game was a fluid and exciting one, with the girls taking Simon and Rod easily—Rachel doing most of the work. Darby sank zero balls in the second game, but she and Rachel still won, thanks again to Rachel. With almost every one of Rachel's skillful shots, Simon remained in awe and silent, while Rod kept uttering the same thing: "Lucky."

"Not luck, man. Skill."

Rachel then challenged Rod and Simon by herself to a game of three-player cutthroat. She let the boys go first. And for added fun, she poked at Rod.

"Hey, Rod. You went to film school, right?"

"Yeah, so?"

"What movie is this from?" Rachel sank one ball and then another, and started quoting the asshole character from Darby's favorite film: *"You are an embarrassment—to the game of pool—and you should be glad—that I even let you play—at my table."*

"You know," Rod said with a tense voice, "I don't think I've seen that one."

Darby jumped in.

"C'mon Rod. *Dazed And Confused.* The scene at the Emporium."

"Haven't seen it."

"What? Rod, that movie's a classic."

"Hardly a classic."

"Dude, see something besides film noir for once."

But Rod was preoccupied getting his ass beat at pool by a

woman. Darby had an idea.

"So, if Rachel sinks the last ball blind, you have to go see *Dazed* with me. Brew 'N' View, Friday, midnight. You pay for admission and beers. Bet?"

"Only if she can trick-shot off the far side," Rod insisted.

No sweat, Rachel said with a nod and a shrug.

"OK, then, one more thing," Darby added. "You have to do my laundry."

"Shit, I don't even do my own laundry," Rod shot back.

"Fine," Darby said, "then send it out, but you pay."

"Fine," Rod said, but he had to raise the stakes too. "And if she misses this shot, Darby, you hand-wash my Lexus."

"Deal."

Simon, previously quiet, then roused Rod. "You're going down, Roddy boy! Down in a ball of flames." Other people in the pool hall stopped their play to watch the big wager.

Rachel, cool and calm, pointed her cue stick down, almost perpendicular to the table, and then shut her eyes. With one downward chop, she hit her cue ball, making it glide straight across the field, rolling softly to the far cushion. The ball then came back left and knocked the 8-ball where she called it into the middle pocket. Boom.

Rod looked away, pissed off and deflated. Half the bar cheered. Darby high-fived Rachel and Simon said what everyone else already knew.

"Roddy boy, don't bet against Darby. It's a fool's gamble, mate."

Box Full of
Letters

OCTOBER 10, 1996

Thursday after work Darby was alone at the loft. She was about to head out for a bite with Rachel. She was also taking her redheaded love to see Dust 'N' Bones, Rachel's favorite Guns 'N' Roses tribute band. "Bones," as Rachel called them, were in from the Twin Cities and playing The Empty Bottle.

Just to accent Rachel's pool hall win, Darby gathered her clothes—all of them—into a big duffel bag, and stuck it by Rod's door. Rod, being an anal-retentive taskmaster, had also left Darby a pile of her mail, organized with a heartfelt message on a yellow sticky note:

D~ Open your mail. Love, Rod

Darby was clearly bad with snail mail at both work and home.

Simon's main use for the mailbox seemed to be for nothing

other than receiving English football mags and letters from his widowed mother. For Rod, the mailbox was a receptacle for monthly style literature: *GQ, Motor Trend,* and *Cigar Aficionado.* There were other trifles that arrived for Rod too, such as the Viagra coupons and adult diaper sample packs that he said came as a prank by a bitter ex-girlfriend who signed him up.

Darby looked at her mail pile, which seemed to repaint a 1990s footprint. There were notices about Election '96, and promotions for wings and "Crazy Bread" which notified her how much she must have eaten out in her middle twenties.

On top was something that looked more important and Darby tore it open. Embossed with the Manhattan School of Management's crest at the top-left, the letter's immediate tone was terse and formal. With a heavy dose of snootiness, it addressed a pressing matter.

Dear Ms. Derrex,
This letter is regarding your prior acceptance to the **Manhattan School's** Master of Business program, 1996 Fall Semester.

Before Darby left Chicago the first time, she had accepted and enrolled, and it had become another excuse to move away and start over after Lina and her split. Now, evidently, the school figured out she wasn't coming and wanted to assert that:

fees paid prior cannot be refunded.

Other tidbits were conveyed in a hard, cover-our-ass timbre of legalese. The institution apparently also wanted to assert the last parting shot in their failed relationship.

After skimming the rest, Darby stopped reading and was

relieved to find out she needn't respond. More importantly, the letter seemed to imply that there was not another Darby Derrex running around Manhattan somewhere, enrolled and matriculating credits in her name.

Another formal-looking mailer in the pile seemed to address other recent business. The car rental place sent a follow-up. Maybe another refund?

```
Dear Loyal Customer,
Reynolds Rent-A-Car™ appreciates your busi-
ness. Enclosed is the final receipt for your
Reynolds Rent-A-Car™ invoice:

1993 Subaru Outback TXL 4-door sport economy

In addition to the promotional rate, other
charges have been assessed.
```

Charges—for what? Darby wondered. She now remembered those parking tickets. *Fuck.*

```
Your credit card on file XXXXXXXXXXXX3020
   has been charged:
City of Chicago parking violation citation
   09-04-1996 - $35
City of Chicago parking violation citation
   09-05-1996 - $35
City of Chicago parking violation citation
   09-07-1996 - $35
City of Chicago parking violation citation
   09-08-1996 - $35
City of Chicago parking violation citation
   09-09-1996 - $35
City of Chicago street cleaning citation 09-
   10-1996 - $60
City of Chicago late fees - $100
Processing fee - $6.25

Thank you for using Reynolds Rent-A-Car™!
```

Darby had never intended to stick it to the fine people of Reynolds Rent-A-Car™ by skipping out on the tickets. Frankly, it hadn't occurred to her that the city would bill the vehicle's owner, and then her as the renter.

Or that her "bullshit, I won't pay!" pronouncement would equal $300-plus in penalties.

She decided then that if she should time travel again, *don't ever rent a car.*

WALKING CONTRADICTION

OCTOBER 11, 1996

Darby took Friday as an out-of-office workday. Both "Casual Friday" and the "working at home" thing were suddenly fresh, new '90s trends. So why not partake?

She'd already spent the late morning sipping black coffee outside Urbanite, watching a steady stream of cyclists and hipsters shoot down Milwaukee Avenue toward their own workdays. With her Sony Discman, pad and pen, Darby took in new releases by The Roots and Wilco, scratching down notes. The sun, coffee, and music made it a great start to the day.

Rachel was off to Washington D.C. for a work trip, and with her out of town, it was a perfect time to skip back onto the Grey Line. But she worried: *what if I like 1991 as much as I like '96 now?* Not likely, but *what if.*

Shortly after noon, she met Rod at Liar's Club for a midday drink, since he was officially out-of-office too, easing into an early weekend after a three-day commercial shoot.

"You're a film guy," Darby probed Rod. "So, random question: If you could go back in time to the Golden Age of movies or whatever, where would you go?" Rod furrowed his brow, interested in the topic. Darby sat quiet, waiting for some explanations from her friend. "I know, unusual question," she said.

"I probably have thoughts about that," Rod said. "What makes you think of that? Going back in film history?"

"I know you're a huge movie buff, that's all," she said. "Just curious."

The question was one suited much more for music people like Darby and Spiro. Music nuts have their legendary concert wishlists. Stuff like The Beatles coming to America, Queen at Live Aid, Hendrix at Woodstock. Live performance moments like that are just their deal. But for the astute pupils of Hitchcock, John Wu, and Tarantino, going back to see a movie shot on-set isn't the same. But Darby wanted to see if Rod had some relatable perspective that might help her feel more comfortable about the idea of skipping back to 1991 for that Nirvana show.

"Now that I think of it," Rod said, extinguishing his cigarette, "in real life, I would have loved to go back in time and kill Hitler. And kill Nazis, just like in *Raiders Of The Lost Ark*. Woulda loved to blow that fucker up. Limbs everywhere. And catch it on film, documentary-style!"

"Excellent."

Rod had other unrelated wishlist ideas.

"But, to really answer your question—I'd really love to see The Great Communicator at work. You know, Ronald Reagan doing his thing. Speaking to the people, inspiring the nation fifteen years ago. Maybe I'd go back and meet him when he was just *actor Ronald Reagan*."

Rod's pre-icon Reagan idea was somewhat, in an odd way,

like Darby wanting to see Nirvana before they became rock legends. Maybe his Reagan gushing came of the same spirit.

Like Tam, Rod was an interesting creature and a mishmash of real things that do not readily go together. Darby tried to make sense of this in her 21st-century frame of mind, as they quietly enjoyed afternoon drinks. Rod, she decided, was very much a dichotomy of the postmodern man, a walking contradiction.

For starters, Rod was a multiracial, second-generation American who had done well in advertising; a pretty corporate setting full of WASPy madmen. He was the son of an up-from-nothing labor Democrat politician, yet as an adult he was nominally a Republican and loved Reagan everything, even participating in the 1990s' first run of Reagan revisionism; one that credited everything from the rising stock market to the fall of Communism to Saint Ronny. Yet, oddly, Rod never criticized Clinton. Darby always assumed that Rod had some appreciation for Slick Willy's womanizing.

Rod sipped the last of his drink and broke the conversation's flow. "So, sorry, D. I gotta bounce. Someone important is coming to town."

"Hot date?" Darby asked.

"Yes, actually," Rod said. "Mackenzie is flying in, in about an hour."

Oh, her. Rod's "Model from Manhattan." The real model of the bunch.

Darby always thought it was weirdly fun to see Rod, barely tall enough for the Gucci loafers on his feet to touch the floor while seated, going out with tall, thoroughbred women. Even Roddy Clark's very hard-boiled detective name seemed to clash with the names of his some-time girlfriends and merry-go-round lovers, with bright names like Abbey and Becki Lynn, others with devilish, alluring names like Nerissa, Kara, Tori, Samantha. Others, suitable to the 1990s, had first names like last names: Hayden, Hunter, Parker, Mackenzie.

"Mack's got a show," Rod said. *"New York Fashion Week In Chicago,* they call it."

"You're going to a fashion show?"

"Yup. I am. She's in it, of course. So I get a front-row seat, kinda." Rod said he hadn't seen Mack since his last New York trip during another commercial shoot. "She's here 'til Monday night. I suspect we'll get along at least until Sunday afternoon."

Rod laid down $20 for the drinks and got up, both his feet hitting the ground like a caped superhero. He also gave his trusty friend Darby a top-handed politician's handshake.

"Might not see you all this weekend. We're staying at The Drake," he said.

But Darby knew either way that Rod would stop home. He'd grab fancier socks, a pack of his Gold Flake cigarettes; change into a nicer shirt, or grab a splash of cologne.

"Have fun at the show," Darby said as Rod walked out. "Tell Carrie Bradshaw I said hi!"

"Who?"

Darby instantly knew she'd have to stop it with the bad anachronisms.

Sex and The City wasn't even out until, like, 1999. Ugh.

"Never mind," she said. "Just have fun."

Destination Universe

OCTOBER 10, 1996

A day before her Casual Friday drink with Rod, Darby had told Tam earlier in the day about her next little project.

"You'll get that concert review from me soon. A band that's no longer with us."

"Ah, it's always music with you, isn't it?" Tam said. "You jump back on the Grey Line... for work? Nerd," Tam said, making fun. "Can't you come back with a winning lottery ticket?"

But Darby's jackpot mindset was long gone. Over it.

"Shit, Tam. Been there, done that. If my life on Wall Street wasn't a damn lottery, then I don't know what that hell is."

The two of them had picked up a little office hobby—besides time travel, as it were—and one that involved no hard alcohol. City Scene's building had a game room downstairs with vending machines, totally underutilized by the staff. It had a pool table and foosball too, and along the back wall were a set of Skee-Ball machines. Whenever their brains were fried from too much writing and editing, Skee-Ball broke the monotony. Today was such a day.

Tam started the game by rolling up a 50-pointer, hitting the impossible hole right in the middle of the board. Darby would trail the entire game.

When it came to music, Tam's tastes fully clashed with Darby's. She was a huge country music fan, and just for fun, she threatened to send Darby back in time to review the decade's country music scene.

"Just think. You could've discovered Billy Ray Cyrus! First-ever review of *Achy Breaky Heart*. Just imagine it!"

"Please... no."

"I could make you review Shania Twain, Faith Hill too. I *am* your boss."

Darby rolled her ball up and couldn't even make the first rail, scoring a zero. Between pool and Skee-Ball, Darby's rep as a girl who liked sports and games didn't amount to much.

"I'm not going back for a scoop," she told Tam. "I *am* curious about our little time-travel universe." Darby also mentioned that she was bothered by one weird thing. That the Grey Line could transport people from one year to the next, yet only locally. "It can't be that you can *only* time travel here in Chicago. And nowhere else in the world? That can't make sense, can it?"

"Don't know." Tam seemed less interested in the whole idea but conceded that it didn't make sense. "Maybe New York has its own version. A special line, to go back to dirty, bombed-out, old 1970s Gotham. Poor New Yorkers."

What was constant was that Chicago was always the center of *its own* little universe. After all, Chicago had the best athlete on the planet, the best hoops team in history, and also spawned the best football team of all time, the '85 Bears. Beyond sports, Chicagoans were told time and again how their city invented the skyscraper, the Ferris wheel, the TV remote, and the dishwasher. Chicago pioneered open-heart surgery, invented cellular phones, figured out the right way to serve a hot dog (everything, no ketchup), and even perfected thick pizza in two ways, with stuffed *and* deep-dish. If this big, great city could accomplish all that and reverse the direction of its river, why wouldn't time travel be another hometown specialty?

"Imagine going back to see how weird the 1980s are."

"Fun. Weird I bet," Tam said, not seeming too interested.

"I'd love to go back the 1960s and '70s too, to see rock's beginnings. See Zeppelin, the Sex Pistols, Talking Heads, maybe The Runaways."

"Wow, you're *serious*," she said. "Just don't get lost in the past."

Tam then rolled a 100 to the top-right corner and this came after her third score in a row. Darby managed to score once, so it was 250-10. Tam claimed victory and then turned up her concern over Darby's next excursion.

"Maybe you should stay put, you know. Just enjoy life where you are for once. Stop searching. You are enjoying yourself, right? With that fly new girl of yours."

"Yes, I am," Darby said. "But I have bands to review! Next issue."

Overall, Darby felt Tam was too nonchalant about time travel and all its possibilities, while Darby had deliberated in the most finite detail before leaving for 1996. She did her research, made lists, packed appropriately, prepped Spacey to take over the shop if she didn't end up coming back. How could Tam be so carefree? Darby had to know.

"So, why did you come back here in the first place?" Darby asked her friend. "Why did you, as you put it, decide to go... off-grid?"

Tam looked at Darby squarely in the face, wondering why she even asked.

"For love. What else?"

City Scene | Music

Latecomers' Reviews by Darby Derrex
October 15, 1996

Starting today, City Scene's new music editor reviews historic Chicago concerts twice monthly in a new column, Latecomers' Reviews. She begins with a band you might know.

Nirvana
Metro 10/12/1991

It's likely that very few of us who are Nirvana fans were there at Metro to see the little-known Aberdeen, Washington, trio 33 days after the release of "Smells Like Teen Spirit."

As we all know now, that first single, written by Kurt Cobain, Krist Novoselic and Dave Grohl, is arguably the keynote song of this decade and one that changed music forever.

You would be very lucky if you were indeed present at the all-ages show on October 12, 1991, as I was. And if you could remember it—or can get a look now at the show's taping—you would see Nirvana at their first Chicago gig exhibiting a new shape of music to come.

From the first strums of their opening song, "Jesus Wants Me For A Sunbeam," a Vaselines cover, to "Teen Spirit" and "On A Plain" (both from *Nevermind*), to the show's final notes, Nirvana roared with a raw energy that floored concertgoers and critics alike.

The Metro show was one that saw Nirvana unleash a burst of energy that today would be considered less characteristic of the band's thoughtful, often sorrowful style. That night, just up the street from Wrigley Field, Nirvana's frontman raged powerfully on vocals and guitar, while exuding a captivating grace rarely seen on stage, and perfected only by other legendary vocalists in the vein of Janis Joplin and Mick Jagger, Robert Plant, and Prince. Meanwhile, Grohl's rimshots and drum pounding swirled with Novoselic's bass, in a fervor that could've woken the dead at Graceland Cemetery three blocks away.

Nirvana took a different turn with *In Utero*, in 1993, exploring another level of songwriting depth, plus a feel for anxiety and depression, within singles like "Heart-Shaped Box," and later in their live *MTV Unplugged* performance. But in October of '91, it was all unabated rage in a riveting performance.

Hopefully anyone present that Saturday knew what they were witnessing. Not just Nirvana being loud and bombastic weeks before they became the biggest band in the world, but a close look at a legendary band in its most flawless form.

Rating: 5/5
Setlist: Jesus Wants Me For A Sunbeam (Vaselines cover), Aneurysm, School, Floyd The Barber, Drain You, Smells Like Teen Spirit, About A Girl, Breed, Polly, Sliver, Pennyroyal Tea, Love Buzz (Shocking Blue cover), Lithium, Been A Son, On A Plain, Negative Creep, Blew, Endless, Nameless

BRICKS ARE HEAVY

OCTOBER 16, 1996

Hammond shot out an email Wednesday morning for another meeting. This electronic inter-office messaging phenomenon was really catching on.

Jake the Intern wasn't in today, so thus far Darby hadn't been called whatever new epithet Jake might have invented and ready. Darby hadn't turned on her Mac yet. But Ms. Holbrook, in the cube across the aisle, printed out a copy of the email sent to everyone and taped it to Darby's computer screen. It read like the usual Hammond blurb with an all-caps headline:

MEETING @ 11AM - ALL MUST ATTEND

Ash circled the subject line with a red Sharpie as if to question Darby's eyesight. Over the past weeks, they had become office buddies and realized they had the same sense of humor.

Darby pulled the taped page off her screen. "Thanks, Ash, forgot my bifocals!"

"Thought that might help. Ever since those horny coed sites shut your Mac down."

Darby looked over at Ash, almost embarrassed. Ash chose to let Darby off the hook.

"We had an intern using your Mac while you were on vacay," Ash explained. "He got fired after like two days, for looking at stuff he shouldn't have."

"What a dumbass."

"Yeah. Too bad," Ash said. "He was super cute."

Darby was 25, and Ash couldn't really have been more than a few years younger. But Darby had forgotten that when you're 21 or 22 years old, just a few years seems like a continental divide. Ash sometimes liked to make it like Darby was a member of some much-older generation that hadn't yet accepted computers as a daily currency.

"I *do* read my email, you know," Darby insisted.

"Sometimes you're so lost in your headphones. What are you reviewing?"

Darby told her: "Soundgarden, Pearl Jam, and Nirvana, actually. A manly man's deluge into the coming year's music. Good though."

At the beginning of October Nirvana's label released *From the Muddy Banks of the Wishkah*, a mostly live album with cuts from early years. Darby could just feel that the album would go No. 1, and it did. Kurt Cobain had been gone two and a half years, and people still wanted more. Other new releases signaled grunge was fading. The Spice Girls and Republica put out popular, very dancey singles, and Snoop followed up 1993's *Doggystyle* with *Tha Doggfather*. Yet the idea of reviewing Marilyn Manson's new disc made Darby feel morose.

"So, what do people your age listen to?" Darby asked her.

"Same stuff as you."

"How old were you when *Nevermind* came out, Ash?"

"I was sixteen, maybe."

"Are you old enough to drink beer—now?"

"Yes. Yes, I am. I'm twenty-one and a half."

"And a half—twenty-one and a half?"

"Need me to get your walker, old lady?"

Just for the old lady jibes, Darby lampooned Ash further.

"Ash... Ashley... That's a very, very common name. When someone says your name in public... *Ashley!* ... do the nearest fifty people turn around?"

"Not everyone can have a J. Crew name like you, Darby."

It was a good thing Ash printed out the meeting notice because Darby would have drifted off to musical La La Land. She had dug in, taking notes on Dave Grohl's drumming patterns and Nirvana's faint blues influences. Then, at five-'til, the whole floor could hear Hammond's billowy pipes from upfront again. This time he sounded less like Robert Stack and more like a sedated Harrison Ford. Darby and Ash got up to head to the mystery meeting.

"Come in, come in, please," Hammond said. "We'll wait 'til everyone else is here."

The room was quieter this time, like a drowsy study hall, with the stale air tainted in a cornucopia of office accents: copier fluid, highlighter pens, generic coffee bonding to Styrofoam cups. People filed in somberly. Hammond spoke up.

"OK, if we can get started: This will be short, but I've called a meeting because we have, unfortunately, less-than-good news."

Darby wondered if the paper was shifting gears and if

they'd all be fired, let go, *downsized*, or whatever it was called now. A return to Wall Street and the business world flashed her mind. *Fuck that.* Darby was having fun here.

But layoffs were not why Hammond called a meeting.

"Turns out we've gotten word on a former colleague of ours," Hammond said. "I realize some of you newly on board may not have known him, our last managing editor."

Terry.

Hammond looked at Darby a split second. "Terry Mills was a good man and a very good editor. If you knew him, you liked him, for sure."

Darby wasn't ready for a eulogy, especially one about someone once a close friend. It was still everyone's assumption at City Scene that the man just up and quit one day.

"He loved his sports teams, loved life, loved to ride motorcycles. Unfortunately, Terry was in a crash, a fatal accident a few weeks ago, unbeknownst to us until now."

Hammond kept talking but Darby didn't hear much more. She thought about Terry, and how they got along because of non-work things. Both being from the East Coast, their preference for New York-style pizza and really good bagels. Their squabbles about the NBA. Darby hadn't seen Terry since that Nerf hoops day.

"For those of you who knew Terry, I'm sorry, and this probably hits like a ton of bricks, and we'll miss him. Take any time today you need."

Hammond adjourned the meeting and people went back to their desks.

Darby couldn't snap back into work or drift off passively into music again. She felt bad—more than bad—that she was too wrapped up in her own little world and hadn't lifted a finger to see what became of Terry. Right after sitting, her desk phone rang.

"What up, punk?" It was Spiro. "Done with class for the day."

"And?"

"Well, I cut, actually. Let's hit some record stores."

"Sorry, Spiro, I can't. Besides, I *am* at work, *so*..." Darby didn't want to dampen Spiro's mood and still needed to process the news. "I'd be a drag anyhow."

When Darby hung up, she felt more lost. Maybe she would go ahead and sulk over that Marilyn Manson disc. The phone rang again, and she wondered what Spiro wanted this time.

"What up, punk?" Darby said.

"Darby?" It was Rachel.

"Oh, hey. Sorry, thought you were Spiro calling twice."

"You call Spiro *punk*?"

"Sometimes. He rang me a minute ago and answered that way—"

"OK, Miss Explainer." Rachel was ready to joke around, as usual, but she noticed Darby's more tranquil tone. "You sound like you're asleep. Food coma?"

"No. Actually, some bad news at work."

"You have to review a Phil Collins album?"

"I wish it was that. Actually, someone I know—knew, anyhow, my old editor, he died."

"Damn. I'm sorry." Rachel asked, "What happened?"

"Wrecked his motorcycle a week or so ago. Nobody here knew, and I found out now."

"That's awful. You OK?"

Now Darby felt guilty about feeling bad too. "We hadn't spoken in a while."

"You should come over later," Rachel said adamantly. "I want to see you."

Darby had little else to offer, saying only "I will," and "I should get back."

She told Rachel she'd be over by 7:30.

After work, Darby still felt listless on the walk over to Rachel's place. She picked up a bottle of wine but didn't remember paying for it. After Rachel buzzed her in, Darby slowly climbed the stairs to see her waiting, door open, standing atop the landing. Rachel's red hair was wild and loose, this time stuffed under a navy-blue Minnesota Twins cap that made her look relaxed like she hadn't left the apartment. Comfortably sexy too, Rachel had on little else but a black tank top with a worn-out Motörhead emblem on it, barely covering her feminine shoulders. Knotted around her waist was a red flannel shirt, which made its own rebellious statement as it dangled over her jean cutoffs, dancing upon her long, beautiful legs.

Rachel greeted her with a sympathetic smile, and Darby walked into her hug.

"You OK? You're *not* OK. I can tell."

"I don't know." Darby knew it was 25 years and then some, and that she hadn't mentioned Terry's name once in the time she started dating Rachel. "I'm not even sure if I have a right to feel bad, missing someone I didn't know was gone."

"Don't be like that. Losing a friend sucks. Doesn't matter if you saw him a week or five years ago." Rachel mentioned a high school friend lost in a car crash, and a guy friend she'd not kept in touch with, lost to AIDS, while in college. "There's never a satisfactory goodbye."

Darby came in and tossed her jacket to Rachel's sofa. Rachel took off her Twins hat, pushed her hair to one side, put her arms around Darby, and then put it on Darby's head.

"You look nice in dark blue. Like my Twin City special?"

"Not really," Darby said, faintly smiling. Sports talk wouldn't cheer her up.

With that, Rachel reclaimed her Twins cap and tossed it aside. She kissed Darby square on the lips, then took her hand, leading her through the dark apartment. No words, only a glance back once with a commiserative, heartening smile.

Once they made it to Rachel's bedroom, they kissed again, as Rachel pulled Darby's T-shirt up and off, and eventually buried her lips upon Darby's shoulder. Darby couldn't help touching Rachel's sultry hair.

"I like it when you play with my hair," she told Darby. Darby embraced Rachel from behind, with both of them facing a large mirror in Rachel's room. "Kiss my shoulders," Rachel said. "I want to watch."

Thoughts of watching roared Darby on. Rachel's skin was soft, probably the most delicate thing about her, and Darby had always fixated on that part of her from afar, from the first time they met. As Darby kissed, she let her fingers trace the random patterns of the dusty freckles upon Rachel's shoulder blades. Each time Darby pressed her lips, Rachel sighed.

Rachel then turned toward Darby, and pushed her down onto her bed, locking eyes. She pulled her tank top up and off, tossing it forward for Darby to catch.

"I think it's cute how you act all polite and respectful."

"Cute?"

"Cute, and frustrating," Rachel said, closing in further, climbing onto the bed, then onto her. "I know you're a little shy and all, but sometimes I wish you'd rip my clothes off."

So far, Darby had never tried to be cute, nor thought of herself as reserved or shy, or trying to be distantly respectful, nor purposely frustrating. Instead, Darby was just being normal for her. Normal, confused, hesitant, broken, the only way she knew how to be.

But Rachel sliced through all of that.

TELLIN' STORIES

Rachel and Darby were hot and a little sweaty. And afterward, Rachel was energized and inquisitive as they lay side by side. Ever since the Dust 'N' Bones show Rachel had started to pick harder at Darby's music brain.

"So, love, why are The Runaways your fave?" Rachel asked her.

Technically Dreaded Letters was Darby's all-time favorite band, but by the fall of '96 they were still mostly unknown. The Runaways were a close second, and they were about as metal as Darby could handle. But the real reason Darby took up the Runaways, Nikki And The Corvettes, and a whole library of vinyl records was that her older brother Cal had left them behind. Right after that car crash in his late teens, listening to and learning to love all his music was the only way that she knew how to grieve.

But Darby wasn't going to talk about that now. Not today.

Rachel kept probing.

"What makes the 'Queens of Noise' your go-to? Got some lifelong crush on Joan Jett?"

Darby had a real answer.

"Everything, really. They're the perfect combination of punk, metal, and glam," Darby explained. "Joan, pure punk; Lita Ford, 100% metal; Cherie Currie, total glam rock. Great rhythm section. Their songs are underrated. And the live stuff, the covers especially, are all good too." Then Darby asked Rachel: "And why do you like hair metal so much?"

Serious question. She wasn't making fun.

"It just rocks," Rachel proclaimed. "I'll have to make you a mixtape."

Darby winced. "I appreciate that, but I guess I just don't get it."

"I like the melodies, pizzazz, the flair. You know—the edge."

"And the poofy hairdos?"

Rachel laughed.

"You should see my high school pictures. Poison and Britny Fox had nothin' on me."

"Long before your days of seducing girls, in Motörhead shirts, I take it."

"Yeah, Lemmy and Motörhead got me off the hair spray look." Rachel was interested in more than music and got to what she really wanted to know. "You never talk about whom *you've* seduced, Darby. About other women. Exes, even boyfriends. Tell me about other loves."

Darby paused before speaking. Her ex-fiancée came first to mind. Alan was a handsome, ambitious, manipulative attorney, back in 21st century New York City, a life she'd left behind. Yet they had nothing in common, and their engagement followed years of dating, breaking up, getting back together and being unhappy; an experience now erased with time travel backward. Darby decided to skip Alan. "What do you want to know?"

"Normal stuff. No incriminating information," Rachel said. "Just a snapshot."

"I don't have anything super exciting to tell, unfortunately."

Over time, Rachel had told Darby about some boyfriends and that she had hooked up with other girls, but never officially dated one. There was 'first kiss boy' in middle school, named Kenny. Kenny, Rachel said, had been Rachel's guy until high school. Then it was Kevin—Rachel joked she had a "letter K fetish"—and Kevin was a standard, strong and silent quarterback type she hung onto until college. After that, her life was a mishmash of "Minnesota-nice boys" and "attractive assholes." Archetypes she said everyone dates.

"I bet young Darby didn't date much. I bet you were shy in high school."

"Well, I talked to you, didn't I?"

"Yes," Rachel said, "but I made it obvious that I *wanted* you to talk to me."

"OK. So, then, high school music nerds make great lovers at age twenty-five?"

"Maybe. I doubt a typical nice, straight guy—a dude—could fuck me like you just did. I mean, *sheesh*. You have an edge."

"Well, I had a friend die on me today. So you got my darker side." Darby's joke fizzled but she continued on. "I *have* had some steadies, you know. And I dated boys, yes, in high school, before I ever knew what I liked."

"So, tell me about it," Rachel said, entwining her long legs between Darby's. It felt safe to talk history, so Darby started backward, with the last lover, or fling, perhaps, she had before moving to New York. Or, not moving to New York now.

"Well, there was Nancy."

"*Nancy*, huh? That's a fancy name, Nancy."

"Maybe a little," she said. "That was an unusual one."

"Why? Was she crazy?"

"Crazy, no. Two decades older than me? *Yes*."

"Whoa, that explains it." Rachel joked. "Wow, you stud.

What was this Nancy like? Was she married?"

"No! Of course not."

"Did she have kids? Was she a hot mom?"

"She had no kids I knew about."

Rachel showed no signs of jealousy but wanted more. "Any other dazzling women have you romanced, Darby Derrex? What about women in bands? Madonna? Sheryl Crow?"

"No. *C'mon.*"

"What about Liz Phair? I'd do Liz Phair. She's hot. I mean, seriously."

Serious or not, Rachel knew there was more to Darby than flings and obligatory boyfriends in the straight world. Darby recounted some embarrassing teenage year episodes.

"My love life was kind of a shit show."

Darby told Rachel about her awkward first kiss with a boy named Steve Carpenter at the 1988 Super Dance for Muscular Dystrophy. That first smooch in the high school gym awarded Darby the designation as Steve's "girlfriend" for a whole two weeks in tenth grade. Then Steve dumped Darby since she wasn't a girl who would put out.

"Tenth grade? Late bloomer! When'd you lose your virginity?"

"I was nineteen. To an older woman in college. While I had a boyfriend, actually."

Then, Darby ran through a list of other men and women she'd gone out with in college, on often miserable but memorable dates. Darby's relationships, if you could call them that, were brief, thanks to them being demanding or her being emotionally unavailable.

There was Jamie, that guy she was newly dating at the University of Chicago when she'd inadvertently slept with Sandy, her Spanish professor. Darby went with Jamie to his fraternity's Western-themed *Holiday Ho-Down.* Drunk Jamie bummed cigarettes from friends and then disappeared for half the party, only to return later, sloshed and smelling like an ashtray. He called Darby "a little bitch" when she didn't want to make out with her smoky, shit-faced date.

"Ouch."

"I had one awkward, post-college relationship too." Not to disappoint, Darby described Melissa, a work colleague who was unusually forward, even more than Rachel ever was. "One Saturday we kissed in her apartment, and she wanted to sexy-up the mood."

That afternoon Melissa put on her "Love Making '94" mixtape, its name suggesting that the compilation might have been broken in on someone else. Right as the infamous Spandau Ballet song "True" came on, Melissa went down on her.

"Now every time I hear smooth jazz. Or saxophone solos," Darby said, "I remember."

"I *already* hate that song," Rachel said. "At least you got some."

Then Darby got to Lina, whom she'd never mentioned before either. Rachel wanted to know the same things about Lina, up to a point. Her personality, the circumstances, how she looked, what music she liked—hopefully not Spandau Ballet. Darby complied again.

"We met through friends," she said, shrugging her shoulders. "We were together for a year-plus. She was smart, not really a music person. Someone who reads a lot."

"An intellectual."

"Yes. But you're an intellectual too."

"Well, thank you!" Rachel said, feigning offense. "I'm more than just long legs and great hair, you know. Anyway, this Lina—what happened?"

"We got in fights over nothing, my fault mostly." *I looked for an escape. And found one,* she thought, silently. "Guess we wanted different things."

Cuddling closer with beautiful, out-of-her-league Rachel, in bed for the first time, Darby felt perfect. Even as Rachel interrogated her, she realized that no moment between them ever seemed contentious or awkward. She felt driven, almost, to tell Rachel she loved her—if that was OK with her. Someday, should the moment arise. Easy.

Darby concluded it all with a non sequitur: "Everything happens for a reason."

"Does it?" Rachel asked, looking her in the eyes, cold, with her signature smirk.

"If not," Darby said, "I wouldn't be here with you."

After the cross-examination, Rachel dozed off, spooning Darby, who was happy, but awake and staring in the dark. She thought about how good she had it now.

Later, seeing that Rachel was asleep, Darby reached down into her jeans on the floor. The time-pass watch was shoved in a pocket, glowing softly. DAYS LEFT: 44 it read.

Darby laid her head back down. Questions flashed. *So why did I leave anyhow?*

A VERY '90S PREQUEL

Bizarre Ride to the Far Side

LATE MARCH 1996, ORDINARY TIME

Long before she ever moved off to New York City, Darby fantasized about living abroad. It wasn't likely something she'd do, but one aimless Saturday she bought a travel guide in a firetrap of a used bookstore that cost $4 and provided an inexpensive, if brief, mind escapade.

Paris For Adventurers came with photo scapes of breathtaking monuments and resplendent cathedrals, plus candid pics of beautiful, quirky French people walking about cobblestone streets. Its poetic words introduced Paris as "a daring mistress," calling it a place that tourists quickly love, providing "the ideal quick and dirty fling." She'd never been to Europe and was somewhat ashamed about that. But Darby was itching to see the outside world and what lay beyond America's suburban, strip mall-laden sprawls.

Spiro had been at DePaul for grad school since the previous August, enrolled in a master's of literature program.

Yet what to do with a literature degree, if anything, was never part of the equation. Nearing May, Spiro's current quarter was nearly over, and he came by the very next day with the Chicago Tribune's travel section in hand.

"I need a vacation," he said.

"Aw. You poor guy," Darby replied.

"Check this out. There are some cheap flights to Europe we could take."

Darby and Lina had just broken up after almost a year and a half, and a trip away somewhere might get her mind off it all. Darby told Spiro she wanted no spring break antics.

"No banana schnapps. No drunken wet T-shirt contests, and no cruises," she told Spiro straight off. "And camping will only work if you want to hear me bitch the whole time."

"Spring break is over. I'm talking about skipping class." Spiro flipped through his newspaper and began pitching bargain airfares in weird, un-sunny places. "Look, $300 to Warsaw."

Darby just gave him an odd look.

"Only $228 to Sarajevo! How 'bout it?"

"How about not. Sarajevo in Yugoslavia?"

"Bosnia-Herzegovina," Spiro corrected her.

"Wasn't a war just there?"

Spiro kept flipping through and didn't answer. Then his usual tangents.

"Here. Prague! Great literary landscape there. We can hit a poetry slam!"

As if American poetry slams aren't bad enough. "OK, but— we can do that here."

The 1990s had evolved into an era of change with exciting history happening daily. The USSR had fallen, but this didn't make its former satellite countries the new Palm Springs. But Spiro's inner Indiana Jones pushed the issue as he talked about a desire for "intrepid adventures," despite these special airfares going to all the wrong places.

Yet once Spiro said, "How about Belfast?" Darby's sadistic humor pangs kicked in. How great it would be to freak out her very Irish-Catholic aunt with an irreverent postcard:

> Dear Aunt Tilly,
> Greetings from Northern Ireland! Only two bombings today.
> Still have my arms & legs... for now. The Orange Order says Hi!
> Love & Shamrocks,
> DARBY

But neither of them knew Northern Ireland from northern Iowa, and what piqued Spiro's inner agitator sounded risky to Darby. She pictured border guards asking for bribes and random guys giving her unwanted attention. Trains that didn't run. Getting stuck behind the old iron curtain. Spiro kept reading off destinations far off and far out.

"Here's one. Hong Kong, $423. Let's party like it's 1997?"

Spiro beamed, but Darby didn't like where this whole idea was going.

Then Simon came to the living room and sat, and Rod pulled up next to Spiro, cocktail in hand. Travel drew their interest. Like most Brits, Simon had been everywhere and spoke.

"Hong Kong? You don't wanna go there, mate. It's a huge, very expensive city." Simon cast off any notions about shoe-string travel there. "Fifty quid might barely get you lunch."

Darby was happy for Simon to butt in and maybe he could steer Spiro right. Besides, she couldn't see a 15-hour flight to Asia. She'd strangle Spiro before landing.

"Hong Kong's fine for business," Simon added. "Rod's been there, too, right?" Rod nodded yes. "But if your work isn't paying the tab, it's not really the place."

"They do have nightclubs. Good nightlife," added Rod. Then Rod, being Rod, took the conversation off-path, talking about the kung fu film circuit—gun battles, heists, action film stuff. Rod mentioned the movie *Hard Boiled* with Chow Yun-fat, where, as Roddy explained:

> Inspector Tequila takes on gun-toting mobsters, fighting them off—all while holding a baby he's rescued. He takes a bullet—the hero, not the baby—and at the end, he puts a gangster through a glass door. He wipes a dead thug's blood off of the baby's head. The baby smiles.

After the film's brief re-creation, Rod imparted a final suggestion before going out for a smoke. "Go instead to Thailand, for the beaches. Or Macao. Great for gambling."

"OK. Thanks, Rod."

Darby now had second thoughts about the whole thing. Maybe Spiro should go alone, and send that Belfast postcard, signed in gun powder and blood, and she could save her vacation days. But other rates Spiro then began reading from the paper sounded better.

"What about Amsterdam? Only $199. Paris too."

"WELL—That's kind of a steal," Simon said.

"What airlines?" Darby asked. "Does it say?"

"Majors. There's no Air Chechnya if that's what you're worried about."

Simon said that the next month before tourist season was perfect, and "because of everything going on in the world, continental Europe is very cheap now." He explained that rich countries like France, Germany, and Luxembourg were busy bickering about a new currency called *the euro*, and about which countries could and couldn't join the new, cool kids club called the European Union. This drama made the dollar "strong," Simon said, and European currencies "weak," so things like lodging, meals, souvenirs, and booze were cheap for Americans. Darby wanted to extinguish any further ideas Spiro had about post-Communist countries or hanging out with "authentic locals" in some shithole tavern in Stalingrad.

"Paris could be fun," she said. "Think of poets and novelists who lived in Paris, Spiro. Hemingway, F. Scott Fitzgerald." Darby couldn't think of any others, but that would do.

"Whoa!" Spiro perked up. "Paris—Fitzgerald! Big Papa! YES!"

Plus, they had a friend to visit. "We can see Ry-Guy while we're there," Darby told him. "He's got that internship nearby, and he can give us a tour."

"OK. Deal!" Spiro replied. "But we have to hit Amsterdam first."

Simon backed this up. "Yeah, you two should fly there, take the EuroRail down to Paris. Cheap stay in the 'Dam, short train ride. Then you see both places."

"They speak English there, don't they?" Darby asked.

"Everyone does in Amsterdam," Simon said. "Come to think of it, that's a good way to start. A place where they can understand you Midwestern yokels."

"I'm *not* from the Midwest," she said.

A week later Darby and Spiro had their trip planned. Their college pal Ryan Nakamoto was working as an architect on a historic preservation fellowship outside Paris. Darby exchanged postcards regularly with Ry-Guy, and he had written that they should "come hang."

Stylistically, Ry-Guy was the polar opposite of Spiro. Well-polished and about 5' 8", his black hair was always perfectly slicked to the side, golf shirts always tucked into crisply pressed pants. Ry wore expensive designer shoes that were never not shiny-as-hell. And despite his clean-cut looks, Ry-Guy had a sharp, sarcastic edge.

The weekend before departure, Darby and Spiro called Ry-Guy international/long distance. Noon in Chicago was evening over there. They put Ry on speakerphone, and the call went like every conversation they'd ever had before with him.

"Yo!" Ry-Guy said, sounding preoccupied yet buoyant as always. "What up, punk?"

Darby said hello. Spiro said, "I'm here too."

"That's why I said *punk*, bitch!" Ry said he was about to head out drinking on the town. "Too bad you're not here now. You coming over, or what?"

"Hitting Amsterdam first."

"Pick me up some weed, bro."

"No can do," Darby said.

"Bullshit. Get me some pot brownies. Spiro—*you's my ganja-bitch!*"

Immediately, they knew that seeing Ry-Guy on the far side of the Atlantic would either make the strange land of Europe more familiar or just outright bizarre.

"So, what do we do when we're there?" Spiro asked.

"Drink and get fucked up. That's just what Americans do in other people's countries."

YOUR OWN PRIVATE
AMSTERDAM

APRIL 15, 1996

Darby never could sleep on airplanes, but persisting with insomnia was one of her expert skills. She would need that and a sense of humor once they left America.

Their flight left Chicago on a Monday night, placing them at Airport Schiphol (pronounced *SKIP-ple*, Spiro said) early next morning, with the ocean blearily forwarding the hours in between. The airplane was loud but stocked with standard comforts. One thing about KLM, the official royal Dutch airline, was that all of their flight attendants were tall and remarkably beautiful. They made safety announcements to passengers in English but spoke to each other in Dutch, an intriguing language that, to Darby, made them sound like they had golf balls in their mouths. Before landing, the in-flight TVs showed classic episodes of *Mr. Bean*.

Prior to departing, Spiro found a list of travel necessities recommended for first-time travelers, which he "downloaded"

from the Internet—meaning he printed it—to help them pack.
It read like a list of summer camp items:

> *A quality jacket and compact umbrella, or a*
> *   raincoat*
> *Travel-size toiletries*
> *Flip-flops, in case the showers are nasty*
> *Comfortable walking shoes*
> *A sleeping bag*
> *Something to read*

A more pragmatic list on a different travel website implored
other things:

> *Your passport and a photocopy of it, in case it*
> *   gets stolen*
> *Cash in foreign currency. For this trip: French*
> *   francs, Dutch guilders*
> *Travelers cheques, in case an ATM eats your*
> *   debit card*
> *Something for carrying your money besides a*
> *   back-pocket wallet*
> *A roll of your own toilet paper*

That same list mentioned things <u>not to bring</u> when traveling
abroad:

> *Pets*
> *Illegal drugs, or any type of drug paraphernalia*
> *Pocket knives or things that can be construed*
> *   as weapons*
> *Big folding maps that scream "Look, I'm a*
> *   tourist!"*

The travel lit also said it was customary to choose hostels upon arrival in the Dutch port city, and Simon corroborated this. Spiro mentioned that they were going to have company for one day. His friend Cecily, really an ex-girlfriend, was still in college at age 28, studying art through the University of Cleveland's exchange abroad program. So, they'd have a knowledgeable Amsterdam guide for at least a day.

Other than a one-time family Cancun trip, it was Darby's first time outside America, and she was once warned by Lina that she might have a huge "holy shit moment." The first real glimpse came after the airport monorail dumped them off at Amsterdam Centraal, the main city train station. It was a courtly building in its own right, with two clock towers spread across its gunwale, facing an open brick plaza. That morning the city was fastidiously minding its own business, with bicycles and jaywalkers zigzagging along crowded, time-charred streets. There were few billboards, no honking cars, and instead of Burger King signs littering skylines, they saw steeples that read "1645" and "AD 1397." There were no in-your-face, 50-story structures named for insurance companies or industry titans. Amsterdam's immediate charm definitely belied the bombastic reputations that big American cities had. During the Carter and Reagan years, America's children were taught that cities—*the inner city* it was called then—were awful, crime-ridden hellholes. Quaint Amsterdam was the opposite.

Spiro had things besides 600-year-old landmarks on his mind.

"Look: Coffee shop!"

They walked down a street called Damrak, away from the station, and there were coffee shops with pun-filled names like Green Belt, Hi-Fidelity, and Bong Jovi, after the band.

"Look, another! Coffee shop!" Spiro sounded like an ornithologist spotting falcons.

"I could use some coffee. Like now," Darby told him. She had probably slept 60 minutes total on the flight over, and no more than 10 of them were consecutive.

"I didn't say cafe," Spiro lectured. "Coffee shops are where you get the ganja!"

Darby told Spiro "I know," and that she had read their travel book on Amsterdam too. "I don't want to get stoned right now. It's seven in the morning."

Darby first wanted to find a place to stay. And coffee, not coffee shops, was what she craved. Besides caffeine, a place to nap would do. She counted back the hours and figured out that in Chicago it was around 1 A.M., and that she would normally be tossing and turning in her own uncomfortable bed about then. Then, their backpacks gave them away.

"Ay, there, Americans. Looking for a room? A hostel, yeah?" A tall guy in an overcoat approached them. He held brochures and seemed on the up and friendly enough, introducing himself as Henry, with a middle-England brogue. His accent and long hair made him seem like a convivial and more articulate Ozzy Osbourne. "Welcome to The Netherlands. First time?"

"Yup."

"Great. You'll be needing a place to stay, then?"

"Yes, we're looking for a hostel," Darby said. She noticed that they weren't the only new arrivals fumbling out of the train station plaza. "Yours in a safe area?"

"Oh, you're safe in Amsterdam," Henry said, "unless you go looking for trouble."

"Well, I'm looking for trouble," Spiro said, "I've got a coffee date soon."

"Ay?" Henry didn't get Spiro's line.

"Never mind. What's the name of your place?" Darby asked, as more clueless American travelers materialized, seeing some getting hit up by scruffy, drugged-out panhandlers.

144

"It's called the Funky Chicken."

Spiro said to Darby that with a name like Funky Chicken it meant they *had* to stay there. "Funky Chicken? Sounds like a dance move I used to do."

"Haha. Yes, I see." Henry wasn't much for Spiro's quips, but was polite about it. "Unusual name, yes, but we have the highest ratings. Big windows in every room. Double locks on the doors. And we take credit cards now." He gave them a rate that sounded reasonable and said they could pay in dollars, British pounds, or guilders. Darby asked Henry what they could do in town that didn't involve cannabis and prostitutes.

"See the Rijksmuseum, the Jewish Museum, any of them, really. Vondelpark, too—it's a beautiful place to walk around, or play footie or hacky-sack."

Eight minutes later they were there. The hostel had a big sign outside, in all caps:

WELCOME TO THE FUNKY CHICKEN

Henry left Darby and Spiro to a college-aged lad and a woman who showed them what the rooms looked like on the first floor. The innkeepers said they could leave their packs in a locker until their room was ready at 11 o'clock, after the hostel's cleaning.

Clean was good. But all Darby wanted to do was sleep. All Spiro wanted to do was blaze a fat doobie at a coffee shop.

"I just need to wake up a little, and get coffee and food," Darby said. She wanted to get to know the place a little before descending into a cannabis haze.

"Fine," Spiro said.

145

Darby woke up a few hours later from a nap that began milliseconds after her head hit the pillow. By then, it was about 3 P.M. local time, and it was the best sleep she'd remember having, perhaps ever. Her eyes stared up at the A-frame ceiling above, and then she got up to look out a window that was wide open with no screen. She could smell that room was clean, thanks to the "Guests: No Smoking / Toking In Rooms" signs stapled onto the walls.

"Good morning, er, *excuse me*—afternoon," Spiro said to Darby, who rubbed her eyes and said good afternoon back. "Can't believe you slept after drinking all that coffee."

Between their Funky Chicken check-in and being let into the room, Spiro and Darby killed a few hours walking around, but she didn't remember more than a few licks of it.

"What did we do?"

"A lot," Spiro told her.

He said that first they stopped into a pub, drank coffee, ate blocks of Dutch cheese.

"Oh, right. I remember."

Spiro said they saw hordes of Dutch parents walking very blond babies in high-design strollers. They passed rows and rows of colonial-era homes before they wandered accidentally into the Red Light District. Scantily clad women stood in windows of the 'Dam's fabled sex shops, next to more 600-year-old churches. Then they strolled into the Rijksmuseum and saw works by Dutch masters.

"You kind of got into it with the door guy," Spiro said of their museum visit.

They had walked the entire first two floors of the place before trying to find the exit, only for Darby to be stopped by a security guard on the way out. The guard, who was very tall but looked like he was 14 years old, took issue with Darby's small backpack, fearing that a quick turnaround might knock over a sculpture.

"You were like, 'Why do I need to check my bag?' and he was like 'Madam, you must relinquish your bag, so as not to damage zees fine works. It would cause much consternation.'"

"Much consternation? He said that?"

"Totally. His English was remarkable! *Anyway*, they thought you'd break something." Spiro hinted that Darby's American brusqueness scared off the baby-faced guard.

On the way back to the hostel, they decided to enter one of those weird sex toy shops, mainly because the store's doors were wide open. Spiro said that made it seem less risqué, as other tourists had a look too. Passersby shuffled through the shop and its long U-shaped aisle, and now Darby remembered the shop owner's English.

"We're not a museum," the shopkeeper yelled to everyone. "Buy something, or have a nice day and get out!"

Right after Darby crashed, Spiro slipped out to use the phone, and to grab some falafel and a few bottles of Gatorade—good for jet lag, he claimed—then read while she slept.

"I got halfway through *this* while you conked out." Spiro held up a battered Howard Zinn paperback. "Got 730 pages here. I'm half done. Hope you're rested."

"Bet you *can* eat pot brownies in here," she said, pointing to the "No Toking" signs.

"I did," Spiro said. "Just a small one—a *fun-size* space cake. Wore off already."

A knock came to the door.

"Sit. I'll get it," Darby said, standing up, grabbing her towel. "I'll go take a shower."

Darby opened the door and a hiply dressed young woman was there.

"Hi, is Alex here?" she said.

Darby had only heard about Cecily in past tense. Spiro once described her as "fun but a little spoiled" and also "nice and spunky but sometimes crazy." Whatever she was, Darby got the door with an open mind.

"You mean Mr. Spiro? Yes, he's hiding in here under a book. I'm Darby."

"Oh, hi." Cecily said, sounding tepid, as if coming by wasn't a good idea or she'd walked in on them. But when she saw Spiro, Cecily's face lit up, as did Spiro's. "Hi, Punkin!" she said to him sweetly, making Spiro blush. Whatever their unfinished business, it was lovey for now.

"I'm Darby," she said again. "I know this clown from college."

"We were in clown college together!" Spiro chirped.

"Sorry. I'm Cecily," she said, embarrassed, which prompted Spiro to return to normal colors. "I'm a little spaced-out today. Amsterdam does that to you."

"That's what I heard," Darby said.

"That's why we're here," Spiro added.

Darby left to let them have a moment. Soon, they had sightseeing to do.

Cecily told the two of them they would "see everything Amsterdam has to offer" if they just walked toward Vondelpark. Together, they passed pubs and more old buildings, slim by American standards, each four or five floors high, with long windows and cursive A-shaped rooftops. The tight, crowded streets were hugged by brick bridges that rose and descended gracefully over each canal. Today's venture would be about just feeling the pace and spirit of Amsterdam.

Cecily's walk was more of a stroll, fitting for the chunky, yellow-stitched punk rock boots she wore. Her slow roll gave her and Spiro a chance to catch up on things that happened in their lives, while Darby took in the sights without excessive description. She noticed Cecily's edgy style and her hair— short, dyed black, pulled to the side and held in place by kitschy, pink girly barrettes. The fact that she was pushing 30 years old didn't take from the trendy bite of her gingham flannel, ripped jeans over black leggings, or the lace choker around her neck. Her look fit the times and the city she lived in and she wasn't faking it by any stretch.

Eventually, she checked on Darby. "You OK back there?"

"I'm good!" Darby appreciated Cecily not wanting her to feel left out.

Spiro brought up coffee shops again.

"Here's a really good one," Cecily said.

A place called Beatrix was named graciously, or perhaps irreverently, after The Kingdom of the Netherlands' Royal Queen. It had a chalkboard sign out front boasting wide selections of cannabis strains and beverages. Cecily said it also had a nice beer garden out back.

"So, people really do this here?" Darby asked, as they walked inside.

"Do what?"

"Partake in smoking weed?"

"Absolutely," Cecily said.

When it came to the selection, Darby let Cecily and Spiro drive. She picked a table out back as the other two looked for something to pack an easy, gradual buzz.

Sitting outside seemed to make the occasion feel less illicit than the other times Darby smoked pot back home. Instead, they were surrounded by people engaging in normal, public place conversations. Cecily sat down and fired up a joint, and after a few tokes, passed it onto Spiro, who stopped to sing to a familiar-sounding 1970s song that came on the outdoor speakers.

"I want you-ooo-ooh. To roll me a jay."

Cecily sang, with Spiro. *"Every day!"*

Spiro sang it louder, line after line, pointing right in Darby's face.

"I want you, you, you. To toke on this jay."

"Stop it," Darby said.

Spiro didn't stop but added some wah-wah pedal and air guitar to ham it up. Cecily sat up perkily and lit a second spliff of her own, laughing and entertained by Spiro's carefree ways and stupid-stoned vaudeville act. Darby smoked a little but mostly watched Cecily and Spiro light up and swallow them down while 1970s hits continued to play.

Darby asked Cecily again about the local pastime, smoking cannabis in coffee shops. She wondered if the practice of it ever became humdrum.

"So... does smoking weed in Amsterdam ever—get old?"

Cecily shrugged her shoulders. "Nope. Why would it?"

After a final round of toking, Spiro stopped singing and Darby wondered more about this Vondelpark everyone spoke of vividly. Cecily and Spiro said they'd both use the restroom, and then they could head over.

Out front of the shop, Darby waited for the other two, for what seemed like a while. It let her look at the sights of Amsterdam's bustling street activity. But as the solitude sank in, Darby started thinking about Lina, missing Lina, wishing she hadn't screwed things up. She couldn't do anything about it right then and there, and Darby remembered that she was on the other side of a fucking ocean.

A minute later, the door swung open fast, almost hitting her. Spiro and Cecily tumbled out of it, chuckling hysterically. Darby smiled, wondering what the deal was.

"You guys go back for seconds? You get flushed down the toilet?"

With that, Cecily burst into more snarling laughter. Spiro looked at Cecily and then Darby, his eyes cashed, cackling like a kid caught binging Halloween candy. Darby shrugged her shoulders and figured they speed-smoked something extra, before they walked on.

About 20 minutes later over a slow, quiet walk to Vondelpark, Darby noticed Spiro and Cecily were acting weird; weird even for stoned people. They let out ridiculous guffaws together in unison every few minutes. Just laughing and no talking. Spiro eventually spoke.

"Tastes like cork!" he said randomly, picking at his tongue.

"What does?" Darby said, and she turned around, to find that a second later Cecily was sitting on a park bench aside the path behind them. Cecily then started rocking forward, laughing harder than before, her eyes out to infinity. "She OK?" Darby asked, getting no answer.

Spiro, in turn, looked at Cecily and then looked at Darby, and then began his own laughing barrage at Cecily, who was laughing hysterically herself.

"Hey, guys? *Guys?*"

Neither uttered anything but giggles, drubbing it out like a spaced-out Beavis & Butt-Head. After several minutes more their laughs swelled down and Cecily got up to walk again. Steps later, an endless patch of grass appeared. As Henry the hostel guide described earlier that day, Vondelpark was active, beautiful, magnificent.

"Check it out." Darby pointed out people playing soccer in the distance, and a small crew of people closer by kicking a hacky-sack. There were clusters of sightseers and students out in the afternoon sun, some reading, others sitting around in clumps of five or ten people.

Cecily sat down again. Once her butt hit the edge of the grass, she gabbled and giggled again uncontrollably. Spiro returned to laughing too.

"Hey! You guys sniff some paint?" Darby's mere question

turned their mouth-bobbling up five notches. Spiro made eye contact while laughing, but Cecily was in her own haze and started rocking again. Then Spiro got a grip long enough to share something.

"We ate some mushrooms," he said to Darby. Spiro elaborated: "We ate... some... hallucinative... magic... mushrooms."

This must have been why it took them so long to leave the coffee shop and why they were acting so damn strange now. Darby was annoyed and suddenly felt like a chaperone.

Luckily, about 50 feet across the grass Darby spotted a man with a coffee cart. "Stay here," she said to the other two, and a minute later Darby came back with three hot cups of coffee. Maybe some caffeine would push the psilocybin giggles out of them, she thought.

Upon receiving his cup, Spiro perked up, saying, "excellent, excellent." Cecily finally made eye contact, and Spiro resumed his singing. This time, a rendition of another familiar 1970s tune:

"You're living in your own... private... Amsterdam."
"You're living in your own private Amsterdam!"

Darby ignored Spiro's singing and looked over to Cecily, whose eyes were pretty red. She tried to make idle conversation to liven up her drugged-out friends, Cecily in particular.

"Great skyline. Nice town ya got here," Darby said to Cecily.

Cecily nodded and then stood up, and after stabilizing both feet, she made an about-face turn toward some hedges behind them. Cecily then vomited loudly into a flowering bush. Spiro registered only a very surprised expression.

After Cecily was done puking, she reclaimed her seat and they sat, saying nothing while looking at the gorgeous sights of Amsterdam's biggest park. Darby had something she wanted to share but didn't want to be a jerk about it. Then again, Cecily probably wouldn't remember.

"For someone who lives in Amsterdam," she said, "you don't hold your drugs well."

WELCOME TO PARIS, FOOL

APRIL 18, 1996

The EuroRail train to Paris felt inherently safe despite its bullet-like speeds, and it reminded Darby of the monorail she once rode at Disney World. She and Spiro watched tiny, zipping Fiats and Peugeots on the highway beside them, failing to match the train's pace.

On the way out of Amsterdam, they caught a view of the Dutch countryside's tulip fields of gold, blue, and magenta. Spinning windmills looked like they were high-fiving each other. And with four hours to Paris, Darby could attempt to nap to the train's hum, while Spiro doodled passages in his leather-bound journal.

Since arriving in the top-left corner of Europe, they had walked a lot and seen a lot of the small city. During their second and third days in Amsterdam, Darby kept them off harsher substances, and Thursday they got up early enough to enjoy real sit-down breakfast before noon in preparation for hitting two other museums and the Amstel Brewery. Each morning after the first day, Darby chose not to partake. Hot caffeine and spring sunshine were enough.

Eventually, they hit that coffee shop called Bong Jovi. Darby wanted to go, only because its name was music-related, while kitschy and ludicrous, and she hoped they might even sell Bong Jovi T-shirts. There, Spiro had a last cannabis fill while Darby people-watched.

The mere speed change from fast to slow woke Darby up as the train slid into Paris. Their promenade into The City of Lights was a sedate crawl and it allowed a comfortable wakeup before they hit the terminal. Once they arrived at Gare du Nord station, Spiro unveiled his "downloaded" directions to their place of accommodation and said the walk would take 20 minutes if they didn't get lost.

The first sights of Paris won Darby over immediately, and she decided straight away that its beauty was not debatable. You could be the most closed-minded, inbred American possible, she thought. You can despise the French, laugh at their berets, hate their tendency to put eggs on everything, hate their snails on a plate or even their crusty bread. But you couldn't dislike the city of Paris if you tried.

As the two of them walked to find their quarters, Spiro looked up repeatedly at each block, for street names on building corners, since there were few American-style street signs on metal posts. Darby again lazily enjoyed the sights as they ambled in and out of tiny, slaloming lanes. They looked for a street called Rue Dumonde, and the number *343* atop a doorway, somewhere down a slight hill. The surrounding paths looked more like alleys, and nothing on Dumonde's sleepy path looked like a hostel or an inn. Then they heard a voice.

"What's up, punks?"

Darby looked up and saw Ry's head pop out a third- or fourth-floor window.

"Oh, hey, Ry-Guy."

"I could totally spit on you two right now," Ry said, in his usual smart-ass way. He continued his warm greetings with fake gags and mucus sounds before deciding to act his age. Ry said he'd heard them talking and sounding lost from above. "Welcome to Paris, fools!"

Ry-Guy made his way downstairs and popped out an old door. They said their hellos, and Darby pointed out an Italian-style eatery across the street, suggesting they get something. At a table outside, they sat and Ry asked about Amsterdam.

"You guys get high? You get *super wasted*?"

"Spiro did, for sure. His ex-girlfriend did too."

"D'you guys go to Amnesia?"

"I did," Spiro said, looking at Darby. "No, I did. While you were napping." Spiro explained that was where he got the "fun size" pot brownies.

After telling Ry what he wanted to hear about coffee shop stops, they ordered food and drank beers, while Ry smoked. Ryan said he'd gotten in late that morning, and he was more dressed down than normal, wearing flip-flops, shorts, and a Depeche Mode T-shirt. Darby, the pickiest music lover of the three, took issue.

"Still listen to terrible bands?"

"F that, man. Depeche rules!"

Just like Darby hated Bon Jovi, Darby hated Depeche Mode and their sullen, moaning singer even more. Darby asked Spiro what he thought and got a typical answer.

"Depeche Mode? Well, they're not Miles Davis or any-thing."

"Miles who?" Ry scoffed, before going back to his main issue. "You bring me ganja?"

"We brought just ourselves," Darby said, "and our love for Jesus."

Ryan replied as expected: "Sheee-it."

After they were done, the trio went for a walk about town. Ry advised they head toward a place called the Jardin du Celaise, a grove surrounded by walls that guarded it against street noise, with hedges cut into cool, artistic shapes. The park's gravel paths crunched under their feet as they walked among trees and blooms in the peaceful garden. Spiro saw it as a place with cover for partaking in other greens. He pulled out a couple of joints he'd bought in Amsterdam, explaining simply, "Thank the ganja gods—open borders!"

"See, told you," Ry said. "You are my ganja-bitches!"

Spiro lit up one of the spliffs like it was no big deal, right as a French couple walked by with two toddlers in tow. The parents glanced disapprovingly at Spiro before their rambunctious kids distracted them by running in circles and falling pants-first into the gravel.

"Hey," Darby said, "don't you guys think you should do that somewhere more discreet?"

"Where?" both asked.

"Anywhere more secluded."

"This is secluded. Look at these big-ass trees!" Ry said.

Once Spiro got the blunt's fire roaring, he sucked down a huge puff and blew it upward, then passed it on to Ry-Guy, as other heads turned.

"Drugs aren't legal here like in Amsterdam. You wanna get arrested?"

"No one cares here," Ry-Guy said. "C'est la vie."

A short walk through a tall sunflower patch let the two of them burn down their joints and blow the smoke upward in secret. Darby had frankly enough of European park benches after Cecily's laugh-in, but Spiro at least stopped singing. Ry lit up a cig and Spiro counted his remaining joints, as they walked out of the sunflowers and back onto the crunchy gravel.

Ten minutes later two darkly dressed people approached. Police.

"Hello, sirs," one of them said in English, as they stopped them in their path.

The officer who spoke first was probably 6' 2" and looked intimidating. Darby had never heard that the French were tall—quite the opposite, actually—but this Frenchman had linebacker shoulders, and his partner, a woman with blond hair wrapped tightly under her rimmed police cap, was also taller than each of them. She alone looked physical enough to tackle any hooligan who might run for it. Clearly, they hadn't appeared to offer sightseeing tips.

"Yes, hello sirs," he said again. "Are you American?" Both Spiro and Darby nodded, looking guilty. "May I ask you just about your stays in Paris today?"

Darby felt nervous and conjured up scenes in her mind of prison films. She stood silently and reconciled that hanging with Spiro and Ry-Guy would be less fun in a grimy jail, or that a French women's prison couldn't be much better. Spiro too was silent and stuck his hands in his pockets. Ry spoke up.

"Bonjour, *officiers*," Ry said, as he introduced himself by name, *Monsieur Nakamoto*. Almost bowing, Ry started talking like a tour guide who was showing his esteemed colleagues around. Darby and Spiro nodded nervously. Both of the cops seemed less-than-impressed with Ry's explanations or credentials. The linebacker policeman spoke again.

"Très bien. Certains résidents ont signalé des comporte-ments illégaux dans ce parc."

"Comme quoi?" Ryan asked back.

Not wanting to trifle with Ry's French, the linebacker cop got to it in English. "We have the report of people engaged in prohibit-teed activities." The policewoman almost smirked as her fellow officer signaled with his handwork that he was talking about smoking something, most definitely cannabis.

"Do you know, that is, cannabis est *illégal?*" said the blond officer.

The words "illegal" and "cannabis" validated Darby's fear. The officers seemed certain to make an arrest of the first Americans they could find. Yet, Ry was prone to make up random shit. Darby just had never heard him do it in French.

He explained: "Mes amis ici, ils sont un peu timides. Mais oui. Certains enfants américains étaient comme, '*Like yo dudes! Wanna buy some weed, bro?*'" Ry described fictional youths with California accents pushing weed. "We are Ameri-can, but we don't do drugs, sir!"

Then the policeman's walkie-talkie went off, signaling a more critical matter. Distracted, the French linebacker cop said, "OK!" and it looked as if they had to depart in haste.

"Bonne journée," said the policewoman, who gave them a long, incredulous look.

Darby felt her heart slow down and thanked their lucky stars. "Holy shit! I thought we were going to jail," she said as she struggled to regain her breath.

But Ry-Guy acted like he had it all figured out from the beginning.

"They don't arrest Americans here. Unless you steal a police car," Ry-Guy said. "Or maybe if you run buck-naked around the Arc de Triomphe with a rifle or something."

"What the hell did you tell them?"

Unfazed by the whole thing, Ry waited until the officers were further away, then broke out into laughter like a TV villain. He lit another cigarette, then answered.

"I told them that some other little American punks, not us, were bothering people."

Spiro was puzzled. "So—you *do* speak French?"

"Sure. A little," Ryan said. "Only when I'm super fucking stoned."

The next morning Spiro wanted to go to Père Lachaise, a famous cemetery best known as the resting place of Jim Morrison. Other accomplished composers such as Chopin, Rossini and Bizet had all beat The Doors' legend there, along with 20th-century vocalist Maria Callas. The literary icons buried in the cemetery's tombs—Oscar Wilde, Proust, and Molière—were a draw for many travelers, and for Spiro too, but he mentioned Morrison first.

"Jim Morrison—who cares?" Ry said, trying to get a rise out of Spiro. "The Doors suck ass. Sounds like church music."

"Like their music or not," Spiro shot back, "Jim Morrison's an icon. A legend!"

"No way man."

"Better than your club-hopping Depeche Mode crap," Spiro said, getting testy.

They passed the cemetery's gates and Spiro taunted Ry by dissing his music. He imitated the jumpy, cheesy *boom-chicka-boom* sounds heard about nightclub dance floors, also making fake organ grunts and *awk! awk!* squeaks. Ry didn't have much of a response.

"Ry-Guy, you listen to techno Euro-trash porno flick music!" Spiro said. "So sad."

"Shut up, fool." That, followed by a din of silence, was Ry's big comeback.

Darby followed the two arguing clowns along, hoping to find some passed-on punk musicians or buried blues artists interred there that she could relate to. Spiro took pictures of graves, while Ry-Guy mocked their names.

"Look! Ball sack!"

"Balzac," Spiro said adamantly. "He was a great novelist and playwright."

Yet Ry kept making fun of the departed. Upon seeing a tombstone naming Jacques MacDonald, Ry asked why it didn't have golden arches on it.

"Wrong spelling, dummy," Spiro said, this time in a ruder tone.

"Don't talk shit about the dead, Ry," Darby said. "They might hear you."

"No way, sucka. C'mon, Spiro. Take your pics of Ronald McDonald and Slim Jim Morrison and let's go. I wanna drink!"

Darby wanted a drink too, and the other two made her need a few. After a half-hour of a slow pace, snapping pics, and arguing, Darby tried to speed things along. "Look, I gotta use the bathroom." She didn't really have to go, but Ry's response was predictable.

"They got trees. Go over there. That looks like a nice oak to pee on."

"I'm not gonna pee in a cemetery, man."

"Aw, c'mon," Ry said. "Give Spiro one real reason to take a picture here."

"OK, F this," Spiro said. "Thanks for ruining it."

The three of them snaked toward the nearest exit, yet right in a lane of mismatched stones and obelisks, Jim Morrison's tomb finally made an appearance. Spiro pulled out his pocket camera again, snapping every angle of it. The singer's resting place was surrounded by handpicked flowers, notes, and mementos from fans and visitors. There were drawings of the singer and a six-pack of beer someone left there, plus dense glass bottles with misshapen, melted candles sticking out of them. Other visitors had left behind postcards from Stockholm, Bellingham, Madrid, Los Angeles, Caracas, and Edmonton.

But Ry-Guy wouldn't let up. "Come on, Spiro! She's gotta pee. And I gotta drink!"

Spiro got his photos and appeared satisfied before they made their way out. Darby hoped to lighten the mood with chitchat. Then like a break in the clouds, Ry-Guy softened the animosity and decided to be somewhat human if not a tolerable Paris guide.

"I'll get the wine and beers. Drinks are on me, punks."

At a bistro a block away, the sunshine settled upon their outdoor seating. At first pour, Darby's buddies no longer poked at each other. The next two hours they boozed and ate bread, and all of it made the day not such a disaster after all.

YANKEE
COCKROACHES

APRIL 21, 1996

Next day was their last full day in Europe, and Darby wanted to make the most of it. The capital's vivid skylines charmed her every step, and the favorable exchange rate let her and her buds fill up on more unnecessary midday booze and baked revelations. Most of the day, Ry and Darby followed Spiro, who took pictures of everything and nothing, while the boys plotted enough time to bicker and make fun of each other's clothes, hair, music, and general existence.

Later, after Sunday evening's wine-bread-dinner trifecta, they zigzagged the Left Bank's tiny streets, while looking for one last thing to do. Ry suggested shooting pool. Spiro talked about coffee, but Darby didn't want to get jacked up on caffeine the night before flying out. From the looming dusk, two young men appeared and wanted attention for reasons unknown.

"Hello! You are American!" said one of them. Ry lit up a

smoke and Spiro nodded.

Both men were smartly dressed like greasers, hair perfectly gelled, looking like they'd stepped off the set of *West Side Story* or out of a 1950s-themed American diner. They wore Marlon Brando leather jackets, jeans, and glossy shoes that reflected the streetlights above.

Greaser #1 spoke again. "I see you *must* be American! Yes, yes."

Harmless, Ry-Guy took these weirdos and their greetings as an opportunity to make fun. He responded, "American, yes! Pizza Hut, yes! Mickey Mouse, yes."

Greaser #2 spoke. "So, you *are* from th' States! Haha, yes, no funny business!"

Ry and Darby looked at each other, not knowing what "no funny business" meant. Maybe a signal that they were not getting robbed.

Spiro detected a German accent and replied: "Wie geht's. Ich sprech' Deutsch."

"Ah yes," said the one with Elvis hair. He was eager for information. "Vee are—how do you say?—looking for some camaraderie!"

Elvis's buddy, very blond like many Germans are, was fashioned more like James Dean, and he launched into some chat only Spiro understood: "Ja—yes, you see, my friend. Wir sind an guten Zeiten interessiert, denn, wissen Sie, heute Abend etwas Spaß."

Spiro thought whatever Elvis and James Dean were talking about was worth a smile.

"We're not from here, but," said Spiro. "Wir sind gerad' im Urlaub, *you know.*"

James Dean said, "Wissen Sie, wo sich der Ort namens 'Renoncule' befindet?—*as you say in American, the butter-cup?*"

Elvis repeated this phrase, *buttercup*, emphatically. "*Le Renon-see-yool.*"

Spiro was trying to be helpful but didn't know what the German boys were talking about. Ry-Guy became impatient, lit up another cigarette, and looked to Darby, equally puzzled. Spiro tried more to sort it out.

"Le Renoncule? Ich weiß nicht. Aber es gibt viele gute Weinbars," Spiro pointed to the street and the bistro they'd just departed from. The German greasers laughed and Elvis pulled out a cigarette. Ry-Guy approached and gave him a light.

"Oh, das tut mir leid. Ich war nicht klar," Elvis said.

James Dean piped in: "Ja. Es ist ein legendäres Bordell."

Spiro laughed. James Dean pulled out a comb to groom his already perfect hair.

"Nein," Spiro responded. "*Sorry*—dass ich nicht helf'n kann." Spiro then shrugged.

It was the end of the discussion and the greasers looked deflated and slightly embarrassed. They gave a gracious wave as they said goodnight, and walked back into the dusk.

"Check ya later!" Ry-Guy yelled.

Darby was curious. "What did you guys talk about?"

"You know, two dudes looking for shit to do." Spiro said this with a huge smile.

Ry-Guy still found their German-ness reason to poke fun. "It's 1950s night in Paris!" Ry-Guy then flexed like Schwarzenegger. "Day vant to pump some iron?"

"Ha, no."

Ryan joked again. "A place to eat some big German wieners?"

"Quite the opposite," Spiro said.

Darby felt drizzle wet her head and wanted to get a move on. Spiro could elaborate further while they walked. "So what did Elvis and the Deaner want?" she asked him.

"Well, they asked me if we'd just patronized an important nearby establishment," Spiro said, laughing. "Some high-class brothel called *The Buttercup*."

"We should find it!" Ry-Guy said. "Let's go."

"Sounds *lovely*," Darby said sarcastically. "But I'm not into brothel girls."

By about 9 P.M. the sun hadn't really retired. Flying over, a nice old lady on the plane had told Darby that Europe's brighter evenings came from the sun's light hitting the earth's curve during spring, making the sun appear to set later. The sun, for sure, seemed unwilling to sleep, wanting to amble the Paris streets and participate in the three friends' evening hijinks. But the skies still dangled the idea of rain in a very flippant, French way, and every other moment Darby felt a spritz unseen fall on her head. They were somewhere between the Seine River and the garden where Ry talked them out of getting arrested, and no one had an umbrella. Darby pulled out a misshapen paper map that had lost its color.

"Put that shit away, man," Ry said. "I know where we are." Ry then said that just up the hill were places to hang out. Spiro added that Ernest Hemingway's one-time residence was ahead too, and pulled out his leather journal to review his notes about the place. A minute later they turned onto a street called Rue Mouffetard, where most inns looked closed for the night.

"Look, they named this street after you," Ry said to Spiro, mispronouncing the name. "Boulevard Moof Tard."

"It's Moovff-a-TAR," Spiro said.

"Well, today it's Moof Tard," Ry said again, pointing at them, "you fuckin' moof tards."

Darby told Ryan she hadn't been called a "tard" since

junior high school.

"Mangling French. Lying to police. Insulting the dead," Darby said to him. "How'd you get in this country, Ry-Guy? Why'd they let you in here?"

Further up the Boulevard Mouffetard, they saw some scant nightlife emerging. Big lights showered down upon a large, painted mural depicting a top-hatted man with a bowling ball in his hand. Its art nouveau script read *Mouffetard République de Bowling*, above a red arrow that curved toward a basement doorway below. Its windows flashed jumping disco lights and social activity. Suddenly then, the skies let loose and it poured rain, very hard and heavy.

"Screw this! Let's bowl," Darby said. Nobody argued and they ducked inside.

The République, or Moof-Tard Bowling, as Ry kept calling it, was hopping for a Sunday, and with people mostly crowding the bar, there were open lanes. Darby, Spiro, and Ry got fitted with scruffy Charles de Gaulle-era bowling shoes, then grabbed a lane. Disco lights flashed, as 1950s classics like "Hound Dog" and "Great Balls of Fire" played. Most of the people there were men, some with girlfriends, none wearing bowling league shirts, but instead decked out as if for a summer formal. One guy with a front-heavy Johnny Depp hairstyle wore a Coca-Cola rugby shirt and fingerless mesh gloves, dipping in his white jeans flamboyantly as he rolled his ball. Spiro pointed out some more Euro-greasers in white tees.

"No sign of Elvis or the Deaner. They must've deflowered The Buttercup," he joked. Bowling seemed the perfect option during torrential rain. "Wonder how many Americans can actually say they've bowled in Paris?" Spiro said.

They played for an hour as Paris poured and poured. Darby won the first game and laughed as Ry-Guy rolled a bunch of gutter balls before getting vocal in his frustration, "Bullshit!" During the second game, Spiro bowled near-perfect, rolling a hedgehog—four strikes in a row—causing Ry to get belligerent, badgering them to leave. By then, the rain had stopped.

Back on the street after rain delays, Big Papa Hemingway was still top on Spiro's list. As they walked up Mouffetard it was inevitable they'd hit its path. Spiro stopped them.

"Home of a great literary mind!" said Spiro.

Ry wasn't impressed. "Looks like a ho-house. No wonder he moved to The Keys."

Spiro snapped photos uselessly in the dark. And as they walked on, Spiro started dropping facts about Hemingway, along with random Spiro-like assertions.

"Hemingway was, ya know, like a cipher, like, the Grandmaster Flash, or maybe like the Run-DMC of early 20th century writers. Dropping knowledge."

"Cool, Spiro. That's totally def," Darby said. She noticed her friend's shoelace had come undone. "Tie your shoe and let's go, trivia man."

Spiro tied his shoe and kept talking about writers as rappers, as Darby rolled her eyes. Ry lit up another smoke, and then Spiro, still babbling, stood up but then stopped walking and kneeled down again, seeing his other shoe untied now. Ry got impatient—*c'mon!* he said—and Darby turned to Ry to give him shit about lighting yet another cigarette and his filthy smoking habit. Then came a huge crash.

Darby turned around and said, "What the fuck was that?"

Ry-Guy dropped his smoke and yelled "Yo!"

Spiro, crouched in fetal position, looked up with a mischievous smile. Surrounding him were shards of terra cotta. It looked like remains of pottery scattered before him. Wherever it fell from, it was obvious that it had missed Spiro's head by inches. Had Spiro been a step further he'd be dead or severely injured. Shrapnel covered the walkway and street and it looked like the aftermath of a mob hit, that is if flowerpots were mob victims.

Darby asked him: "Man, are you OK?"

"Think so."

"Well, shit, I'm glad you tied your shoe again," she said, relieved. "Lucky you're in one piece, my friend."

Ry-Guy then jumped in. "Watch where you walk! Stop talking about poets and pay attention," he implored Spiro. "Always knew you were a pothead, fool."

Spiro took some pictures of the smashed ceramic and mangled flowers on the pavement. Darby pointed upward to three strings swinging in the wind. He took a few photos of the tethers that had held the flowerpot that nearly crushed him.

Up the street, Spiro said there was a square where Monet and other masters painted Impressionist classics. The Place de la Contrescarpe looked like nothing special at first, just a small fountain in a square that was really a circle. The cobblestone area was encircled by restaurants and outdoor seating areas under posh awnings. People had come out to dine, drink wine, and enjoy the last remnants of the weekend under the stars. Darby followed Ry and Spiro to a corner and they stopped and stood there, as Spiro pulled out his journal to begin writing something. Ry lit up yet again and Darby fixed her eyes on some people huddled up.

"Check out that guy," Darby said. She pointed out what looked like a guy in his twenties, standing up suddenly, emerging from a hump of sleeping men.

Ry said, "Kind of preppy for a bum."

"Homeless person," Spiro corrected him.

Whatever you'd call the man, he looked utterly wasted. Probably 5' 11" and husky, he looked like an average American, wearing a brown J. Crew barn jacket, maybe a Carhartt, and a Boston Red Sox cap, which seemed to affirm stateside origins.

Ry-Guy took delight at the man's exaggerated stupor.

"That guy's super-wasted!" Ry's talk caused Spiro to stop writing and start laughing. This drunk American stumbled forward and back, nearly stepping on another sleeping man's head.

"Wonder if he has any idea where he is." Darby surmised that the guy wasn't with the other sleeping men on the edge of the fountain. She noticed that the intoxicated Red Sox fan wasn't covered in dirt or sunburned in the way that a lot of unfortunate street people are. Whoever he was, the guy was a very long way from Fenway Park.

"Bet somebody got him trashed and ditched him," Ry said. "See, told you. Come to other people's countries, get fucked up."

Darby suggested asking the guy if he needed help.

"I'm not talkin' to that sucka," Ry said. "Fuck that noise."

An instant later, the drunk man managed some steps forward, but then stopped and dropped his pants. Then he lowered his stance.

"Holy shit!" Spiro said.

"Yep, I think you're right," Darby said. "Something you don't see every day."

Ry started to laugh hysterically. "Look at this fool!"

Now in the middle of this cultured part of Paris, no one seemed bothered by the unseemliness of a drunk person going to the bathroom in a square where writers penned literary milestones and painters founded a movement. No police came, no one looked over except the three Americans. It was very French perhaps that no Parisian here literally gave a shit.

They watched the stupidity at a sensible distance away for

a few moments, as the drunk American did his business, pulled up his pants, and then wrestled with his belt. He stumbled more, nearly tripping forward then unfailingly backward, stepping right into the pile he'd just dispatched. It was so ridiculous that Darby wondered if it was a prank, and looked around for a film crew doing up a *Candid Camera* episode, a theatrical commentary on America's excess and standing at the 20th century's end.

Then they were interrupted.

A middle-aged man speaking French walked right up to Ry-Guy. Roly-poly, with a friendly smile on his never-shaven face, this disheveled French version of Spiro's roommate Pete saw Ry puffing up a cigarette and wanted one. He looked non-threatening but odd, even though nothing in Paris seemed odd to them anymore. To top it all off, the man had overly large breasts for a man and he was holding a pet ferret.

"Bonsoir, jeune homme, là," the man said. "Voulez-vous me donner un' cigarette?"

Ry pretended at first to ignore him, but then answered the Frenchman.

"What do you want, fool?"

"Pourriez-vous épargner un' fumée?"

"I don't speak Korean, man. Whatchu want from me?"

Darby told Ry that the guy wanted a smoke, but Ry remained obstinate. The French ferret man got impatient and started signaling with his fingers a simulated act of smoking.

"C'est bon et poli de partager une cigarette avec un bon garçon."

"No way, man!"

"Une cigarette! S'il vous plaît."

"Get lost, homie!"

"O, s'il vous plaît!" The man scolded Ryan and shouted a litany of things that called into question his ethics as a fellow smoker. "Ne sois pas avare, bâtard pas cher!" he shouted, calling Ry a *bastard*, poking him in the shoulder. Ry raised a fist at the Frenchman.

"Listen," he said, smirking like a cruel jester, "I don't know what you want, punk," which was a lie, "so you best step off, bitch!"

The Frenchman yelled again, while his ferret squirmed, waving *to hell with you*. He then waddled away slowly, spewing an angry monologue.

"That wasn't nice," Darby said. "Can't share your cancer fumes with the gentleman?"

Ryan said nothing at the Frenchman's vexation. By the time he was a few feet away, Darby turned her head and noticed that the drunk American had escaped his circle of hell, and was moving. Spiro began speaking but Darby stopped him.

"Shut up for a second. Look."

They watched for a moment, as the two men faced.

The Frenchman waddled, busy grumbling to himself and his ferret, too angered to notice the oncoming drunk. In turn, the American with turds on his shoes was too hazed to see that he was about to walk into the French ferret man's path. They approached closer at a slow pace, and somehow, absent of speed, the men collided into each other.

Their bumping shoulders went unnoticed by the ferret man, still grumbling. But the impact sent the drunk American falling, with his loose arm backhanding a server holding a tray of appetizers. Dishes and food crashed, and the Red Sox fan's body barreled into a table of patrons, who started yelling.

"Fais attention!" one said.

"Stupide putain américain!" said another.

Ry laughed loudly at the clumsiness. Darby and Spiro thought it was funny too. But the wine-drinking patrons, covered in their Bordeaux and buttery foods, were not amused. They noticed the three friends laughing and redirected their ire from the sloshed Red Sox fan onto them.

"You laugh? Fuck you, Am-ree-CAN ass-*HOLES*!" said one man.

"Go away, you, you... Yankee cock-ROACH-*EZ*!" said another.

One continued shouting and gesticulating angrily at them, while the other picked a curled piece of shrimp off his shirt and hurled it at Darby's head.

"Hey, asshole!" Darby shouted back.

A moment later, a cathedral clock tower behind them struck its bells, signaling a very late hour. The clangs reminded Darby of another movie scene, one from *European Vacation,* calling for Clark Griswold's execution. She took it as a warning.

"Seems to me," Darby said, "we should get the hell out of here."

DISINTEGRATION

APRIL 22, 1996

The morning after being called cockroaches by French wine drinkers, Ry, Darby, and Spiro would have one last, quick look at beautiful Paris and head home.

The night before Darby couldn't really sleep. Maybe it was their weird interactions. The German greasers, rain and bowling, plus Spiro almost losing his head were pretty exciting episodes. But Darby had tossed and turned while thinking more about Lina. She hoped she could grab Spiro's ear and talk it out after Ryan split.

At dawn, Ry-Guy needed to head back first thing to work on architectural drawings he said he'd put off. So, they went quickly across the street to grab croissants and coffee, again outside in the morning sun. It was barely 8 A.M. and the Chicago duo didn't have to fly until 4 P.M., so Darby sipped casually and listened as Ry lit up and recapped their days in Paris.

"What if we found that Buttercup place?" Ry said.

"What if? I wouldn't have gone in," Darby said. "Not into that sort of thing."

"C'mon, Darby," Ry said. "You like girls too."

"Apparently not the kind of skanks you're into." Now Ry was getting on her nerves.

"What if—this would be funny," Ry continued, "what if we busted in and said we were undercover cops, like—*Put Your Hands Up! Everyone is under arrest!*"

"You don't look like a cop," said Spiro.

"And we don't have police badges, guns, or handcuffs," Darby added.

"Oh yeah. That's true."

Their few days in Europe together produced some fun times and good stories for future catch-up conversations. But as always, Ry-Guy seethed for more mayhem.

"What if I had to punch that guy? He wasn't gonna leave me alone."

"The guy with the man-boobs?" Darby said.

"YEAH!"

"If he didn't have to carry his ferret you woulda been toast." Diffusing Ry's tough guy act was almost a hobby for Darby. "He was like fifty. Harmless. Couldn't give him a cig?"

"No way, man."

"Why not? Isn't there some *You got my back / I got yours* thing among you smokers?"

"I don't know."

"Bullshit, Ry. I've known smokers," Darby said. "I live with one. When you're short a smoke, someone gives you one. When a fellow smoker needs one, you give back."

"We're in France though."

"It's supposed to be anywhere in the world, I think." Darby was never a smoker but knew that to be true. "It's a club mentality. You dissed the brotherhood last night, my friend."

"Ha, yeah, I know," Ry-Guy said. "I just like to fuck with people. Parisians, especially. Come to Paris, mess with the locals. Get asked for a cigarette, say no!"

Ryan Nakamoto clearly hadn't shaken his jerk-like tendencies since college, or since leaving America's shores. Even a new country couldn't change that.

"A'right guys. It's been real," Ry said. "Gotta head back."

They got up and gave handshakes. Ry said he might be back in Chi-Town for Thanksgiving or Christmas, and proposed hanging out again then.

Once Ry was gone, Darby and Spiro still had tall cups of coffee to finish. Spiro became quiet, and Darby was too, just enjoying the early sun and breezes. With Lina on her mind, she was about to speak up. She wasn't seeking advice per se, but Spiro got up and said, "getting more coffee," then he came back with two more tall cups. Picking up even a cheap coffee tab was something that the penny-pinching grad student rarely did.

"Last hours here," Darby said. She mentioned the Eiffel Tower but had something bigger on her mind. "Was gonna say something, though," she started.

"Me too," Spiro said, then pausing. "So—I told Ry yesterday. Figured now I'd tell you."

"Tell me what?"

Spiro fiddled with his notebook and then fidgeted in his chair. His normal pep faded into guilt and soft-spoken, short sentences.

"So, I'm staying. In Europe. For just a little while. Perhaps longer. So, just so you know, I'm not heading back with you today. Sorry, Darby."

Darby didn't have a reaction at first. And it didn't sound feasible. Spiro had just started school and life in Chicago. Last she checked, Spiro didn't have a trust fund or an internship abroad as Ry-Guy did. But as Spiro sat like a punished teenager, Darby mustered a response.

"When did this come up?"

"I don't know." Spiro looked up at the sights and smiled.

"I just can't leave."

"I doubt you can change your flight. How are you going to get back?" Darby realized she sounded like Spiro's mother. "Don't you have class next week?"

"Well, the current session's over. I'm gonna call and make arrangements," he said.

"Sounds like you're planning a funeral. You're not quitting school, are you?"

"Definitely not."

"OK, what then?"

Spiro mapped out his plans verbally: Call the registrar to postpone until fall quarter, maybe a year; He'd also quit his part-time jobs by phone. He still had "a little moolah saved," he said, from graduation, mowing lawns and washing dishes back in Dayton. He trifled with the idea of studies in Europe. He would improvise, but it would be for the better.

"I'm not quitting. Just a sabbatical, perhaps."

Spiro said he could stay in Paris for a couple of days, write a little, eat as much cheap French bread as he could find, and then head back to Amsterdam. He said he could stay at Cecily's place until he planned out the rest of his trip.

"Don't worry," Spiro said, "I'm not going to blow my student loans on weed."

"I'm not worried about weed. Maybe mushrooms and ex-girlfriends."

"Ha. No, I'm not *with* Cecily," he said adamantly. "Just gonna crash there. It's OK, man! I'll be fine. Too bad you can't stay too, having a real job and all."

Darby tried to keep it positive and proposed an early send-off at a pub down the road, and then grabbing a train to see the Eiffel Tower. A one-off going away party.

"I'm good. Probably need to save some cash, now," Spiro said. "But, sorry, what were you going to say—you said you were gonna say something too."

With her friend's new news that he was staying, Darby dropped it. All of a sudden she didn't feel like talking about missing Lina. It would only bring her down another notch too far.

"Nothing, really," she said. "This was fun. I had a really good time."

Now, stories about their trip, new inside jokes, and their wild adventures would be postponed. She feared their friendship set aside would disintegrate slowly with time. Spiro had chosen whatever was next in Europe over what was next with his best friend. He had new and exciting paths ahead, new friends to meet, new stories to collect over old ones.

Perhaps this was the way it was: Long-time friends moving on.

DECEMBER

DECEMBER 1994, ORDINARY TIME

On a Friday night, Darby made way to her circle of friends'
annual winter holiday party. An old college friend named Erin,
whom Darby knew from her U of C's college radio station DJ
days, hosted and kept the tradition alive after college. For
those who stayed in town after their tenure at the University
of Chicago, the annual white elephant party was a must-go
event. Darby brought along Spiro and Ry-Guy, who hadn't left
for France yet, and each of the three of them came with
kitschy/offensive gifts worth no more than the $15 limit.

Ry-Guy brought some boxy thing, placed in gift wrap that
read "You're Expecting!"

"Mine's a bottle of Malört!" Spiro proclaimed very proudly.
He'd even used his arts and crafts talents to wrap it up to look
like a Soviet missile, USSR insignia and all.

Darby couldn't think of anything good and didn't want the
embarrassing experience of venturing to a sex shop like some
partygoers did each year to buy their gag gifts. So, she decided
on a pack of the most pretentious-sounding specialty beer she
could find. With the help of Adam the snarky beer guy at the

Clark Street Chalet, she walked out with a boxed tallboy set of something called Skeevy Steve's 'Super Horny Toad' Stout. The store even wrapped it in candy cane wrap and a festive green bow. The pricey beer felt like it weighed a ton.

That night, the three of them settled in at Erin's and caught up with old college friends and saw a bunch of new faces too. The host called for the kickoff of festivities and the 30 or so people took numbers from a pail. As luck would have it, Darby drew the number one card.

Darby didn't like being put on the spot, starting it all off, but her willingness to be a good sport and the prospect of grabbing something funny pushed her along. Pressured on by partygoers, Darby opted in haste for a gift wrapped curiously in an oversized red velvet bow.

It was one of the larger boxes there and it captured her curiosity too, as people cheered and yelled out random things. Once Darby got the wrap off of the box's exterior, the object inside was still well hidden and wrapped in several layers of multicolored tissue paper.

Partygoers prodded, "What is it?" But it would be at least a few minutes of unraveling suspense. More and more red and white tissue paper. Then Darby unveiled it.

In keeping with the gag gift theme, gift number one of the night was a long rubber penis.

"Awesome," Darby said, very deadpan.

The following 29 gag gifts included Spiro's bottle of Jeppson's Malört, a *Kama Sutra For Dummies* book, plus Ry-Guy's gift, which was a Costco 54-count box of Twinkies. There were half a dozen sex-related books and other gag gifts, and also a set of *Friends* shot glasses—one each for Joey, Chandler, Ross, Phoebe, Monica, and Rachel too. The guy who got Darby's pretentious beer loved it. But Darby was annoyed no one wanted to shift gifts and steal her fake rubber penis gift as per the rules, and so she'd have to dump it off later somewhere. But each time she left her gag gift sitting on a table or counter someone—Ry-Guy, Erin, other friends, and random people—all reminded her, "Don't forget your penis."

Then after socializing and spending half the party as its punchline, Darby noticed an alluring, dark-haired woman smirking across the room. She saw her again later in Erin's kitchen when she went to refill her beer. This girl and her friend with her snickered at Darby.

"What?" Darby said, looking at them.

"Nothing," her friend said. "Tough luck on your pick."

"Guess I'll have to regift this," she said, trying to show humor. "The real-life Steely Dan." Darby thought nothing of her obtuse literary reference, not to Steely Dan the band, but the inanimate dildo "character" in the book *Naked Lunch*. Darby saw the dark-haired girl's eyes light up, which puzzled her a little.

"Don't think too many people would get that," said the beauty with the dark hair. "I love books, especially weird ones. *Naked Lunch* is one of my all-time favorites."

Lina introduced herself and her friend, Donna, who said hello and then told Lina "I'll come back," going off to let Lina talk to Darby. Lina said she was a librarian and explained she had a *fetish* (her word, actually) for Burroughs, the Beat writers, and their subversive novels.

Darby and Lina morphed their initial chat about literature into normal conversations full of the usual *what do you do? / who do you know here?* stuff. And after nearly an hour of talking with Lina, Darby got her number and even found a nice place to leave Steely Dan, in the pocket of someone's long, fluffy winter coat by the front door.

From the first date after the white elephant party, Darby and Lina quickly became a thing. Darby had kissed a few women in college and slept with just one—her Spanish 205 professor.

Yet with Lina it was exhilarating, feeling just cozy and easygoing. More than anything, Darby enjoyed Lina's company, along with her subtle flirtations and Lina's thoughtful, sometimes innocent girl-next-door ways. They saw movies together despite their very different tastes. Lina managed to get Darby to go see *Interview With A Vampire* in its second run at Brew & View, since she'd read the book (twice, she said), while Darby got Lina to come along to see well-known Chicago alt-rock bands Lina had never heard of like Fig Dish, Shellac, and The Wesley Willis Fiasco. Darby went to Lina's first *Tonight With A Writer* presentation, scoring major girlfriend points. And they went on double dates with Tam and her on-and-off girlfriend at the time, and one with Darby's roommate Deighv and his perky girlfriend Jenna. Once too, Lina and Darby tagged along to a fancy new hotel bar's launch party with Rod and a modelesque woman named Claire. Yet, a lot of time they stayed in at Lina's place.

Right around Valentine's Day, Lina's library had a month-long program called "Foundation Film Fest," and because of it, Lina gained a new addiction to silent films. So Darby found herself watching black and white works of yesteryear. She liked the Charlie Chaplin films—kind of funny actually—but *Metropolis* felt pretentious.

By the time Lina had her watch Georges Méliès' *A Trip To The Moon*, Darby had had enough. Maybe it was the moon with a face, or the crashed rocket sticking out of his eye.

"What the hell is this?" she said, softening it with a smile so as not to sound like a dick. Darby hated it. "What the hell are we watching?" Darby asked Lina.

"This is—a *classic* film," Lina said.

"Says who?" To Darby, the half-hour mess was like the

most terrible of early MTV music videos. It was just weird and creepy. "The moon is talking. And it has Mick Jagger lips!"

"The moon is beautiful and alive, if you look at it the right way," Lina told her. "Haven't you ever seen a face like that in the moon?"

"Not really," Darby said. "Nope."

"It does if you stop and really look at it."

"Maybe to you, but I just don't see it. To me, it doesn't look like a moon, but an angry talking piece of cheese." Darby got up to pour them some more wine. "I'm gonna need more red to get through this 'classic film' or whatever it is. And, you?"

"Yes, more, please."

"OK, Moon Star, gimme your glass."

But Darby's fussing didn't bother Lina. She was more interested in warming up to her random new nickname. "Moon Star—I like that. You're sweet. I knew I liked you."

By the time summer of 1995 became fall 1995, staying in almost every weekend for Darby and Lina had become routine. But it never got old. Cuddling up on her couch, talking, drinking wine alone was what Lina liked best. She was a true homebody and her inquisitive nature also became routine. Lina often probed Darby into deep conversations or tried to, about both important and mundane things, one of which was Darby's first love, music.

"Why do you like bands so much?" Lina asked her.

"Why do you like books so much?" Darby replied.

"You can't answer my question with a question," Lina said. "I asked first. You tell first."

"OK, so, I really like music, because—I don't know. *I just do.*"

"But why the specific music you listen to? Clearly, you don't just listen to the radio. Seems like the bands you find take a lot of work. Why Superchunk and not Phil Collins?"

As if Phil Collins wasn't a simple enough reason not to like Phil Collins. Anyhow...

"Quality is one thing. Then there's authenticity. Just as important." Darby likened it, as much as she could for her librarian girlfriend, to picking up on good poetry or literature, or searching for the best in what's underrated. "Just like the way the written word sounds good to you—to me, it's guitar riffs, bass lines, and countermelodies, innovative drumming patterns. Certain things just sound good to me."

"But why?" Lina asked her.

"OK, so Stephen King—you said you love his books, right?"

"*Yes*, I do," Lina said, all bright-eyed.

"Well—some bands that make music the same way. The Ramones, for example. Their songs are short, hard-hitting, straight to the point. They deliver their fury quickly," she explained. "Then—just like a good book chapter—song's over, and you want the next one."

Mind blown. Sort of.

"You make that up?" Lina hinted Darby was embellishing, bluffing.

"Yes. I did make that up, just now. But that's how I see music."

But for Darby, it seemed like second nature to link favorite musicians to their literary counterparts like a historian or social scientist would. Darby explained that she saw artists like Iggy Pop and The Stooges, Nina Simone, even Throwing Muses, in the same context as important writers and literary giants that Lina said she liked.

"You've got Led Zeppelin," Darby continued, "and they are pretty much the combination of Melville and Edgar Allan Poe, but of rock 'n' roll. Kinda dark, not overly emotional. They even have a song called Moby Dick, and it's a famous one. You know that one?"

"No. I don't know." Lina was starting to sound convinced.

"OK, fair. What else?"

"There's Morrissey, and his old band, too, The Smiths. Morrissey is without a doubt a music version of Oscar Wilde."

"I know him. I think J.D. Salinger," Lina weighed in, "but, OK, go on. More, please."

"There's Public Enemy, basically rap music's Tennyson. *Cannons to the left, cannons to the right. Stormed at by shot and shell!* Same thing as their song 'Prophets of Rage.'"

"Public Enemy?"

"And then Bob Dylan. I'm not a huge fan, but he's pretty much the George Steinbeck—"

"*John* Steinbeck."

"Right, *John* Steinbeck—of modern music. And Patti Smith, passionate, brainy, and sorrowful, just like Virginia Woolf. Radiohead, sort of Aldous Huxley in a band, with their despondent lyrics about a lost society. Or Pink Floyd, same angle, but more like Orwell—"

"Hmm—"

"Then, Nirvana. Definitely Kafka-esque. And Carly Simon. I mean, 'You're So Vain' pretty much *Dorian Gray* in a song."

"Wow, Darby. I guess you *have* thought a lot about this," Lina said, with a lovey smile. She wasn't necessarily sold on Darby's logic or her tit-for-tat comparisons. But the enthusiasm and careful thought behind it moved Darby's brainy girlfriend.

Seeing that their wine glasses were empty yet again, spinning out of another conversation, Darby got up to open another bottle she'd brought. Lina had a summary thought. "So, I hope you weren't trying to impress me with your music-as-literature talk," she said. "Or with more wine and your artistic analogies. I hope you're not trying to seduce me."

Darby paused awkwardly. Lina stared up at her with her green eyes.

"Why's that?" Darby asked her.

"Because it's totally working."

DEBUT

JANUARY 1996, ORDINARY TIME

"My sister has these Grinnell College friends," Lina said. "They're in this band. And they're playing here next week, Darby, and I think we should go see them."

For Lina, it was the most out of the ordinary kind of statement. It was also a little devoid of detail; also uncharacteristic for Darby's very left-brained girlfriend. She just blurted it out as they sat silently, over dinner one night.

On top of that, Lina wasn't much of a music fan and generally didn't care about new bands of any sort. But her sister had said something apparently important about "this band," as Lina kept calling them. Over winter break, the sisters' conversations had made it important enough to tell Darby. Then again, she knew Darby was all about the newest bands.

Darby said: "Next week... when?"

"Well, Tuesday, actually. It's in a couple of days," she told her.

The first few days of 1996 were so cold that they hadn't left Lina's new place for two days. Darby loved the quality

187

girlfriend time and braved the bitter cold one Friday night to pick up some vegetarian fare from Lina's favorite Mediterranean spot. The next morning after that they slept in nearly until noon after staying up to watch all three hours of *Hoop Dreams*, Darby's favorite sports documentary. Then when it was Lina's turn to pick movies again, they did a day-long binge of '80s films from Lina's John Hughes movie collection, from *Sixteen Candles* to *Weird Science*. Before Darby left to go home Sunday, Lina brought it up again.

"She's not going back up 'til next weekend."

"Who?"

"My sister, back up to school. Joan says this band, Dreaded Letters—"

"Dreaded Letters?"

"Yup—anyway—they're supposed to be good. So, go with me. I wanna hang out with Joan before she heads back. And you get to see some music from a hot new band."

If this hot new band was so hot then why hadn't Darby ever heard of them? Sure, college towns like Athens, Georgia, and Olympia, Washington, had spawned most of the last decade's best bands, and even mega-famous ones like R.E.M. But in Darby's mind, nothing noteworthy had ever come from central Iowa except corn and minor league baseball.

That following Tuesday it was still bone-chilling cold, and Darby didn't really want to go out. But after work, she hailed a warm cab to meet up with Lina and her sister Joan. City Scene had her doing less-inspiring tasks like fact checks and updating the concert calendar then, and Dreaded Letters' two scheduled shows hadn't registered with the local papers. They truly were unknown.

When Darby got to Lounge Ax, the place was nearly dead. She passed through the door, that time with no bouncers present, to see Lina sitting at the bar, looking gorgeous, snuggled up in a black wool sweater.

"Hi, love." Lina gave her a kiss.

"Where's your sis?"

"Over there—with the band."

Lina pointed out Joan with her three college friends, crammed into Lounge Ax's photo booth machine. Two of them hung halfway out of it, with its velvet curtain half-draped over them. Photo booth flashes shot Darby in the eyes four times, as the four girls laughed and cheered while getting their pictures taken. Joan then joined Lina and Darby at the bar, and the others went to the stage to tune their instruments. Joan gave Darby a greeting hug.

"Nice to see you again, Darby." She then went on, "So, yeah, these are my friends in the band. Thanks for coming." And with the first few guitar clangs, Darby got a sense that the three musicians were more than the sum of their parts. A roar of guitars, and a smack of the drums and bass in unison, set the tone for Tuesday's little music revolution. Lina had to tug hard on Darby's sleeve to gain back her attention.

"Hey."

"Hey what?" Darby said.

"We should get a picture. Photo booth time. We've never gotten a picture together."

That couldn't be true, she thought. But Darby realized she couldn't think of a time so far when they were together that she'd stood next to Lina in front of a flashing camera.

Lina took Darby's hand. "Come on, it'll be fun."

Darby plugged in a few quarters and the two of them ducked into the booth, with Lina giggling like a child climbing into a rollercoaster. A warning light blinked and Lina put her arms around Darby and leaned the side of her head into Darby's. The photo booth did its thing.

Photo 1: Darby and Lina look around confused. The flash blasts.

Photo 2: Darby says in Lina's ear, "Great, I'm blind now." Lina finds this funny.

Photo 3: Lina looks right at Darby's face and says, "Yeah, me too."

Photo 4: Lina puts her hand up over the camera lens, and kisses Darby hard on the lips.

After four snaps were completed, Darby and Lina stayed for a long moment in the booth, making it an impromptu kissing booth, mashing furiously. Then a man and woman outside made it known that they were waiting their turn, as the guy fake-coughed and gave a knock-knock on the side of the machine to catch their attention. Darby was unsettled, yet exhilarated about getting caught kissing passionately with Lina in public.

"Sorry," Lina said, smiling, as they got out.

The woman there then stopped them to remind Darby and Lina not to forget their pics. The slot outside had two photo strips ready for the taking.

A few songs into the start of Dreaded Letters' first set, Darby knew right away that they were not college just kids with a so-so band. Even if they didn't have a record or a tour manager to put their names in the paper, their live debut at sleepy Lounge Ax was really something.

"Great, aren't they?" Joan said.

"Yes, for sure," Darby nodded. She didn't really want to alter her attention from the music, even a minute, for fear she'd miss a note.

Lina went on conversing with her sister, talking about books and Joan's studies at Grinnell. Darby was happy she had come along and enjoyed the ride both for the band and Lina. And that they'd finally got a picture of the two of them together.

SPARKLE + FADE

MARCH 1996, ORDINARY TIME

Darby knew she was a fickle, sometimes ornery sort of woman. She wasn't Ms. Positive nor Ms. Cynical. And if you asked her about it, she'd probably say that, just like her much more negative and caustic father, she had an ever-present sense of skepticism about the world and relationships too. It was something that she had never remedied.

And yet she knew that this predisposition made her not the most ideal candidate to be anyone's partner in anything, especially the girlfriend of an incredibly kind, intelligent woman. Separate from that, Lina brought up that thing called the future.

"So, Darby," Lina said one morning. "What are your goals for us?"

"Goals?"

"Yeah, you know. Relationship goals."

Darby's only goal so far today was to get enough coffee to wake up after a night of tossing and turning. Their server at Clarke's Diner kept filling Darby's cup but it was barely making dents in her lack of sleep. Yet Lina knew Darby was awake enough to provide some coherent answer, even if she didn't have any "goals" or anything that remotely sounded like a marking point of any measure. Darby didn't naturally associate *goals* and dating someone.

"Well," Darby said, "I met and found you. That's a pretty nice thing and—I guess—a decent goal, as life goes. Isn't it?"

"Yes, I guess you've struck gold, haven't you?" Lina said with a smile.

Lina could roll with it when she needed to. But today she wasn't searching for a short and cute, witty answer. Lina was serious. Maybe it was because she was just a little older than Darby, 27 to be exact. So she was a little more past "the dating for fun thing" than most.

"So, that's fine, what you said," Lina said. "But that's not what I meant. What's your goal—or goals—for us, I mean. Don't be all aloof. You *are* allowed to be emotional, you know."

Darby could see that Lina was fishing for something; maybe Darby's heart and soul. It didn't wig her out entirely, but she paused, not wanting to say the wrong thing.

"I don't know, but I probably have some thoughts about that."

"OK, good. Like?"

The server came by a fifth time and filled Darby's coffee.

"Well, I like being with you a lot, so that's a good thing."

"It is. I love our time together," Lina said.

"Me too," she said, right as the server came back and their pancakes hit the table. Darby then got flustered, and her OCD and its immediate, spread-the-butter-before-it-melts tendencies kicked in. "Can we discuss this later?"

"Later? OK."

Lina seemed miffed. Perhaps she wasn't as excited about the steaming breakfast plates as Darby was. But Darby couldn't leave it like that.

"So, no, I do have some goals for us. *Sure I do.* Just wanna get it right. Explain it right."

"OK."

"Your question—what are our relationship goals? That's, I guess, a big question," Darby said to her. "And it deserves a big answer."

"All right. That's fair."

With that, Lina smiled, and shifted her hips on her side of the diner booth, seeming suddenly at ease, brighter, more comfortable. She looked down at her pancakes, looked up at Darby again and smiled, then picked up her fork to dig into their breakfast adventure.

At age 24 Darby couldn't boast about any kind of success in relationships, especially long-term ones. Unless you considered two-month dating arrangements or casual flings "long-term." But Lina was a catch, and Darby knew this.

Yet lately, maybe being out of college and living like a so-called grownup for two years now—Darby started to worry about that *future*. She'd made it through college and comfortably far enough away from the drama and dismay of her family life back home in New Jersey. And in only Darby's second session with her therapist, or "the shrink" as she liked to call Dr. Vriedmann to herself, Darby began to open up about this.

"How old were you when your mother left?" Dr. Vriedmann asked.

"Maybe eight or nine," Darby said. "It was a week or so after my ninth birthday, probably. My mother told my father she was leaving."

"And how'd that make you feel?"

It wasn't a dumb question, nor invasive. But for Darby, hard-hitting questions about her mother and home life didn't conjure feelings. *Mother* and *home life* were dormant things, ancient history. She couldn't conjure a memory of how it felt or any emotion of it.

"I must have been sad, but I don't remember it. Blacked it out, perhaps."

"And how did it come about," the doctor asked, "how you found out she was leaving?"

"Well, my mom and dad had been fighting—arguing, not fighting—having serious and unpleasant conversations, sometimes yelling. And I was up very early one Saturday to watch morning cartoons, and sneak an extra bowl of Count Chocula before they could see."

"The kid's cereal?"

"Yup. I loved that stuff," Darby told her. "Anyhow, it was before 6 A.M., and I was up."

Darby said that that morning her mother had left a note behind. That early morning, little Darby had read the handwritten thing her mother left for her father. It wasn't for her to see.

"Guess I was supposed to have it explained to me later. But I saw the note—and read it. My father never knew this, because I went back to bed, pretending to sleep."

"Hmm."

"I lost my appetite for sugared cereal that day."

It was that morning that Darby's mother had also made her own necessary life change. She told Dr. Vriedmann that her mother "ran off" with a biker guy from Queens. A neighbor from down the street that Darby met a few times, as you do in the suburbs. And that when the neighbor moved out and back to New York or onto wherever his Harley would take him, Darby's mother went along with him.

The doctor advised Darby to talk it out, and just listened.

"After they split up, it wasn't the usual split-up. No two-apartment life, or weekdays with mom and weekends with dad. Dad didn't get remarried nor did I gain any cheery half-siblings. My mom, one day, just left to do her own thing."

On the way over to Dr. Vriedmann's office, Darby was thinking about her older brother and all of the records she had inherited from him. The Runaways, The Clash, and a few other rock albums eventually became Darby's only because her older brother was gone.

After Cal died in a car crash one night along with two other teenage friends, Darby remembered not much, only that everything felt black. People around her, even her parents, spoke hushed, very little. And at the funeral a week later, Darby sat in her grandmother's lap in a formal-looking Easter dress, only to be whisked away by Grandma right when the service ended, to do other things—little kid and grandma things—while the grownups grieved. Cal was almost ten years older and had much more time with Darby's mother. It made sense to Darby now that her mother never really recovered from that loss. Her parents' relationship also never recovered, leaving Darby in its wake.

"Parents who lose a child have a high divorce rate," Dr. Vriedmann told Darby.

Perhaps that's all it was. Eldest child dies, marriage goes sideways, daughter gets a record collection as consolation. The odds were against her. At least the records Cal left behind for her were good ones.

The next weekend, Lina was moving. Not moving in with Darby, but on her own, into an older house. The place she was moving to was a cute frame two-flat that looked like something out of a Tim Burton flick. The sofas, bed and TV, and other heavy items were already in, thanks to movers. Lina was good at saving money and managed to buy a home. For Lina, being 27 already came with a grown-up sense of responsibility—one that partly eluded Darby.

As the two of them moved Lina's last few boxes in from her hatchback to the upstairs quarters, Darby wanted to be helpful. Lina placed the last box on the floor by her kitchen and caught her breath.

"So. *Darby.* The big question, you said, deserves a big answer."

"What are we talking about?" Darby asked Lina.

"What I brought up before. I've been patient and you've had enough time to think it out, I think. Relationship goals."

"Oh, that."

"What's that mean? *Oh, that.*"

Darby felt caught off guard and thought moving Lina in would be followed by cuddling and watching a thoughtful documentary. She thought she'd earned more good girlfriend points but didn't have that answer.

"I guess I'm still thinking about that."

Thereafter Darby went home, and it was clear that her answer, or lack of one, put Lina out of the mood for any cuddling and movies. *Just let it lie. She'll calm down,* Darby thought, while walking over a random bridge and the Chicago River, homeward. It wasn't the first time Lina had gotten a little irritated with her about something Darby said or didn't say.

But one thing was true; there was a new dynamic at work. They had started getting on each other's nerves for different reasons. Maybe the sparkle was beginning to wane, the way it just does in relationships, Darby began to think. There were normal things that were less fun and felt like more work. Alas, maybe Darby's inability to answer the damn question—*what relationship goals do you have for us?*—was indeed a big deal, a bigger deal than she thought, and that it soured Lina's outlook.

When Darby got home she wanted to smooth things over and called Lina.

"Hey, how are you?"

"Fine. Same as before," Lina said back.

"I wanted to stay over but you seemed mad at me." Darby also reminded Lina she was off the next week, for Europe with Spiro. "I don't want you mad at me while I'm gone."

"I'm not mad, maybe just disappointed. Besides," she said, "I thought if I asked you a simple question about us, you could give me a simple answer."

Darby said she was still thinking exactly how to answer.

"Fine, think about it, Darby. But since you can't answer it now, we should take a break."

"A break?"

"Yes, a break," Lina said. "If you don't know how you feel about this relationship, or me, then think about it, but I'm breaking up with you, at least until you know. Thanks for the help moving. Have a great trip."

Click.

HELLO

MAY 1996, ORDINARY TIME

On the evening journey back home from Paris, Darby had been a little perturbed—not angry, not feeling totally betrayed, but definitely annoyed—that Spiro basically ditched her. Whether he was staying back to enjoy more Paris alone and in peace, or out to get some action with Cecily, it felt shitty. It was a small consolation for Darby that she got the window seat and an empty spot beside her. The flight back to Chicago wasn't particularly crowded.

After getting pushed aside by Lina and then by her best bud, it felt like all her meaningful relationships were suddenly on hold. Sure, Darby couldn't disparage anyone for wanting more of Paris. It was beautiful, and Spiro had the time and freedom to see the world before responsibilities and real adulthood took hold. Darby also knew that she wasn't a great traveler. By the end of the trip, she was irritable and starting to miss mundane routines back home.

On top of that work wasn't going great.

Hootie And The Blowfish had released their debut album two years earlier, yet it was still a huge hit. Celebrity news mags like *US* and *People* loved Hootie, as did late-night TV hosts, especially David Letterman, who had them on every chance he could. Hootie's debut album sold 10 million copies in 1995 alone and sat for a year at #1. And when City Scene got the follow-up Darby was delegated (or, perhaps relegated to) the task of writing the review. Her writeup of *Fairweather Johnson* wasn't the way to kick off a music critic's career, she feared.

Worse yet, writing about the band made Darby feel like a fraud, like one of those tobacco company "scientists" who sell their expertise to make cigarettes more addictive. Yet for much of the nation, Hootie And The Blowfish were addictive. This made Darby want to puke.

Weeks later, Darby would notice Nancy's own Hootie And The Blowfish CD on her living room mantle. Darby decided to say nothing about it, just like Darby never asked Nancy about her precise age, even knowing she was definitely at least half if not a full a generation older.

Memorial Day 1996 seemed like just a typical Monday off, another reason to sleep in, do nothing. The weekend before it everyone was gone. Simon was back in the UK on business and to visit his widowed mother. Rod was visiting a girl in Miami. Only Deighv and his girlfriend Jenna were around, and at about noon they stopped in so that Deighv could change clothes and grab his beloved sunglasses. That day Jenna was dressed in all white, in a sweater wrapped around her neck, as if she and Deighv were heading to a tennis club. Darby had no plans.

"You should come with us!" Jenna said. "There's a shindig

at my friend's place. Nancy's my boss, but she's cool. The more the merrier." Darby didn't want to impose, but Jenna insisted, "Come with. Don't be lame."

"What's it like to hang with your boss?" Darby asked, reserving judgment. But Jenna made clear it wasn't about career moves.

"She's more of a friend, and you'll like her. She's cool. It will be grand."

The word "grand" scared Darby, and it sounded like a grownup's party. But Darby didn't want to be bored all day. If this shindig—or soirée, Jenna had also called it—was dull then Darby could slip out, leave early. She could say, *long day tomorrow, thanks for having me.*

"Guess I can drink wine with grownups," Darby acquiesced. "Do I need to dress up?"

"No. She's just trying to impress her boss," Deighv said. Jenna looked over at him and stuck out her tongue, before giving him a lovey smile. "Just don't talk politics," he added.

Darby said, "I won't. Why would I?"

"We're all liberal, here," said Jenna. "Some of her friends don't like Bill Clinton. If you get them started, they'll go on and on and on, and you'll want to drink yourself under." But Jenna said not to worry and hinted that the venue would be worth it. "She's got this place Uptown on the lake. Amazing view."

Deighv said they needed to run out and grab some wine at the shop down the street.

"Be ready when we get back, OK?" he said. "Ten minutes."

Just that spring that Darby had begun facing the inevitability of growing up. Becoming "a citizen" was what her dad had called it one time over the phone while criticizing her career choice. Soon enough, Darby had started a GMAT course and pondered the possibility of grad school or a move, sublimating in order to get Lina off her mind. She found herself going out less. Being "productive" on weekends. Taking things seriously became a motto. So did looking and dressing the part. By age 24, she'd started, albeit reluctantly, buying shoes that weren't Vans, as well as classier, professional clothes. Respectable garments that weren't concert shirts or jeans slowly became the norm. She had to "grow up," be more mature, whatever that was. Soon Darby would find Nancy wanted to reverse that, undoing her in little ways.

That day, Darby wanted to look cute but casual. She put on a semi-fancy trim-cut Nirvana T-shirt she'd had a while, with some sexy dark blue jeans she'd bought once for a date with Lina, early on in their relationship. It was warm out and this outfit wasn't summer wear, but she wasn't going to the beach. Just a drink or two, mostly with strangers.

When Jenna and Deighv came back from the wine run, Deighv yelled from the street below with uncharacteristic authority. Jenna honked.

"D, Let's go!"

Darby grabbed her keys and a pocket-sized clutch purse for no reason and ran out.

Jenna was spot-on that Nancy's place was spectacular. Her place on the 27th floor of a glitzy deco high-rise was situated on the cusp of Foster Beach, with a southbound view of the lake and the city's great skyline.

"Hello, there!" Nancy said as she and Jenna gave each other excited hugs before Nancy gave Darby her own welcome hug and some attention. Nancy's wedges made her seem tall, and the elevation made Darby spurt out a snap compliment.

"Excellent view you have," Darby said, looking down for a moment. "Great shoes, too."

"Thank you!" Nancy was more grateful about the shoes. "I got to meet Jimmy Choo."

"Jimmy Who?"

"That's the designer's name—of the shoes. I work in glamor, so I get fun perks."

Darby looked down again at her pumps, those Jimmy Choos, which looked comfortable enough, and noticed how pretty Nancy's feet were. "I don't know anything about designers, but they look fun." Darby looked up again and Nancy's very direct eye contact almost knocked her over. The host then turned toward the small crowd in her front room of people talking, inviting everyone to pour drinks and get comfortable. She looked back over at Darby.

"Well, thanks for noticing." That extra moment wasn't about designers or shoes.

Eventually, something chilled and bubbly ended up in everyone's hands, but instead of making conversations, Darby found herself pleasantly polite and quiet, starting to obsess about Nancy. The back of her neck, her shoulders, her skin. The parabolic slope of her hips, and the way her lively Spanish-looking, frilly, yellow dress hugged them and taunted Darby about having her undivided attention. There was the way Nancy held her wineglass, daintily pointing out her pinky finger. Her ornate jewelry, made up of bangles and Arabesque earrings, bounced and swayed, showcasing her whimsical nature. Darby would fixate subtly and silently, but Nancy was on to her.

Most of the guests there, Darby figured, were in pairs, if not couples, and many seemed to be principally business-related contacts who had become friends. Darby could tell by the context of their conversations that Nancy won friends easily with her charm. These "grownups" Darby wanted to call them, talked provincial politics, and opined about art and film, while the sunrays danced and gradually faded from the skyline view. Closer to dusk Darby caught Nancy alone in her kitchen when she went for a bubbly refill.

"How long have you been here?" she said.

"Going on three years," Nancy told her. "I'm not here enough, but I love my place. Moved in after my divorce got settled. It was, you know, a way to invest the settlement—from my ex-husband—and minimize taxes." Nancy stirred a cocktail she threw together with the tip of her finger. "You could say the skyline view was a little self-indulgence."

Darby was all ears.

"A little splurge isn't a bad thing. I wanted to buy a place, and this," Nancy said pointing to her skyline, "this was a late 40th birthday treat to myself."

"Great birthday present."

"I moved in two years ago, last summer. I'm a Gemini."

Darby sensed she liked to brag just a little, but that Nancy was a curious person too.

"So, what do you do? Tell me about you," she asked Darby.

Darby told her she was a writer and aspiring rock music critic, as she worked to sound out some confidence. "I cover new music, concerts, for a local paper. Fun, as jobs go."

Nancy jumped in: "I love music. What kind do you like? I'm mostly an '80s girl."

"All kinds," Darby said. "Variety comes with the territory. Alternative, reggae, trip-hop, punk rock, cowpunk, a little bit of old country."

"Country, huh?" Nancy kept finger-stirring her drink. "No one admits they like country."

Darby put out her beef with music writers and the fact that many of them come off as judgmental snots just to sound cultured. "I'm just one person," she said to Nancy, "but it's about finding something in a record. You just listen—with an open mind."

"I like open minds," Nancy said. "So you're open-minded, are you?"

"Yes, probably." *Where was she going with this*, Darby wondered. "Why, are you?"

"Very much so."

Nancy smiled and decided to stop putting Darby on the spot with her seduction. She shifted back to the music part.

"I love all kinds of music too." Nancy added that she had seen The Police, Isaac Hayes, U2, and Patti Smith all perform live. She also mentioned loving Miles Davis, said that her first-ever concert was Elvis, whom she said she saw in Las Vegas with her parents.

"So—Who was your first?" Nancy asked Darby.

Jenna and another woman walked into the kitchen, and this made Darby stop as they looked at her, puzzled. A provocative question.

"Ha, not like that," Nancy said, with a giggle. "Who was the first band you ever saw?"

Darby took a breath and calmed down inside.

"Well, I was thirteen," she started to explain, which made it still sound for a moment like they were, indeed, talking about losing virginity. "Huey Lewis and The News. That was my first show." *Not very punk, Darby.* "Huey Lewis. With my Aunt Tilly. Yup."

Nancy's brushed away any fears of being judged uncool.

"I bet that was super fun."

Nancy then hinted that she should get back to her company, and nodded toward the living room. "Keep me in mind if you know of something else fun—if you want a partner." She touched Darby's hand while making it appear accidental, on the down-low. "Join me out there," she said, handing Darby a full bottle of white, and insisting "thanks for helping," then moving toward the living room. She looked back over her shoulder just like the first time.

An hour later, company had dwindled down to just four: Darby and Deighv listening, Nancy and Jenna telling stories and having a laugh about their business trip debacles in different cities. One Nancy story was about a near disaster when fifty pounds of cosmetics melted on a hot day just before an important fashion show. "Another designer, not Jimmy Choo," Nancy said. It prompted a second story about Nancy and Jenna being hit on by younger guys at the hotel bar. One guy told Jenna "you and your mom are so hot," while Jenna tried not to laugh. His sidekick tried buttering up Nancy with "you're so beautiful, just like your daughter."

Once nine o'clock came, so did a bid good-night. Darby, Jenna, and Deighv got ready to leave, collecting more Nancy hugs and thank-yous for coming over. They were out the door with Jenna by the elevator when Nancy told Darby to hold on. With the curl of her finger—*come here*—Darby was drawn back inside.

"You forgot something!" Darby's tiny clutch purse had popped out of her back pocket onto Nancy's couch. "Yours?"

"Oh, yes. Not sure why I brought that."

"Very stylish!" Nancy said to her, handing it to Darby, while also giving her something else. That something else was a business card with some handwriting. Nancy shouted goodbyes again to the others and mouthed silently to Darby, "Call me," as she shut the door.

Darby had made it through nearly 25 years of her life without ever taking someone's business card. She doubted forty-something Nancy really wanted a twenty-something's concert recommendations. And she knew they would never do any sort of legitimate business together. When Darby got home she just looked at it:

Nancy Lynn Booker
Executive Vice President & National Accounts Manager
Fashion Associates, Inc.

Gold Star ^{SM} Sales Leader

The card had two addresses on the front; one was at the Sears Tower, bottom left, and opposite of it was her company's world headquarters at *Avenue of the Americas*, in New York. Phone numbers on each side ended in solid zeros.

Scrawled on the back: "Call me ♥"—plus a handwritten number.

She smelled the card and took in its seductive aroma, Nancy's exact scent from that evening. Darby would smell it twice a day in the days that followed. It kept her buzzing.

The first time they'd shared Nancy's bed, they talked about their origins and Nancy said she was from the Old South, or "a little parish in central Looz-iana." Lying beside her mess of blond hair, Darby joked that Nancy was from "the original South Central." Nancy's lack of response to the comment registered that she didn't know who or what "South Central" was. A generational difference, in Darby's mind.

But Nancy's southern provenance stoked a sense of pageantry. She loved to dress up and show off, and she'd use it to entice Darby and display her prowess.

Nancy's bedroom hideaway had long, dark red curtains and white carpeting, which perfectly framed the look of the room, from floor to ceiling. The bedroom's windows had more of that breathtaking view, a more private angle of her skyline. And when Darby and Nancy secretly started seeing each other, the fun and games began.

The first time Nancy insisted, "kiss me here," pulling her hair up and out of the way, demanding Darby place her lips on the back of her neck and the soft spot under her hairline.

"I so wanted you to do that the first night you were here," Nancy said. "I thought about it the whole next day. That and other, dirty little things."

Darby admitted to Nancy, "I didn't really think you'd be interested in me." Or that Nancy, a classy older woman who had once had a husband, wouldn't be into other girls. Either way, Darby admitted that that night she was immediately obsessed with her.

"Yeah, I could tell," Nancy replied, "I like that you like me too. But I was pretty sure I was going to have you either way."

"So," Darby said, "I had no say in the matter?"

"As soon as you complimented my shoes—I caught you looking at my legs—I knew I had you hooked."

Darby still couldn't really believe Nancy was into her, as they cuddled together in bed.

"So, what now?"

"Well," Nancy said to her, "it looks like you're in for a long, hot summer."

SATURATION

Life training for modern single guys in the 1980s and '90s apparently came with one important rule. That rule: Never to call too soon.

Darby thought it sounded like boneheaded nonsense. Pseudo-wisdom at best. But that's what Spiro, Rod, and even Simon had told Darby at least a few times before when they talked about their experiences with women. And even shy, nice-guy Deighv said he went through it when he first asked out Jenna. To Darby, this ritual that her guy friends said they did, always seemed like typical ego-driven male bullshit.

But now she knew what they were talking about, feeling it, as she fiddled with Nancy's business card with her hand-written home number on it. Yet, the idea of sorting out what was too soon or too long was a little maddening. Ever since the Memorial Day shindig, she thought lots about Nancy. She wondered if she could legitimately "date" an older woman. What would they do? Go to a movie? Wine bars? *More soirées?* Practical plans didn't matter, as Darby daydreamed about Nancy's bare shoulders and the tan lines on her curvy, sun-kissed body.

That following Monday Darby sat at home, flipping

through TV channels, waiting for Deighv to leave the loft to go over to Jenna's place, as he did each Monday after stopping in from work. Darby wanted a quiet place without distractions to call from, with Nancy's prior whispers making obvious it would likely be a secret affair. Approximately 34 minutes later Deighv shoved off, and Darby took a leap. She dialed Nancy up.

"Hello? Nancy Booker." It sounded like she was outside, on a cordless phone.

"Hi, it's Darby."

"Oh, hi, you!" Nancy's heightened sounds of familiarity made it like they had spoken many times before. She asked Darby to hold, then asked how she was doing. She then said she was alone, sitting on her balcony, drinking red wine, wondering if Darby would ever call.

"I wanted to wait," she said, trying to joke, "until the smell of your perfume faded."

"Oh, so you love my scent? It's Chanel N°5, love."

"Speaking of," Darby replied, "how often do you give your business card out like that?"

"All the time. I'm a professional!"

"No, I mean—to girls you like. With your Chanel scent and 'call me, cutie' on the back?"

"Oh! Never before."

"*Right.*"

"That's a first," Nancy insisted. "Honest!"

Darby didn't totally buy it, but maybe she was the first of Nancy's female prey.

"And, so, you date girls now? Have you ever before? You said you were married or had a husband once." Darby felt like she was letting her mouth run. "Sorry, don't mean to be nosy, but I'm just trying to figure all this out."

But Nancy was cool about it.

"Yes, I was married. It was what it was, and I don't want

to talk about him," Nancy said. "I haven't dated a lot of women. Just a little." Then she got coy. "Maybe you had something special."

To Darby, that sounded good enough. "OK, what are you
doing this week?"

Nancy said that she had to go out of town for a day, but
that she'd be back from L.A. day-after-next. "After that, I'll
need downtime. Might want some company. If you're around."

So, tonight was out, but Nancy had an open dance card for
later in the week.

"I can come by if that's what you want," Darby said.

"That's what I want. But, that's not *all* that I want."

Nancy was laying it on pretty thick. As someone who had
only ever dated people her age—more than half of whom were
guys who couldn't get the simplest things right—Darby wasn't
used to the candor. Nancy's take-no-prisoners candidness
about the endgame was refreshing. If Nancy was one-tenth as
persuasive in her career, she was setting the world on fire.

"Same time as now, but on Thursday?" Darby asked
Nancy.

"Yes, please." Nancy said Darby couldn't stay over. "Call
first. But that would be grand."

Thursday, it was the same time, same situation: Darby waiting
to call, quickly getting impatient with her guy roommates not
leaving the damn loft. Rod said he was meeting Simon to see
Buddha Knievel at the Empty Bottle, then got up and left, but
not without coming back, first to change his coat, then to refill
his metal cigarette case. Deighv had not yet left either. Just
when Darby was about to say *the hell with it,* Deighv got up.

"Going over to Jenna's. See ya."

The moment the door closed, Darby grabbed the phone and blazed Nancy's number. It felt both exciting and scary, dripping with anticipation.

Darby hoped Nancy's flight back wasn't delayed or her business trip extended. For a moment, she pictured Nancy somewhere else, poolside in Hollywood, being fawned over by a business contact. A tall, glamorous man, a millionaire lover. But it rang only twice.

"Hello, there? Is that you?" Nancy said, as though expecting Darby's call.

"Hey there, yes it *is* me, Darby, here."

Nancy told her little nothings about her day, airport nonsense, how it was cooler in L.A. than in Chicago, and that she was glad to be home. Darby heard purring in the background.

"Is that your cat?"

"Yes, that's Marsha," Nancy responded. "But you're right, I'm purring too." She went on saying, "Too bad you're not here yet, because I wanted your opinion on something, but it can wait," winding it up with an innuendoed pause. "You remember where I live, right?"

"Yes," Darby said, and asked if she should bring wine, but Nancy said she had plenty.

Then she asked: "Do you like red?"

"Sure. Yes. Whatever you're drinking."

"No, I meant—I'm slipping into something cozy. What do you like better: Red or black?"

Red and black were Darby's high school colors, she remembered. But mentioning that would be idiotic and bungle the moment. "Either is great."

Done buttering her up, Nancy now asked firmly, "So, are you coming over?"

"Yes!"

Darby hung up and thought about calling a cab. But she realized she had no cash on hand and would have to walk five blocks to hit the ATM, *then* hail a cab on Clark Street or Broadway on a night the Cubs were in town. That would add a half-hour if she was lucky. And Darby didn't want to borrow Deighv's car unannounced. That could tip off questions.

Yet Darby felt a sudden sense of urgency. She thought about their flirtations over the phone, not wanting that heat to wane, even a little. She imagined how much more intense and wild it would be in person, touching Nancy. She thought about Nancy in her underwear. Or lingerie—black or red? *Fuck it,* she decided. *I'll ride my bike.*

Chicago was always known as "the Windy City" for a few reasons. Some said shifty local politics conjured up the name in the 1920s. Most assume it was from the lake effect air. But much more threatening than the town's winds was the ever-looming premonition of sudden rain. Whenever you tempted Chicago's schizophrenic skies, they followed through with their menacing threats. Darby, in a rush, forgot about all that.

Running down to the basement, she wrestled to unlock her Trek mountain bike and then rode toward Foster Beach quickly until the last quarter-mile. Outside Nancy's high-rise, Darby rushed to lock her bike to a post, seeing dark clouds in the sky follow and then convene upon her. Fifty feet from the building's glass doors, rains poured mercilessly, soaking Darby from her collar down to her socks.

Once Nancy buzzed her in, Darby rode the up-bound elevator to Nancy's floor, soddening its posh deco carpeting. She could taste in her mouth the bitter hair product she'd put in before leaving home, just trying to look good.

Arriving at Nancy's floor, the elevator doors opened and Darby felt the weight of her clothes times ten. Countering this, she could smell Nancy's scent before the door opened.

"Oh, look at you," Nancy said, hurrying her in.

"Sorry, I'm wet." She started to saturate the doorway too, but Nancy didn't mind. Nancy had on a very comfortable set of shimmery black silk pajamas and atop her shoulders a classy-looking but faint halter top. Darby said, "So, you went with black. I like black."

"Matches those dark skies, doesn't it?" Nancy replied.

Nancy then kissed Darby provocatively, sucking drops of rain off her lips. Darby reached to touch her hair, hoping to play with it. But Nancy halted her for a moment.

"Let me get you dry." Nancy walked away as Darby dripped more, kicking off her shoes. Nancy returned with an oversized towel over her bare forearms. "No, let me. Let me take this off you," she said, unbuttoning Darby's sopping wet shirt. Silently, Nancy pressed her lips wherever she could. She pulled Darby closer, scraping her fingernails across her lower back.

Darby could see over Nancy's shoulder the lights dimmed in her place. Rain hit the windows in sheets of terror, making its jealous presence known, as Darby put her hands around Nancy's waist. Nancy began playing with Darby's long, soaking hair, pulling it softly.

"I've been thinking of you, young lady," she said, still playing with Darby's wet hair. "Meet me in the bedroom, when you've dried off a little more." Nancy walked away and then opened a little door to a kitchen stackable. "Throw your stuff in the dryer." She picked up a glass of wine for herself and she poured another for Darby. "I'll be waiting for you."

Nancy's room had flickering candles buried into sconces high on the wall. But Darby's eyes were drawn to Nancy's voluptuous legs, the same ones she savored that first night. In the darkness, she walked in, to see Nancy's red lips, peering blue eyes and shadowed face, along with the arcs of her body.

"I'm all dry now," Darby said softly.

"Not for long," Nancy said back, with heavy eyes.

She turned toward the window and skyline. When Darby approached, Nancy backed into her embrace. Looking over the other shoulder, Nancy grabbed a kiss from Darby's lips. Nancy's scant clothes came off easily but slowly, one piece at a time. Darby loved Nancy's skin, kissing it and telling her so. Meanwhile, the faint tan lines across Nancy's body accentuated her shape—and pointed to the other places where Nancy wanted Darby to touch her.

At the end of what felt like two hours of lusty sex, the two of them tumbled accidentally onto the floor. But Nancy climbed on top of her, slipping her legs between Darby's to satisfy herself, as Darby looked over at the sight of their bodies in the mirrors across her wall.

Later, lying on the floor, saturated with passion and sweat, they pulled pillows off the bed, onto the floor with them. Darby and Nancy talked and recounted their adventures, tired, looking up at the ceiling.

"We should grab a shower," Nancy said.

"Bonus fun," Darby agreed.

Darby pictured what it would look like—the water tumbling off Nancy's hips and down the curve of her back, even further down her fantastic, round ass. She thought about the splash cascading down the two of them together. Then she pictured her wallet and keys, left in her jeans, now tumbling around the inside of Nancy's dryer.

Great, she thought to herself, before speaking again.

"So what is it you like about me? Not to be vain," Darby

asked Nancy, "but I'm genuinely curious. Why me? Why not another man like your ex. Or some tall, leggy blond?"

Nancy said, "A lot of things. I think you're cute. And sometimes I think you're hot."

"So it's about looks?"

"No, but that's a draw." Nancy said she knew they had an instant, simple connection when they first met. "I could tell then that you're real, Darby. Something about that is sexy."

One Hot Minute

AUGUST 1996, ORDINARY TIME

On another Thursday, Darby was working a little on the late side at City Scene's cozy office. Her boss Terry had tickets to the Cubs-Mets game and offered to take her with. Darby had told Terry that she had to say no thank you.

"Sorry, but I have plans that day, so I can't."

"Suit yourself," Terry said to her. "Go Mets!"

Darby's reason for declining was a simple if secret one. She had been saving this weekday for Nancy, ever since their adventures began earlier that summer. But rolling into mid-August, Darby hadn't heard from Nancy in over a week. And as she sat at work, toiling over updates to the fall concert calendar, she started to envision this hot fling simmering down. She was starting to feel lonely again. And she hadn't heard from Spiro either—not even a postcard since Paris. Darby hadn't seen Lina since before Europe, but she was starting to think about her a lot. With that, an impulse made Darby ring Lina up.

"Lina, hey."

"Hi. Darby? Well, isn't this a surprise?" Lina said this

matter-of-fact but in her usual mellow voice. "I wasn't sure when I'd hear from you again. How was Europe?"

"Fine. Great. Pretty good, but Spiro almost got us arrested in Paris, but—"

"Arrested, huh? You bad girl."

"Well, but not really. It was fine." Darby tried to focus. "I was thinking about you."

"Oh yeah?"

"Well, how you are, and all that."

"I'm good, Darby."

"So, would you wanna get a bite or something?"

"*Darby...*"

"Or a glass of wine, if you already ate dinner already. I'm still at work, but done, basically. So, anyway—I could meet you for a bite, or a snack, or wine or whatever. But, I could do either."

Darby could hear Lina's smile as she rambled a touch too much.

"It's not hot outside. Beautiful evening out there, you know, Lina."

Right there Darby stopped and shut up long enough to listen and let Lina respond. It was almost as if her zero-to-60 ramp-up in the conversation made them both need to catch their breath. But Lina dispatched the tension.

"Well, I thought I'd go do a spin class," she said, "but I guess now I have an excuse not to go. I'll just be bad now. Thanks to you. Bad girl, just like you."

An hour later, Darby met Lina out on Milwaukee Avenue, just down from the Damen train stop. They met in front of Reckless Records, only because Milwaukee had easily half a dozen different restaurants that served wine. They were all terrific, fairly cheap, and a little art-district swanky. It was just a matter of which had open outdoor seats.

Darby saw Lina standing, looking at the record store

window. For whatever reason she dug out an old nickname to greet her.

"Hey there, Moon Star."

"Hi, there. That's a blast from the past," Lina said. Darby felt suddenly like she was being overfamiliar, and Lina jabbed back. "I'm not here to record shop with you tonight, just so you know."

After a short stroll up the block, the two of them found outdoor seating at Cap & Cork, and they sat in the glow of the sun's last fleeting rays. They ordered a bottle of red, nothing fancy, and both Darby and Lina were slow to talk, slow to find words.

Darby didn't really want to talk about Europe, and she sensed Lina probably didn't want to talk about them and the way things were. So, small talk it was.

"How is your work?" Lina asked.

"Fine. Paper just got bought, but I still have a job, as far as I know. Maybe they'll let me write a little more someday," Darby said, not complaining but not convinced.

Then she went back to her nervous, rapid-fire style of questioning from before.

"So—how's your work? Meet new authors? Any good ones?"

"Good, yes, and they're all good." Lina's job wasn't really ever about meeting or interviewing any bad or shitty authors. Darby knew that and kept barreling on.

"So what's going on?" she said. "How's your house? Are you still a vegetarian?"

"Yes, Darby." Lina smiled, amused by Darby's minor rabble-mania. "You still ask a lot of questions. I always thought that was a funny thing about you."

"Funny, huh? OK. I'm sorry."

"No, it's fine. Funny and kinda cute, that's all. Cute, in a neurotic sort of way, I guess."

Lina brightened up and sat up straighter, then took a sip of her wine and looked around at the beautiful evening air. And with that shot called out, Darby stopped being neurotic and lightened up too, finally sipping her own glass of wine.

As the shades of the evening got darker, Darby and Lina got tipsier. And when Darby finally let up and told stories about the Europe trip, each short tale about the German greaser boys and being yelled at by French people, about being chased by rain into bowling alleys, and having pottery almost decapitate Spiro, Lina dialed in and laughed about her adventures with her college guy friends. Darby never thought of herself as entertaining, and Lina was never one who needed to be entertained. But the reacquaintance made the two of them feel like they hadn't really parted.

"Walk me to a cab, up the street, OK?"

"Sure," Darby said, as she settled up. She knew Lina wouldn't invite her back and wouldn't think about asking. It wasn't their style.

But as Darby walked Lina up Milwaukee Avenue, she opened up possibilities.

"Should we do this again? I'm around next week—"

"That sounds like it might be nice," she told Darby. "Send me an email and we'll see."

Lina waved for a cab. Darby said, "Good to see you." Lina gave Darby a loose hug.

A week later they started emailing each other during work hours. Lina started it:

> Darby,
> Thanks for getting me out for wine the

other night. It was a much-needed
break. Now I'll have to do more spin
classes. Thanks a lot.
XO, Lina

All the emails were about nothing, but good fun. *Bored at work. What are you up to? I saw an old black-and-white movie you'd hate.* Darby didn't know if it was going anywhere but felt like she had a pen pal, if not her girlfriend back quite yet. They threw around the idea of getting together again with no definite plans. Eventually, Lina suggested the second install-ment of Thursday night wine. It was Monday, but she hinted she might be free later that week.

Darby,
Up for a rematch?   Cap & Cork on
Thursday?
XO, Lina

Hey Lina,
Yes, OK good. I have some concert
reviews due soon but can see you there.
Lemme email you tmrw about it.
D

Wednesday Darby skipped out of the office to see a show. She didn't particularly love "stadium rock" shows nor the giant venue called the Rosemont Horizon, out by the airport. But the Stone Temple Pilots were on tour, and people still needed their grunge fix.

Darby was all dressed up rock 'n' roll style for the night. Her hair had grown longer since Memorial Day since Nancy liked to play with it, especially Darby's grey streak in the front.

For the show, she clipped her hair up and put on jeans and long boots that went perfectly with her black leather jacket. Darby had her pad, pen, and Dictaphone stuffed in her jacket pockets, ready to go when the phone at home rang.

"Hey you," the voice said. That sexy, flirtatious voice was Nancy.

Darby felt something inside her tremble and spark.

"Oh. Hi!" She didn't know really what to say. "Nice to hear from you—once again."

It had now been nearly three weeks since she'd seen Nancy, but Nancy was no less forceful than she had been before.

"So. I've been thinking about you, sexy girl."

"You have?"

"Oh, yes. Yes, I have, Darby. Been thinking about your face, your fine arms, and playing with that hair of yours." Nancy said she was "at home... alone," just her and her cat Marsha and a bottle of Zin. "You should come by this evening."

"I can't—love to but I can't," she said, trying to soften it. "I'm off to review a concert."

"Ooh. Lucky you."

"You should have told me you were back. Been wondering what you've been up to, Nancy."

"I'm sorry, sweetie. Work's been sending me all over the place." Nancy lamented her trips to New York, L.A., and London, but claimed that the time away from her love nest put her in a spicy mood. "I'm home for a few days. Come tomorrow, then." Nancy softly implored her a different way. "I went shopping again in L.A. and, you could say, I found something alluring that I bet you'd love to take off of me."

A few seconds of silence over the phone went by, and squeezed into it, snapshots of Darby's summer escapades with Nancy filled her head. Private, clandestine stuff:

Nancy removing her red stockings from her long

legs, slowly, one at a time. Making Darby watch and wait. Later, the two of them together, their bodies mingled on the ottoman Nancy placed purposely in front of the windows.

Gripping, kissing, tasting, softly biting Darby's shoulders, running her lips across her collarbone, as she kissed and smelled Darby's neck.

"So? What about tomorrow? Thursday. Seven-ish. Won't you come by?"

It only took another split second for Darby to accept Nancy's sly invitation.

The next night at seven-ish Darby appeared at Nancy's door. All she could conjure was thoughts of hot passion, the smells of Nancy and sex, perfume and sweat, the essence of them together. Primal things.

"So did you miss me?" Nancy asked, lying beside her.

It had been a while since their last tryst, and she felt like she had to catch her breath.

"Yes, I did."

"What did you miss about me, Darby, love?"

"Everything," she said. "Seeing you. Hearing your voice. Your face. And I miss the way you smell." Darby leaned into her, smelling her hair and perfume, and Nancy giggled.

"Aw, you're sweet. Bet you missed the sex too," Nancy said. "I know I certainly did."

Yeah, that too.

Darby wanted Nancy to talk about where she had been. And when she mentioned New York, L.A., and London again, it sounded like something out of an Indigo Girls song, but Darby wanted to know what she was doing and what fun she had without her. But Nancy took control and spoke first.

"So, Darby. Do you see other women?"

"I mean—I have."

Darby was wondering where this would go, but Nancy soon enough disarmed her.

"I'm not jealous, just a little curious about you," Nancy said.

"Curious?"

"Sure. I'm just wondering who else you see, what other women you've romanced."

Darby wasn't sure what she should divulge but had nothing much to report.

"No one currently."

"No?"

"I had a girlfriend for a while, but, you know we kinda broke up. Or—we took a break or something. Anyhow, so, no. Not right now. Just you."

Nancy smiled but wasn't totally satisfied with that answer.

"Well, I wouldn't have thought that. You're so pretty, so I was thinking on the flight back what women your age you might be with." Nancy planted a kiss on Darby's cheek, then spoke again. "Or, I was thinking—what other older women like me you've seduced so expertly."

"Just you, sexy Nancy. And I don't know—I think you seduced me."

Nancy then said she had some news, and there was a bigger reason she had summoned Darby so hastily that evening. "So, something's come up, Darby. I got a promotion at work. And I'll be moving soon, out to L.A."

"Oh." Darby was puzzled. "How'd this come about?"

"Well, the company knows what I'm really worth to them. When it comes right down to it, I'm their rainmaker.

Company's relocating me, expenses and all." Nancy said she was putting her skyline condo up for sale Monday and would be flying out again after that. "I'll miss living here. And I'll miss you. This has been really fun and exciting, and I'll never forget it."

Darby wasn't mad, she said, and it felt like tonight was a bit of a send-off, that final escapade with her sexy older woman. Yet, Darby felt like she could ask Nancy questions too.

"So, am I the first woman you've ever slept with?"

"Well, now that you've brought it up," Nancy said, "*yes.*"

"Wow. I'm a little flattered, to think I'm your first female lover."

"And a great lover." Nancy added that she'd dated "younger people" before. "Ever since I kicked my husband out. But they've been, you know, men. One was a semi-serious, the other was just a boy toy, you could say."

Darby had to know more. "So, once you get settled in L.A. are you gonna look for a new girl to play with? Someone like me?"

"I'd love to," Nancy said, "but there's another reason I'm there. Not just work."

Darby didn't want to act jealous. This was a fling. They both knew that.

Nancy explained further: "I got back together with someone who was in the picture long ago. And now again."

"Your ex?"

"My ex-husband? *Hell* no. No way. No, this is someone different. Michael is like an old flame, but we haven't known each other that long, really. But we have one of those cosmic connections."

Michael? Darby's mind went to what dazzling Michaels from Los Angeles might have enough game to make Nancy sell her condo and its beloved skyline view and make her move. Could it be a celebrity? Michael Douglas? Michael Keaton?

Hopefully not Michael Bolton. Michael J. Fox was probably too short for Nancy, she thought.

"Is he an actor? Some movie star?"

Nancy smiled, charmed, playing with Darby's hair once again.

"No, I met him a year ago, so random."

"So who is he? Some robber baron cosmetics mogul?"

"You're so funny. My boyfriend's an architect, actually."

When Nancy said 'architect' Darby envisioned old college friends. Sleep-deprived, analytical zombies in lousy cable-knit sweaters, constantly drinking Mountain Dew. Guys with no manners, like Ry-Guy. *How could one of them steal my Nancy?* Darby thought.

"Not that it matters," Darby asked, "but how old is Michael? He's not my age, is he?"

"Well, you're hardly a relic of yesteryear," Nancy said. "What are you, twenty-nine?"

"Try twenty-four."

Nancy laughed and pulled the sheets above her face, feigning shame. "Well, there ya go. Guess you're right. I have a hobby, I guess."

"What?"

"I like them a little young. It seems, even more than I thought."

"Why, how old is this guy?"

Nancy's face hauled a big grin, again feigning shame. "Michael's twenty-nine."

Before 10 P.M. rolled around, Nancy and Darby talked more in bed, savoring last moments before they kissed at Nancy's

door. Then in customary fashion, Darby went on home.

She was more tired than normal, not just from two hours of acrobatics with Nancy, but also from not sleeping well and the STP concert going late the night before. She felt her feet dragging and wanted to hit the hay. And as she approached the loft, she saw someone leaving from the doorstep, who then stopped, and turned around, facing her.

"Darby?"

Lina. *Shit, can't believe I forgot. Shit.*

"Darby, hey."

"Hey."

"Wasn't sure if we had a wine date or not, but I thought we did. Were you out?" Lina hinted that maybe they missed each other. "I went to Cap & Cork, looked into Reckless too."

"I'm sorry, Lina. I forgot to email. I was out all today and yesterday."

"Out where?"

"Out of the office. I had a concert last night. Boss gave me a review to write."

"Oh, nice, how'd it go?"

Lina stepped closer, approaching at *more-than-friends* range. Darby froze, but her mouth didn't.

"Good, fine. It went well. Loud concert, the show ran late with two encores."

"Darby?"

"It was Stone Temple Pilots—you know them, I think—kinda grunge, kinda slow rock."

"Darby?"

"What?"

"You smell awful pretty."

"I do?" she said nervously. "Well, thanks."

"Too pretty. For *you*, especially. A little flowery."

"Flowery? Maybe."

"Since when do you wear Chanel N°5, Darby?"

I'm so busted.

Lina suddenly looked angry, "If you were seeing someone, you could've just told me."

"But—"

But, all the *buts* and stuttering in the world wouldn't help Darby now. Lina got more indignant, more pissed off by the thought of it all.

"You know, I don't appreciate being warmed up and then blown off," Lina said, "pretty much stood up on a *date* tonight, or whatever the hell we're doing. For you to see someone else and not be up front about that."

Darby wanted to explain that it just happened, or *had been* happening—for a while—but it was over now. But that would sound terrible, even if she could explain it. Darby needed to say that she *meant to* follow up with Lina, and *meant to* be with her tonight. But Nancy crept up again, reeled her in. She couldn't resist—or didn't.

"I don't know what to say, Lina. Something odd just happened."

"Odd, huh?"

"I'm sorry."

"The only thing that's odd is I'm wasting my time with you. Go be with your Chanel babe, whoever she is."

"Lina?"

"Forget it. Goodbye."

Darby stood there as Lina walked off.

Driveway to Driveway

SEPTEMBER 2, 1996, ORDINARY TIME

Darby told no one that September 2 was her birthday. But birthdays were holidays too, and she kinda hated them all. Whether it was turkey, wrapped gifts under a tree, birthday cakes—it didn't matter. She was fine to forgo all the fanfare, thank you very much. At least Memorial Day drinks led to some fun escapades with Nancy. Then again, look how that turned out.

She opened up a piece of mail that had arrived a week earlier—one that she'd neglected to take a look at. It had a jubilant message inside:

Dear Ms. Derrex,

Congratulations on your acceptance to the Manhattan School of Management! MSM's faculty and staff look forward to

you joining us and our growing Master
of Business Administration program.

It was an invitation to Darby into a new business school in
New York City, and principally an invitation to an opportunity; an opportunity for another life. Sure, MSM wasn't exactly
Columbia or NYU. Having applied on a whim after she and
Lina broke up, she didn't know much about it. But it was "an
out" if not a do-over for someone still searching for some
direction.

Darby packed up over the course of her last day and a half
in town, after picking up the Subaru from the rental place.
First in were things she'd need to take back home to store for
the short term. A few housewares, books, and other eventually
useful keepsakes would have to hang out in her dad's garage
back in New Jersey until Darby could find a place in
Manhattan. Next into the hatchback went vinyl albums she
held onto but never played. The Runaways' debut album and
some Bob Marleys, plus other '80s picks from The Cars and
Billy Squier were ones she also hadn't listened to in ages, since
she didn't have an old school record player anymore. But they
were still important, having belonged to her brother once. She
packed CDs in old Adidas and Vans shoe boxes, along with
some Stephen Kings and Kerouacs, plus the Rock Log that
Martin gave her. After that, a maroon polyester U of C blanket
pulled over it would assure no one would see belongings inside
her car.

Deighv, turning the corner en route back to the loft, saw
Darby close up the car.

"Hey, Darby. You off?"

"Yeah, but not 'til tomorrow."

"Sure you got everything?"

"Pretty much," Darby said nonchalantly. "Gonna get up
and head off pretty early, so…"

Darby still felt sore about screwing it all up with Lina, only to see Nancy move away for her supposed soul mate. And she still hadn't heard from Spiro; not a phone call, nor even a postcard. Her old friend must have really been loving Paris. Perhaps he'd shacked up with Cecily, or, knowing Spiro, maybe he was toppling corporate dictators across Eastern Europe, spearheading a new age revolution of coffeehouse poetry slams for all.

"No one's around," Deighv said. "Rod's in the 'burbs with family. Big Labor Day cookout. And who knows where Simon is."

"Probably off in a soccer pub, somewhere."

"Maybe you're right." Deighv then said he was heading over to Jenna's. "Gotta get my sunglasses, change clothes. You know, look good, for my other half. But I'm glad I caught ya. I wanted to say goodbye. Goodbye, at least for now."

"Thanks, Dave. I appreciate that."

"And good luck with New York, and the grad school thing—if that's the plan."

"Think that's the plan," Darby said. "Guess I should tell 'em I'm coming."

After gathering a few things, Deighv was out for the evening. It looked like Darby would have the loft to herself once again, reconciled that she was fine with a night of solitude and relaxation. Besides, she didn't feel cheery enough for a send-off drink, even if the guys or Tam had been around. Plus, she could come back and visit.

The next morning Darby got up at six, showered, threw the last of a few things in a bag, and jumped into the rental Subaru. It was all gassed up and she had old cassettes she wanted to listen to first upfront. Some Lemonheads and 7 Seconds' *Soulforce Revolution*. Plus, reaching for her more girly emotions about leaving, Darby had some Go-Go's and Ani DiFranco handy too. Before she buckled her seatbelt, she drove up slowly to a blue street mailbox and shoved a sealed envelope with her acceptance slip into it. All she needed on the way out of town was a very large coffee.

Monday's drive was dull, as Darby held her nose from the oil and gas stench of Gary, Indiana, only to be bored by the rest of the state's flatness. After putting down at a Motel 6 somewhere in Ohio for the night, the next day, she rolled across Pennsylvania for a long day through everything that sat between Pittsburgh and Philly, then onto New Jersey.

When she arrived at her dad's house in Cherry Hill, Darby envisioned the last time she'd left that driveway, to head off for her last year at U of C and Chicago, where she'd stay for a while, back when she thought that was forever. Darby didn't expect a birthday card or a cake from her quiet dad. Barely a firm welcome back would be in order. But she had a place to crash for a few days.

BACK TO
BACK-IN-TIME

TAPE TYPE THING, OR REBEL GIRL

OCTOBER 20, 1996. BACK IN TIME.

One of the last things Rachel said that first night they spent together was about a mixtape she would make. Instead, she made Darby a double mixtape.

It wasn't so much the music Darby was excited about. She was feeling starry-eyed and possibly in love, or just appreciated, by Rachel's two 60-minute Memorex tapes, which also aimed to soften up Darby's inner music snob. Giving it a first listen, Darby made notes in pencil aside the song lists Rachel diligently typed up, with the names of the songs and artists.

Tape 1 — "Metal Mix 96"
Side 1
1. Guns N' Roses — Knockin' On Heaven's Door, from *Use Your Illusion II*. 1991 GOOD (OVER
2. Slayer — Raining Blood, from *Reign In Blood*. 1986 \ M /

3. Queensryche — Dirty Lil Secret, from *Empire.* 1990
   FITTING

4. Motley Crüe — Don't Go Away Mad (Just Go Away), from
   Dr. Feelgood. 1990

5. Guns N' Roses — Live And Let Die, from *Use Your Illusion
   I.* 1991   **CLASSIC**

6. Every Mother's Nightmare — Love Will Make You Blind,
   eponymous. 1990   **ALSO FITTING**

Side 2

1. Guns N' Roses — Paradise City, from *Appetite For
   Destruction.* 1987

2. Van Halen— Cabo Wabo, from *OU812.* 1988
   VAN HAGAR NOT HALEN

3. Type O Negative — Cinnamon Girl, from *October Rust.*
   1996

4. Warrant — Down Boys, from *Dirty Rotten Filthy Stinking
   Rich.* 1989   **NOPE**

5. Def Leppard — Photograph, from *Pyromania.* 1983

6. Public Enemy & Anthrax — Bring The Noise, from *Attack
   of the Killer B's.* 1991   **YEAH BOYEEE!**

"Metal Mix 96"—Darby had to give her props on the title—
had no songs from 1996, unless you counted Type O's Neil
Young cover. The second tape was more contemporary and
alternative, showcasing tastes Darby never knew Rachel had.

Tape 2 — "X/Y"
Side 1— XY aka dude music

1. Big Star — September Gurls, from *Radio City.* 1972

2. Bob Mould — See A Little Light, from *Workbook.* 1989
   MINNESOTA

3. The Replacements — Left Of The Dial, from *Tim*. 1985
   MORE MINNESOTA

4. Spacehog — In the Meantime, from *Resident Alien*. 1995
   NEO-GLAM

5. Green Day — 80, from *Kerplunk!* 1992

6. A Tribe Called Quest — Oh My God, from *Midnight Marauders*. 1993

Side 2 — XX aka songs by/for the ladies

1. Bratmobile — Bitch Theme, from *Pottymouth*. 1993

2. Sleater-Kinney — Heart Attack, from *Call The Doctor*. 1996. **SOUNDS LIKE...?**

3. L7 — Pretend We're Dead, from *Bricks Are Heavy*. 1992
   THE BEST

4. Babes In Toyland — Here's My Thing, from *Spanking Machine*. 1990 **MORE MINNESOTA !!!**

5. X-Ray Spex — Warrior In Woolworth, single. 1976

6. The Runaways — American Nights, eponymous. 1976

7. Bikini Kill — Rebel Girl, from Pussywhipped. 1993

That last track was put there on purpose. Not because Darby was pussy-whipped. (Was she?) Rather, the song title referenced something important, a moment between them.

The weekend before, Rachel and Darby were pleasantly wasting another Saturday. The plan that Saturday was to hit Uncle Martin's store and then visit the Lincoln Park Zoo. The two of them got up later than planned. And so they decided to hit the zoo first and maybe Revolver Records after that. But the girls never made it to the zoo, getting lost in other things.

On the walk in the park nearby, Rachel spotted a public park swing set.

"I wanna swing," she said on sight, and her enthusiasm made them ditch the slow stroll. "Come on! Let's do this," she insisted.

Before Darby got on, Rachel was up in the air, swinging and flying back and forth, which made her black beanie fall off in the wind.

"You're like a little kid," Darby said to her, catching her hat.

"Yeah, so?" Rachel answered, her joy beautiful to watch.

Rachel continued her child's play when they resumed their walk around the park. She talked about growing up and going to summer camp as they walked past ducks floating upon the south lagoon. After the ducks passed, Rachel asked Darby, "You know how to skip stones?" She picked up all the flat rocks she could find and started chucking them.

"What's the point of this?" Darby asked.

"To try to get the rock as far across the water as you can," she said, "without sinking."

"But they always sink."

"Not if you throw them right. Not if you skip 'em to the other side. Watch!"

Rachel rick-shotted her stones and made the first few almost to the water's other end. With each score, Rachel cheered like a champ. Then Darby just said it.

"You're a maniac, a rebel girl."

"Aw. I like that."

"What, that you're a maniac?"

"No, rebel girl. Call me that again."

"Rebel Girl."

With those words, Rachel dropped her stones and landed a kiss on Darby's face.

Later, before it got dark the two of them hit RJ Grunt's for an early dinner, and after that Darby and Rachel met up with Michael-Leslie and her new guy at the Rock-N-Bowl.

Throughout that evening, Darby and Rachel crashed balls into pins, not really keeping score. Rachel's verve contrasted Michael-Leslie's usual lack of expression. Darby joked that her new beau—*Bram or Igor or whatever his name is*—seemed to be having fun, but unwilling to show it, perfect goth fashion. Their lull made Rachel more bombastic and she kept saying her new nickname.

"Rebel Girl's turn!" she said before hitting a strike. "Rebel Girl up." She even changed the TV screen scoreboard above to reflect the new byline: REBLGIRL.

That day Darby had done something terribly right.

SHE'S ELECTRIC

NOVEMBER 2, 1996

Darby stopped wearing the time-pass watch by the end of October. She didn't want anyone asking about it, but didn't want to lose it. It could come in handy, even just once more, for hopping the Grey Line to more vintage concerts. Sure, she had thoughts about going back to the 21st century, seeing Spacey again and Revolver Records, but Revolver was safe in Spacey's hands. Her time-pass read DAYS LEFT: 29. For safe-keeping, she hid it under her bed.

Yet Darby decided ditching out on her "past life" in the future or the old present—whatever it was—was perhaps not such a crazy option. She was still mulling over staying versus going back to the 21st century but knew she had a good thing going here and didn't want to walk out on that, and Rachel. She didn't want to fuck up anything. She'd done that before.

Just after noon that Saturday, Spiro called Darby about grabbing a cheap late lunch. His favorite Thai food spot called Penelope's had delicious dishes, and Darby had once been a fan. The slick little eatery gathered decent dinner crowds for reasons besides its cuisine, courting a big slice of what you

240

might call the Bridget Jones economy: cosmopolitan, social, single women who go out often (perhaps every evening) doing so in droves to get their fix of nightlife, and in this case, sweet sticky satay and aromatic dishes like Pad Thai. The female crowd, in turn, brought a bevy of bros who came for ample views of future potential dates.

Lunchtime it was usually dead, and the place offered a $4 lunch special 'til 4. But at 2 P.M., almost approaching 2:15 P.M., Darby didn't mind that she was waiting. The lull gave her a few moments of peace and quiet—another simple moment before Hurricane Spiro would whirl in. She got a pot of tea, which arrived at the table way too hot to drink. And on the way in, she grabbed Friday's City Scene so she could read the second installment of *Latecomers' Reviews*. It was only the second time she got a chance to see this project in print:

City Scene | Music
Latecomers' Reviews by Darby Derrex
November 1, 1996

Our music editor Darby Derrex reviews historic Chicago concerts twice monthly.

Oasis
Metro 10/15/1994

In the fall of 1994, only the most diehard American anglophiles had heard of Oasis. But that year the Manchester, England, quintet essentially tore down music's infrastructure in Britain, much in the way that Nirvana did in America three years earlier with *Nevermind*.

Prior to that, it looked as if the UK's rock and roll fury had been smothered away forever with 1970s records by The Who and the Sex Pistols, or the '80s works of Madness and

The Police. The greatest aspects of British music had aged with greying mods and ex-punks. New British music was the stuff of shy art students dancing to the beats of EMF.

But the August 1994 Oasis debut record, *Definitely Maybe*, changed all that. Still, it wasn't until their follow-up *(What's the Story) Morning Glory?* and the single "Wonderwall" that American radio got the memo that Oasis had come to conquer the U.S. and the world.

For as much good and bad press that the band has gotten, from battles between brothers Liam and Noel Gallagher, to arrests and trashed hotel rooms, to proclaiming their musical superiority over the Beatles, there *is* a lot to like about Oasis. The band's tunes do trend Beatleseque, yet Liam Gallagher's sharp, serrated vocals shred the rafters of auditorium halls like a Johnny Rotten love child. At the same time, lead songwriter and guitarist Noel Gallagher is by no means Jimi Hendrix, but his fretwork projects the band's anthemic songs with a furor like AC DC with some of the songwriting poise of Lennon & McCartney.

Almost the entirety of the band's October '94 performance was made up of songs found on that first album. The Gallagher Brothers' loud clangs and provocative sneer make those songs—namely "Live Forever" and "Cigarettes & Alcohol"—sail hard and sink in.

If you're inclined to see Oasis now or in the near future, here's a fair warning: the band doesn't move around much. If you want acrobatics, there's the Red Hot Chili Peppers, and if you want revolution go see Rage Against The Machine. Instead, Oasis will make you love the traditions of rock music again just as much as they'll make you want to swill beer, walk with more swagger, or—strangely—swear out loud in your newfound Manchester accent.

Rating: 4/5
Setlist: Rock 'N' Roll Star, Columbia, Fade Away, Digsy's Dinner, Shakermaker, Live Forever, Bring It On Down, Up In The Sky, Slide Away, Cigarettes & Alcohol, Married With Children, Supersonic, I Am The Walrus (Beatles cover).

Not bad, Darby thought. She knew that whether or not readers liked the band she had portrayed their first Chicago show accurately, without bias. And after she put down the paper she noticed one more thing about 1996, now, that was new. She couldn't smell.

Ever since falling on her head at Lounge Ax, Darby's olfactory functions weren't right. She realized that she couldn't grasp the smells of morning coffee, and today she couldn't conjure the nutty bouquet of blanched peanuts or fresh Thai cilantro she thought would be there.

Outside the restaurant's windows, Darby looked and saw people dressed for the weekend's Halloween festivities. Some Spice Girls walked past scurrilously, as did two different Unabombers; one in a grey hoodie, mustache and aviator sunglasses; the other, post-arrest, in messy hair and an orange jumpsuit. The unusually warm 70-degree day brought out sexy devils, sexy postal workers but also a round guy in a red sweater dressed like Eric Cartman.

Spiro finally then arrived for lunch.

"Yo, D-Smoove."

"Hey. I haven't been here in ages," Darby said. She pointed out the restaurant's walls, adorned with shelves stocked with 1980s ephemera like PEZ dispensers and vintage lunch boxes. Between golden Buddhas sat pictures of revered people. "Wonder who that is," Darby said, pointing to a photo on the wall.

Spiro looked to the side and said, "Shanti."

"His name is Shanti?"

"No. That's *her* name," Spiro nodded toward a young woman and the only server in the restaurant. She walked by, saying, "Be right with you," prompting a "No rush!" from Spiro. Darby wondered how she missed seeing this young woman the first time.

"She's radiant," Spiro said. "Absolutely electric."

"Yeah, she's pretty," Darby said back. Just like at Lounge Ax, it came to Darby that this Shanti was the real reason they were there and that great Thai food was an extra. Darby could tell her friend was obsessed, as Shanti the server zipped across the small restaurant, with her luxurious, spiral-curly dark hair bouncing. A few times she sent darling smiles at Spiro.

"Think she likes you," Darby said. "How do you know her name?"

"Nametag."

"Oh. Right. You've talked to her?"

"Just a little. I don't want to be a stalker though."

"You're pretty non-threatening, as guys go, I think, Spiro."

"Maybe. You could say I'm a regular now," Spiro said, concocting a little story. "I'm one with a taste for exotic things. Just spent some time traveling abroad."

"Thai food isn't exactly unusual. It's everywhere here."

"True. But still a little out there," Spiro insisted.

"Uh-huh."

"I stop in every Tuesday after my Romantic Lit seminar."

"That'll do it," Darby concluded.

Either way, Spiro's tastes in women were evolving. Darby could tell just by looking at Shanti that she seemed both friendly and intelligent.

Once Shanti dropped off another menu at the table, issuing another "Be right with you," she ducked into the kitchen and Spiro took an opportunity to obsess vocally. He spoke about "her opulent hair" and her name. "Shanti means 'inner peace' or 'calmness' in Sanskrit." Spiro then mentioned an epic poem by T.S. Eliot, *The Wasteland*, and its 430-some lines of chant. "Makes me want to say it too. Shanti, Shanti, Shanti."

"Bet she'd appreciate you know about her name."

"Yeah, but how many people do you think say that? Like, '*Oh I love your name. Are you named after that T.S. Eliot* poem?' I bet *a lot.*"

"Dude, I bet *none,*" Darby rebutted. "I mean, it's not like the Average Joe knows ancient words or anything intelligent in general. She probably just gets hit on by football-crazed idiots, with bad pickup lines. Trust your gut."

Shanti returned and smiled at Spiro again, saying hello once more. Spiro ordered his "*usual,*" saying that the splendid Pad Prik was why he comes to Penelope's so often.

"Yeah, it's good," Shanti said, touching her hair. "You live on the block?"

"Yes, moved back just recently from travels abroad," Spiro said to her. "I told my friend here, I said, you can't get Thai like this everywhere."

Shanti was interested in Spiro's travels. "Travels? Where?"

Ohio and other normal, boring places, Darby thought.

"Amsterdam. Germany. Paris. Slovenia, a little bit," Spiro said, none of which included Thailand. "Just some shoestring travel."

"So cool, me too," Shanti said. "I just got back from Tel Aviv for the summer. It was beautiful. I love the sun. Tan's faded now," Shanti said with a giggle, looking at her bare arms. "I mean, I barely tan." They exchanged school affiliations and Shanti said that she just started grad school uptown at Loyola. "Jewish girl at a Catholic university. Weird, I know."

Darby listened to them rap about higher ed and smiled, knowing that—finally—there was a nice young, scholarly woman out there for Spiro; one who probably wouldn't mind Spiro's quirks and him being habitually broke. Once they finished talking coursework, Shanti acknowledged Darby, who ordered the Panang Curry extra spicy. Darby was fine not being noticed by Shanti. Yet her glances over to Spiro made him kinetic in conversation. He wouldn't shut up.

"You should see *Basquiat*—David Bowie was in it! Random thought: There's a poetry slam I wanna hit. Another thing, I'm on a *Led Zeppelin II* kick right now."

Spring rolls arrived at the table, not by Shanti but by Penny, the place's septuagenarian owner. As Shanti became tasked with other pop-Thai food lovers coming in, Spiro seemed distracted, worried about losing her.

"So, what happened with Michael-Leslie?" Darby asked, point-blank.

Spiro answered point-blank. "I don't think she's into guys like me. She likes hip jerks. Ethan Hawke knockoffs, with their fake bad-boy attitudes. And, they *have to be* in a band."

"No offense," Darby said, "but I don't get her mystique. And I don't even get why she and Rachel are friends." She added that, in so many words, she found Michael-Leslie snotty. "She's a snappy dresser. Attractive, smart obviously. But it's like she's too cool for everybody."

Spiro shrugged his shoulders and didn't disagree. "It's that *muse* thing. Sometimes with beautiful, creative women, I get taken." Despite Michael-Leslie's love of poetry, Spiro began to acknowledge that not much else was there. "Either we have nothing in common, or she's not who she seems." Spiro hinted moving on, mostly, "I still like her, though."

Darby put it straight: "Musical tastes, art, taste in film, all that, when it comes down it—maybe this is just me—they don't matter. I think it's not *what you like*, it's what you *are like*. How you're brought up, what your values are and how you connect with people." Darby said this now, like some girlfriend expert. "You can have a connection and *not* like the same music."

"Weird to hear that from you." Spiro leaned in. "What does Rachel like?"

"Well, I'm working on her, and she doesn't hate what I like. But Rachel likes, you know, hard rock and metal. Old glam stuff too."

"Like what?"

"Metallica and The Cult, New York Dolls. And Motörhead—a lot."

"That's cool."

"Def Leppard. Cheap Trick."

"That's OK, sometimes."

"Stuff like REO Speedwagon."

"No..."

"Styx too."

"Ew. No."

"See what I mean? She even made me a mixtape."

"Really? Big step. With what on it?" Spiro asked.

"Motley Crüe, Queensryche—"

"Oh, no."

"Point is, doesn't matter. I mean, it's not all my kind of stuff. But it's the thought that counts."

Entree plates arrived, and in a snap, famished, they dug in and then finished up. Later, a silent busboy took their plates. Penny then waddled over to thank them, with the bill and some tamarind candies—but no more Shanti. Spiro grabbed one of the sweets, unwrapping and re-wrapping it, fidgeting to talk more to his new prospective muse. He made small talk about Jenna's Halloween bash later that night, more about his Zeppelin II kick, how much he respects Metallica and hates Styx, how much French press coffee is better than drip. He kept marveling at his favorite server, trying to court her attention while not making it look so. Eventually, she noticed and came over, probably thinking Spiro wanted tea.

"You guys good? Need anything else?" She looked at him with a delighted smile, and Darby could see Spiro winding up, in a rush to engage her further.

"So, Shanti. That's a kinda—unique name," Spiro said.

"Yes. Maybe a little," she said, again touching her hair.

Darby saw Spiro ready to pull out a joke, and thought *No. Don't.*

"So, then," Spiro smiled big, "are your parents like hippies or something?"

Shanti's smile flattened, and she looked surprised by the comment, but not in a good way. Darby wanted to kick Spiro under the table. Shanti squinted at Spiro as if she couldn't believe he'd said something so knuckleheaded.

"No, actually, my parents are well-read. My mom is a teacher and my dad is a history professor. Shanti—was the only name they said they could agree on, so that's how I got it." Shanti then closed out her fleeting interest in Spiro. "*I love my name*," she said proudly.

Spiro's face became a rush of firetruck red, embarrassed and uncomfortable.

"If you wanna pay Penny, that's cool with me," Shanti said. "Thanks for coming in."

It made no sense to counsel Spiro on his mistake.

"I won't say anything," Darby said, grabbing the bill. "I got this one."

SERENDIPITY

Later, after Spiro's Thai restaurant disaster, they were in Rod's car, en route to Jenna's "after-Halloween" Halloween party. Darby rode shotgun, Spiro silent in the back. Rod began honking.

"Fucking idiots!" Rod yelled. "Just a little rain and everyone forgets how to drive."

The summer-like skies had rained hard, but only for five minutes about two hours earlier. Yet long after the rain passed, it bred the usual idle, stupid-ass Chicago traffic. Rod's complaints didn't help. It became apparent the car was one place where his lesser-refined roots came out.

"Come on, Beemer boy," Rob blasted again. "Chop chop! Let's go!"

Spiro and Darby were happy to hitch a ride with Rod in his newish Lexus. But instead of music, they both listened to Rod's diatribes about luxury cars and bad drivers.

"Ever since they released the new BMW 3 Series, what— two years ago?"

"I don't know," Darby said. "No idea."

"Well, anyway, once the 318i came out—that whole low-priced BMW series, really—every yuppie dipshit with credit goes out and gets one. They're all rear-wheel drive and their drivers are *so* afraid to get a scratch. So they drive super slow. It's like a country club vomited its membership all over the streets here."

Darby never thought of the city's overstock of fancy new cars as a cause for social strife. But for now, they'd have to weather Chicago's gridlock and Rod's ire.

"Move it! Move, or go back to the suburbs! Come on, golf caddy!" *Honk.*

Foul language aside, Rod was dressed perfectly as James Bond and he said his date was going tonight as his "Bond Girl." Darby and Spiro had decided to coordinate costumes too. Spiro first suggested that they "go political" with a stoner version of the 1996 Republican presidential ticket, Bob Dole and Jack Kemp as "*Roll / Hemp '96.*" After that, Spiro's other idea was a spin on the trending *human genome* news story. He suggested they go as gangsta rap gnomes, with N.W.A. shirts and red pointy hats, basically gangsta gnomes—or "G gnomes."

"No one will get that pun," Darby had told him.

So, instead, they settled as a pair of masked bank robbers portrayed in the new Camp Lo rap video on *BET*. So, it was suits with red ties and black gloves, a sack of fake loot with dollar signs drawn onto it. Propped atop Darby's head was a Richard Nixon mask. She looked back at Spiro, who had on a gingery, flabby-faced Donald Trump mask.

If only these guys knew what's coming in 2016, Darby thought.

Rachel had said she'd meet Darby at the party, but wouldn't divulge her costume of the night. After a half-mile of slow gridlock traffic, Rod stopped and double-parked, then jumped out to get his date. Rod told Darby to hop in the back so that Serenity could sit upfront.

"Serenity? That's her name?" Another—brand new girl.

"No Mackenzie this weekend?" Darby asked him.

Rod stopped and did an about-face, and then opened up the car door again. He leaned in, cracking a tense voice. "Do *not* mention other women tonight. Please."

"Uh, OK. *No problem.*"

Rod adjusted his cufflinks, pushed back his hair, and shut the car door. Spiro, still searing from blowing it that afternoon, spoke up.

"How is it that he's got a different girl every week? I like Rod. I'm not dissing on him. But he's like, what, 5' 2"?"

"Claims he's 5' 4", but I don't believe him."

"Right. Well, anyway, he gets to date all these towering, gorgeous women, and I don't know how he does it! What's his superpower, here?"

Darby knew Spiro was being hard on himself since sticking his foot in his mouth at the Thai place. But he was being hard on Rod too.

"I guess it's his confidence or a way he has with words. Maybe persuasive gifts we don't hear about, because he's not trying to get *us* into bed." Darby reminded Spiro that it's not all it seems. "You've met them. They ever seem interesting to you?"

"*No.*"

"OK, think about courting them, wining, and dining them. There's a cost to his lifestyle."

"So, it's money?"

"No, but Rod has certain tastes. So do his girly girls. Most often they don't come with a brain or a personality, but there's still a price. Bad return on investment, if you ask me."

They then saw Rod's new date appear at the door of her building. "Serendipity" is what Darby wanted to call her, the way she just popped up; a ready-made match for Rod's costume choice. She and Spiro peered out the rain-stained windows of Rod's SUV, watching them tread very slowly, because of her impressive but cumbersome stiletto heels.

"OK, so, take the long legs off her. Put her in a bad sweater," Darby said. "Try to have an intelligent conversation about Victor Hugo or whatever you're reading. Have fun with that."

"But, she *is* wearing glasses," Spiro said, noticing her big horn rims and how they complemented her high cheekbones.

Rod and his date approached the car.

"Maybe he got a smart one this time."

"Shh," Darby said.

Rod opened the passenger door for his date.

"Serenity: That's Alex," Rod said, "And, Darby there, holding the Nixon mask."

"Hello! Hello!" Rod's new girl gushed friendliness as she settled in. "Nice to meet you. Darby's a cool name," Serenity then said. "Is that a family name or something?"

"No. Just one of those W.A.S.P.-y Ralph Lauren names. Very 1990s, I guess."

Darby returned the interest and asked about her name: "Serenity, that's kinda unique."

"Well, my parents were flower children, kinda. It was the one name they both liked."

"Interesting," said Darby.

Spiro winced.

"Anyway," she continued, "with a name like Serenity I joke that I should've been a Prince backup singer. Missed my chance," she said, feigning a frown face.

Just the pop culture reference boosted her stock in Darby's mind. She could tell Serendipity, er, Serenity, whatever her name was, wasn't Rod's usual arm candy. And when Darby asked what she did, she said she did "a little modeling"—not surprising—and TV commercials, which was how Rod met her, but that she was studying pre-med at Northwestern. "In case the acting thing doesn't work out," she said.

A woman who was pretty, funny, and intelligent. Maybe Rod was evolving too.

Once Rod parked outside Jenna's place they could hear a bustling crowd inside from the third-floor open windows. The party buzz brightened Spiro up a little.

Inside, people were sprawled into the hallway. Jenna's front door was wide open, and there stood Deighv, holding a Pabst tallboy. He had his hair slicked in a 1950s way, wearing a plain white tee and jeans just as the German greasers wore in France. Deighv was tipsy and more talkative than usual. He greeted them mightily.

"Yo, lofties!"

"Hey there, greaser Dave. Nice getup." Darby asked Deighv where he'd been all week.

"Need you ask?" Deighv responded. *Nope.*

Spiro spotted Michael-Leslie and floated away immediately. Rod then took Serenity's hand and darted off too, probably to see if Jenna had Scotch. Deighv leaned toward Darby to ask about the tall girl in stilettos.

"Seems refined for Rod's tastes," Deighv said. "Hope he can handle it."

Darby patted Deighv on the shoulder, and with a flinch, he smiled and spoke again.

"Ow. So—check it out! Jenna and I got inked." Deighv slid up his sleeve to show a bright new tattoo of a green Pontiac GTO with rolling wheels and shooting flames. "It was Jenna's idea," Deighv said. "We were just feeling it. She got a red Corvette."

Neither Deighv nor Jenna had ever before seemed spontaneous, or much the tattoo type. So the decision to get "inked" seemed impressive and daring to Darby. Darby knew Jenna was a Prince fan too; so maybe there was a 'little red Corvette' reference there. And she decided Jenna would, as such, have to meet Rod's date at some point this evening. Darby was also pleased that Deighv's tattoo wasn't just a lame-o heart with Jenna's name on it.

Looking around the crowd, more people were wearing timely outfits. There was yet another Unabomber, and a Hannibal Lecter wearing a restraint mask, holding a bottle of Chianti. There were members of The Village People next to all five Spice Girls. And there, in a Guns N' Roses T-shirt, red bandanna, jeans, and black boots was Rachel, dressed as Axl Rose.

Darby walked over to her rock chick. "Hey, stranger."

She grabbed Darby's tie and pulled her closer for a kiss.

"Like it? Good use for my hair," Rachel said. "Bank robber, ay? For a minute I thought you were a Chicago politician."

HYPERTEXTUAL

Darby passively listened to partygoers around them, and to talkative Rachel conversing with newly made party pals about arbitrary things. Content to be all ears, Darby observed the smattering of 1990s randoms enjoying a kitschy American holiday.

Now even more people in timely Halloween costumes filled Jenna's apartment. Joining the Unabomber and the Spice Girls was a soccer mom with stone-washed jeans and felt soccer balls pinned to an ill-fitting, chintzy "Disney University" amusement park souvenir sweatshirt. There was a guy dressed as a can of Red Bull, standing very appropriately next to a guy in workout tights and a ponytail dressed as Tony Little, the spastic TV infomercial pitchman. Another woman in a hot pink wig wore a #91 Chicago Bulls jersey over a teal pants suit; ostensibly "Hillary *Rodman* Clinton." Each was a mascot for the decade at hand.

Meanwhile, every byte of dialog seemed hyperlinked to the next. Ten feet away, Spiro stood with Michael-Leslie, in a one-sided exchange. She mentioned her on-and-off boyfriend, the one who, she said, went to Princeton, but works "paradoxically" at a record store. For the moment, Michael-Leslie and her boyfriend are just friends:

> "I took Darrell to this record release thing," she told Spiro.
>
> "Cool, what band?"
>
> "Pharaoh Head. They're industrial. Kind of a Wax Trax sound."
>
> "Nice."
>
> "Invite only. My best girl used to date Steve Albini, so—"
>
> "How was the music?"
>
> "Good. Darrell and I got in a fight, though. He wanted to leave early."
>
> "Why's that?" Spiro asked.
>
> "He wanted to watch some *Melrose Place* TV marathon."
>
> "Seriously?"
>
> "He loves that show. Won't admit it. Says he watches it for 'ironic' reasons."
>
> "I don't know what that means," Spiro said.

Darby grew bored eavesdropping on Michael-Leslie's self-absorbed histories and gross misuse of both "paradox" and "irony." In another direction stood '50s Deighv and movie spy Rod.

> "One thing the '90s does better than the other decades—"
>
> "Action movies." Rod interrupted. Hopefully, he might let Deighv finish.
>
> "I was gonna say movie soundtracks."

"Totally."

"*Singles. Reality Bites.* Even bad movies like *Sliver—*"

"Ooh, Sharon Stone."

"*Bill & Ted 2, Empire Records,* not great movies, any of them. But good motion picture soundtracks. And yes, your film noir stuff, *Pulp Fiction, Lost Highway,* all great ones too. It's a movie score for our time," Deighv said passionately.

Across the room, a familiar-looking trio of dudes were listing *Things To Do Before You Die.* Loud and trying to court attention, the trio resembled a troika of hobos getting warm over a fire. To Darby, their list sounded like *Things Guys Without Girlfriends Talk About At Parties:*

"Spend the whole weekend drunk."

"Spend a whole weekend naked!"

"I wanna date a hot mom!" one said.

"I'd do my ex-girlfriend's mom," said another.

"I wanna go skydiving," said the third one of them.

Good one, they all agreed.

"Maybe skydiving naked. Sky streaking. Naked, except for my parachute."

"I've always wanted to be in a band," said the longhaired one.

"I should learn guitar," lamented whole-weekend-drunk guy.

"Or, get a tattoo," the longhaired one said.

"I already got three," bragged the streaking enthusiast.

He peeled up his sleeve to show the other two his Bart Simpson tattoo on one shoulder, and on the other was Greek fraternity letters. He then lifted up his pant leg to reveal a bottle of Jägermeister. Clearly, he hoped others took notice, including two vampish women nearby.

But the two spunky young women in black talked about the advanced ink work on their bodies; real artistry and not stupid frat symbols or cartoons. One of them gave 'Jäger guy' a glance of disapproval before turning back to talk about tattoo art.

> "I'm glad the art form's progressed beyond hearts and skulls."
>
> "Right? I'll only do original art. Where do you go?"
>
> "I use Bavmorda. She's part-time at Belmont Ink."
>
> "No way. *Love* her work."
>
> "I can see if she's taking clients. Prob'aly is."
>
> "Awesome. All mine were done before I moved here, up in Madison."
>
> "Bav's cool. I hear DJ Scary Lady Sarah uses her."
>
> "Sweet. I just saw her spin at *Neo* on Thursday."

The two women introduced themselves to each other as Scintilla and Pam, then headed to Jenna's kitchenette for more party punch. Sudden dead air led Darby's ears behind her, where Jenna and Rod's date were talking TV and older men.

> "Prince was on the *Late Show* Wednesday night but I missed him," Jenna said.
>
> "On Letterman? He was great," Serenity/Serendipity concluded.
>
> "Though Letterman is kinda mean now."

"But he's my old man-crush."

"Mine's Sean Connery," said Jenna.

"Good one. Hot!"

By now Rod had switched topics on Deighv, forcibly, to James Bond films. But the segue wasn't difficult since Rod was dressed as 007, albeit the shortest 007 ever. Rod said which Bond he preferred, and Darby was surprised to hear him say Moore over Connery.

"George Lazenby, in my opinion, was the worst James Bond."

"Was he the hairy one?"

"Yup. Did only one film. *Her Majesty's Secret Service.*"

"Never saw it."

"Don't bother," Rod advised.

Rod looked over at Serenity, still with Jenna, and grabbed a cig from his metal case to head to the balcony. He then looked over at Darby because he and Darby both noticed another one of Rod's on-and-off flings, a woman named Quinn, approaching to say hello. Quinn's long, auburn hair was knotted seductively to match her geisha costume. Dangerous.

Rachel noticed Darby looking lost in space: "Hey, you!"

"Yeah, I'm here."

A familiar voice then appeared behind them. It was Simon in a snazzy 1960s suit and a white ascot around his neck. "Yeah, baby!" Simon said.

"You came as yourself?"

"No—Austin Powers, baby!" Everyone by now had seen the trailers. Simon bought into the character, a sort of caricature of himself. "Groovy, baby... yeah!"

Deighv piped in: "That's not much of a costume, you know, Simon."

Simon leaned over to high-five Rachel and slapped Deighv on the shoulder where his new ink seared. Darby watched Rod walk out to the balcony with Quinn.

Over another hour, more drinks circulated in the center of Jenna's place. Empty cups piled up, marking the gradual departure of guests. Jenna and Deighv told everyone the long version of their tattoo story. After a few more chinwags, they heard arguing.

Rod's date stormed in from the balcony, and then turned back and yelled. Her stiletto heels clicked against the floor in a quick, angry staccato as she ran out. A moment later Rod followed behind her, swiftly and trying to act calm.

"Hmm, that looks a little dramatic," Rachel said. "Wonder what's up."

Rachel then threw in her own version of Spiro's interjections, that:

    a) Rod is short, and that

    b) All the women Rod dates are supermodels
       that tower over him.

"How does he get these babes anyhow?"

"I know, right?" Spiro said. "Persuasion, I guess."

"Are they having a fight?" Rachel asked out loud. "What's she mad about?"

Quinn reappeared. Darby leaned over, voice lowered. "See that geisha?"

"Yeah? She's so cute."

"That's Rod's other woman, or *one* of his other women, I should say."

"*Oh.* Damn, smooth Roddy."

"Serendipity probably felt a little neglected or something." Darby said this, realizing she didn't even have the girl's name straight. But 'Serendipity' stuck.

"That's her name?" Rachel asked. "Serendipity?"

"Serendipity? Seriously?" Deighv said. "Typical Rod."

"What a cool name," Jenna frowned. "Too bad for Rod. I was just starting to like her."

FILE UNDER EASY LISTENING

NOVEMBER 22, 1996

Ryan Nakamoto was back in America, home very early for Thanksgiving. How did Darby know? A note on the dry-erase whiteboard up front provided real-time updates:

> D — *Guy who says ur music sucks called. Will call back.*

Friday, the week before Thanksgiving, Spiro came over in the afternoon, awaiting Ry-Guy to turn up. Ryan had convinced Darby that they should see one of his favorite bands, an oddball industrial act called Peter Meter, of all things. Right at 6 P.M. Ry rang Darby's doorbell, and after Darby first buzzed him in, Ry kept punching the doorbell repeatedly, just to be annoying.

"Dude, I buzzed you in," Darby said to Ry-Guy. "Are you deaf?"

"I think I'm hard of hearing now," Spiro said to them.

"You'll both be deaf by later tonight. Peter Meter is *the shit!*" Ry then asked Darby, "Where's your girl?"

She told Ry he could meet her later if they didn't throw him off the roof. Not only would Rachel meeting Ry-Guy be a hoot, but Darby also loved that some live industrial music would totally blow her wholesome metalhead girlfriend's mind.

The three of them hadn't seen each other since Europe. It was a perfect welcome from a guy Darby hadn't seen since bluffing French cops and getting called a 'cockroach' by locals.

Later, at The Vic, the venue's lighted marquee blasted the band's name. Rachel was there, standing and waiting. From 50 feet away she shined luminescent, her long red hair shooting out playfully from under a black beanie, suitably rock 'n' roll once again, in jeans and a KISS T-shirt under her jacket. Darby spotted her first and noticed how the men waiting in line were looking Rachel over. Ry-Guy echoed their sentiment.

"*Damn.*"

"That's Rachel," Spiro said, "D's big squeeze."

She spotted them and hurried over with, "Hey, dudes."

"Rachel Murray, you know Spiro," Darby said, "and this is *the* legendary Ry-Guy. Ryan Nakamoto, the lost fugitive hiding in France."

"Hey there," Ry said to Rachel. "How'd you end up with this fool?"

"I wonder myself sometimes. She's got good taste in music, so I hold her fully responsible for our selection tonight."

"This was my idea," Ry said. "Unless they suck. Then it's D's fault."

"No crowd surfing tonight," Rachel told Darby.

The four slipped into a side door marked for staff and guest list attendees. Darby, for the first time ever, had worked her City Scene contacts to get in on a guest list.

As lights flickered and flashed, Darby passed out some earplugs she'd brought, but Ry-Guy batted them away: "Put that shit away, man."

Once they were inside, an electronic thunder calmed to a silence. Lights went down to pitch-black, and the crowd inside screamed cheerily. The Vic was much bigger than Lounge Ax, commanding a sizable crowd for Peter Meter, even though Darby never heard of them.

"These guys are huge in Europe!" Ry told Rachel.

"Just like the Doors are," Spiro backhanded Ry-Guy.

The band appeared on stage and looked the part of Euro-techno rockstars. Three mean-looking, bald guys in spiked and shiny PVC outfits raised a fist and grabbed their warlock-styled instruments. As they began rocking out, another band member, a very tall woman, stood at center stage in an elevated DJ booth, bouncing to the loud music while shooting out her arms with the beats, kung-fu action-style. Together, their onslaught of lights and sound thrashed from the stage, while the four friends pushed up front, closer to the band.

While Ry got his Euro-trash music fill, Darby, Rachel, and Spiro took in the show's fun vibe. Raving with the beats, brightly dressed club kids danced and shuffled, whipping around fluorescent glow sticks. Some blew whistles, which few could hear above the music.

Right after the show, Ry looked satisfied but sweaty and spent, like a tornado hit him, his hair un-gelled, hilariously in every direction. On Ry's urging, they hit Pontero's on Belmont to order up pizza, while Rachel got her fix of the orange Fanta that seemed to color her hair.

Happy and hungry, Ry-Guy weighed in: "Chicago 'za, bitch!"

Darby decided to translate for Rachel: "Ry-Guy here calls pizza "'za." No one else here calls it that. Ry-Guy can't say the whole word."

"Technically this pizzeria is East Coast style," Spiro asserted.

"'Za is 'za!" Ry-Guy insisted. "Chicago pizza, bitches."

"Well, it's not cut into stupid little squares, is it?" Darby said back.

Rachel tempered their rising pizza hostility and put Ry on the spot. "I notice you say *bitch* a lot, Ryan. I mean, I'm not offended or anything, but is that a Chicago thing?"

Ryan put on a devilish smile. "I use the word *bitch* because that's *his name*," pointing at Spiro. "Last year in Europe he was my *ganja bitch*. Now you's my *'za bitch*, bitch!"

"It's not a Chicago thing," Darby insisted. "He's from the suburbs. He's not even technically from Chicago. He's from Arlington Heights. Ry-Guy is just trying to be a badass."

"Sheeeit, bitch."

"See."

Darby knew Ry-Guy was understandably stoked to be home, chowing down on classic American fare that he'd missed after two years in France.

When the topic of Thanksgiving came up, Ry talked about Nakamoto traditions.

"Best part of being Japanese at Thanksgiving is our turkey comes with homemade gyoza. Deep-fried! What are you guys up to?"

"Rachel's heading back to Minnesota and I'm staying here. Spiro's visiting his divorced parents and I'm avoiding mine," Darby said. "I have work to do and I hate holidays anyway."

Rachel looked at Darby with sympathetic eyes, over her family-related despondence, saying that it would be OK. Shared holiday melancholy was something bonding them, a generation of divorce children holding on together.

"At least you don't have to share turkey with this sucka," Ry joked to Rachel.

"Well, that's true," Rachel said with a smirk.

Redeeming himself for his usual barrage of *bitch*, *sucka*, and other insults, Ry-Guy proclaimed that he'd pick up the tab. "It's great to be home. Thanks, guys," Ry said.

Like Rachel, Darby wasn't offended by Ry-Guy's barbs. Instead, she was heartened just to see her obnoxious friend in the flesh, being himself again after so many years.

PERFECT FROM NOW ON

NOVEMBER 29, 1996

Tuesday after Thanksgiving would be a big day, the day Dreaded Letters' first album hit stores. The news was that the band had signed a one-album deal with a small indie label. The label issued no promotional copies of the album, so Darby and City Scene couldn't get their hands on it early. But Darby knew the music inside out. There was also another silver lining. They had a show in Chicago on Black Friday. At Lounge Ax again, of all places.

But in the meantime, Darby had some work to do and resolved to make the most of her Thanksgiving Day alone. A few days before Peter Meter's show, Darby skipped off to 1994 to catch the Green Day performance at The Aragon. Another review to write.

The Chicago date of their *Dookie! Tour* was one MTV famously broadcast under the title "Jaded In Chicago" and it was exactly the kind of show ideal for Latecomers' Reviews; a famous band at a medium-sized venue, still edgy in its look and feel, in an era before Green Day would sell out 30,000-seat sports arenas.

Darby sat in the loft along with take-out fried rice, tapping a clunky Compaq loaner laptop from City Scene. She was having an uncharacteristic difficulty chronicling the show:

Latecomers' Reviews

Green Day
Aragon Ballroom 11/18/1994
(Opening band: Pansy Division)

Both old and new punk rock fans squabble over whether Green Day should get credit for bringing punk back to the mainstream. ...

With two hours before the Dreaded Letters show, Darby pounded at the keyboard, but nothing monumental. She looked at her time-pass, which read DAYS LEFT: 4.

She stopped working and decided to get ready for the evening out. It would be dark at the club, and she was going by herself. But she wanted to look good, maybe just for the ceremony of it. So she put on jeans, high leather boots, and her favorite leather jacket. Almost a uniform now. She looked at her time-pass again and took it off her wrist.

Darby then stopped to reflect. Things were good. She had a girlfriend and a good job that she liked too. Plus, her favorite band was playing tonight.

Darby tossed the time-pass onto the easy chair in her room and got ready to leave.

Later, at the door of Lounge Ax, no bouncers looked her over, and no one spotted her as that nutjob who fell on her head back in September. At the bar, she ordered up a beer and turned toward the stage, which was dimly lit from the sides with a hovering glare. Across the big rock 'n' roll living room, toward the left of the stage, she saw the familiar shape of a woman's hair. It was Lina.

She knew now it would be silly to try to duck and ignore her, or worse yet awkward if straightforward Lina caught Darby pretending not to see her. Darby would have to face the music and decided to do so before Dreaded Letters' own great music started. But Darby couldn't pretend she didn't see another woman by Lina's side.

"Lina!" she said, ducking into her view. "Hi."

"*Darby.* Hello." Lina was caught off guard but warm. "Should've known you'd be here."

"Well, they are my favorite band."

Darby acknowledged Lina's guest, a tall girl in a cream-sicle-colored polo shirt standing stiffly next to Lina. She looked like a lost golfer.

"Hello, I'm Darby."

"Tanya. Nice to meet you."

Lina said that her friend Tanya had never been to Lounge Ax and that she wanted to take her out. Lina's parents, who had come down from Michigan for Thanksgiving, were already pooped, and lights-out for the night, back at her place.

"I thought this band was great when you made me come last time," Lina said to Darby.

"Actually, you brought me," Darby reminded Lina.

As Lina smiled, Tanya also smiled blankly and awkwardly. "Anyhow, Tanya's not much of a music fan, but I'm working on her."

Explains the middle-aged yacht crew look, Darby thought to herself.

"Well, anyway, I saw you and didn't want *not* to say hi," Darby said. "And I'm glad you like the band. I think they're gonna be huge someday. Save the ticket stub."

Darby looked back to her seat at the bar as she walked over to it, knowing that it was the very same spot where she first met Rachel that September night when The Enlightenment played. Even though the crowd surfing incident happened that night too, she had to hand it to herself for making it all right. More than all right. Perfect, even.

And as more and more people filled Lounge Ax, the crowd was tall enough and noisy enough that it drowned out any sight of Lina and Tanya by the stage.

Darby always thought herself a second-rate pick for Lina anyway—and possibly the same for Rachel too. But she thought she was evolving into a better if not an impossibly perfect version of herself. She would try to keep that going from now on.

City Scene | Music

Latecomers' Reviews by Darby Derrex
December 3, 1996

City Scene's Music Editor reviews historic 1990s concerts twice monthly in this column.

Dreaded Letters
Lounge Ax. Jan. 9, 1996 and Nov. 29, 1996

Twelve people—OK, maybe 17 if you count the bar staff—were present at Dreaded Letters' first ever gig, which took place in Chicago last January. Despite frigid temperatures, the weather couldn't suffice as an excuse for missing that show. Luckily, a friend tipped me off and I had my act together enough to get there. (Yes, I'm bragging a bit.)

Today, this newly Chicago-based band's debut album called *Velvet Mourning* hits stores. While some might assume the record is a good first taste, their day-after-Thanksgiving show demonstrated how a band that is neither grunge nor punk can thrive in the 1990s. Give it time: Dreaded Letters will succeed in capturing hearts. (I have seen the future. Believe me.)

The trio made up of Shawne O'Connell (guitar/vocals), Kira Szymanski (bass) and Kerry Pales (drums) began both January 1996 shows and last week's gig with the title track of their first album. Word around the scene last year was that Dreaded Letters were once three Grinnell College students experimenting with new sounds. By their third song in, last Friday, anyone in the audience could see they're not just a new act, but three maestros expanding musical boundaries and the limits of what could be done with a guitar, post-Jimi Hendrix.

O'Connell sings with the same raw power that most notable punk bands of our era (think Fugazi, Bikini Kill) boast, while her solo guitar gives a nod to progressive rock at a time when any song over three minutes seems an apostasy.

Moreover, the band's rhythm section could be described as perfectly 'minimalist' in the same way that Ringo Starr's drumming complemented the Beatles' internal competing ambitions of Paul McCartney and John Lennon. Like The Police did on their first albums, Dreaded Letters' lyrics tap every issue—from war and globalization to gender—inviting listeners to think, without bashing them over the head.

If you pick up *Velvet Mourning* this week, you'll be witness to how three women rocket their fuzzy riffs into music that makes sense of our times. It's also a glimpse of what the future of music—and the future at large—might hold.

Safe to say, if you stayed in last January because of the cold, or missed Black Friday's show because you were tired from shopping, you missed out big. Someday soon, your best option to see this band will be a stadium. Just an early warning, friends.

Rating: 5/5
Setlist: Velvet Mourning, Yankee Cockroaches, Hypertextual, Silent, Fire, Mantle, Never Again, Horses (Patti Smith cover), Far Side, Welcome To Paris Fools, C'mon, Let's Go, Serendipity.

LAST SPLASH

DECEMBER 1996. BACK IN TIME.

Right after the Dreaded Letters write-up went to print in Tuesday's edition, Darby got a dozen emails from people who were at the same Black Friday show. Some asked when the band was back again. Some hailed the band. Others proclaimed someday they'd be rock history.

With the Thanksgiving holiday passed, Darby felt like she hadn't seen Rachel in weeks, and Rachel had said during a quick phone call that she had plenty going on back home in Minnesota. The early snow lent itself to skiing—one of her family's more normal activities, and one that Rachel said helped temporarily keep the peace.

"Hey—When are you back?" Darby asked.

"Not until Tuesday," Rachel had said.

Rachel told Darby about a slope just over the Canada border, and Darby tried to picture Rachel schussing down a powdered mountain in black leather and an AC DC hat.

That morning, Darby had a public radio interview to talk about new band releases and live shows. The radio station was uptown, so it worked out that Rachel wanted to meet for coffee after lunch. Darby craved a splash of affection since they hadn't had a date out in a while. But things had been going well, Darby thought.

After the radio interview, Darby made it to Buzz a tad early, while soft snows had started blanketing Chicago. Darby ordered, and right as the server dropped off a large mug, she looked up and saw Rachel appear at the door, dressed head-to-toe in black. She had a heavy scarf and dark sweater under it, standing in chunky winter boots. The snow outside made the sunlight fulminate behind Rachel. Darby stood up.

"Finally, you're back."

"Yup. Long drive." Rachel said. "Thanks for meeting here."

In the face, Rachel looked a little stressed, probably from the awful drive, and Rachel didn't address her in the usual ways. No hug, or "dream girl," no "Hey, you."

"How were the slopes? You the only one in black?" Darby joked, pointing to her leather.

"No, ha. I do have a black CB ski coat. Have to have one," Rachel said, looking down. She started chatting about the cool trails and alpine views. She explained to Darby what a *piste* was, and how fun Falcon Ridge was to ski, even with her emotionally tiring family.

Darby could tell she was affected, different.

"So," Rachel said abruptly, "I have something to share with you."

Either it was nothing, or something not good. Perhaps Rachel had lost her lease and wanted to move in together. Or someone back home died. Maybe she finally worked up the resolve to tell Darby that she hated her music—and they had to talk about that.

"You know I hate surprises myself. No one's died or anything," Rachel assured her.

"Oh—"

"No, it's—well, I've had fun with you. I like you, Darby. But some changes are afoot."

Afoot? Odd word to use. "What's that mean?"

"I think we're mostly good for each other," Rachel continued. "It's, I guess you could say, more involved than that. And I'm moving. Moving away."

"Moving?" Darby asked incredulously. "Where?"

"To Washington, D.C.," Rachel said. "I have a work opportunity. It's kind of a big deal, a big thing for me." Rachel worked in government, she reminded Darby, and as she looked away and around the cafe, Rachel then explained that she'd been "poached" for something extraordinary, something perfect for her talents. Someone she worked for back in the Twin Cities had moved onto K Street, Washington's lobbying capital, and wanted her on board. "It's consulting work, in the arts. You know, I love the arts, the humanities. All that."

Since when was there a National Heavy Metal Institute in Washington? *Why must they take my girlfriend away?* Darby thought. Then she snapped to the first thing she could think of; a solution to this new, impending problem.

"We can do the distance thing," Darby insisted.

After all, her time pass ran out, and over the holiday weekend Darby decided, albeit silently and secretly, to stay in 1996. Rachel was a big reason. Maybe the only reason. Her sacrifice was one she couldn't tell Rachel about.

But Rachel's reply was immediate. "No."

And why not? Washington, D.C., wasn't far. A short flight, Midway to National. Easy.

"We can—just see how it goes. Hell, D.C. has a great music scene." Legendary punk bands. City papers too. Darby had never had a girlfriend in another city but wasn't opposed to it now. She could find a job. It would be fine. "I'd love to visit you, once you settle in."

"No," Rachel said again. "It's not that simple. I didn't plan it this way. Not trying to kick you to the curb. But, things happened when I got home. I ended up meeting someone again. You don't know him."

"Him?"

"Yes, a *him*."

"Kenny?"

Rachel laughed. "No."

Darby struggled to conjure up names of Rachel's other Minnesota-nice boys. And a shiny thing sat on Rachel's finger. "Nice ring. Early Christmas present?"

"No, it's just a piece of jewelry. Anyway, I'm moving the week after next."

"Did you get engaged or something?"

No. No, no, Rachel protested. But she admitted that, yes, it was from a guy, someone with a name that didn't sound like a name. Not a real name, at least.

"Sky-what? Sky Who? A Sky-*ler*? Schuyler?"

"Yes, Skylar," Rachel said, spelling it out, "Skylar is *his* name." It is a *he,* she said. "We went out for a while in college and after that, I caught up with him again, and accidentally, inadvertently, he got in touch with me, things happened. Things happen to people."

Darby saw that this conversation wasn't entirely about career moves. Was this Skylar guy one of those "attractive assholes" she mentioned she used to date?

"Well, no, but he's different now." Rachel was getting testy.

Darby pictured this Skylar—*sorry, what kind of name was that?*—in the image of a beach guy, surfboard in hand. *Skylar,* a churlish mess of blond who says "dude" and "S'up?" Any minute now, he'd roll up in a Jeep with a "H4NG LooS" license plate, blasting Dave Matthews from the woofers. Skylar, the *Grinch Who Stole Darby's Girlfriend,* and it wasn't even Christmas yet, goddammit. Her brain couldn't intervene in what her mouth did next.

"Skylar, huh? Very 1990s name," she said. "Very preppy."

"Preppy? *Like, Darby,* you mean?" Rachel went on, her face wincing displeasure. "Look, let's not fight. There'd be no use now. I like you, but, frankly, I didn't think you were *into this.*"

"What do you mean by—*this*?"

"*This*, meaning *us,*" Rachel said. "You're aloof sometimes, and I don't know what to make of it. But that's just you, I think. Skylar loves me, and I'm sure you'll find someone great."

It wasn't the first time that Darby had been told she was indifferent, not dialed-in, not invested, or in this case, that she was "aloof" in a relationship. Alan had said it, and Lina too. Now Rachel. The theme was the same, no matter what anyone called it.

Darby wanted to flee sooner than the check could arrive. So, she laid down $10, got up, and said to Rachel, "Goodbye and good luck." But one more thing. A weak parting shot. "Have to admit... I really hated your taste in music."

STUCK...
BACK-IN-TIME

Uncle
Anesthesia

DECEMBER 7, 1996. BACK IN TIME.

Darby hadn't thought too much about resuming her life in the 21st century. That was before her time-pass expired. Now its battery was totally dead, and Darby was stuck in 1996 whether she liked it or not. But her mind was lodged in the present. Being dumped by Rachel saw to that.

She didn't advertise the big breakup to roommates and friends. But when she stopped going out and spent hours in her room with the door shut, listening to music louder than usual, Deighv, Simon, and Rod just assumed. Darby didn't want to burden anyone or become an emotional slug. Like the drama-filled rock operas of old, her way of dealing with her personal drama came in stages. And it played out just like another mixtape in Darby's music-filled head.

Stage 1:
A spell of defiance sinks in. So do "don't care" three-chord

anthems. Loud percussion and guitars soothe the pain or mask it, at least. The first Oasis album and its songs "Rock 'N' Roll Star," and "Cigarettes & Alcohol" offer titles as defiant as their rhythms. The album's distant older cousin *Never Mind The Bollocks It's The Sex Pistols*, kept denial highs going for a day.

Stage 2:
"Easy," the famous Lionel Richie tune—almost as good covered by Faith No More—balances ups and downs. Following that, writhing poetics by Morrissey, the smug solo artist who probably explores failed relationships better than anyone, followed by brainless power-pop—think Billy Idol's "Mony Mony"—helps stave off a bigger downward spiral.

Stage 3:
A few days later, Rachel was, yes, still gone. Darby finally left her room, but only to go to work or to sift through stacks at a nearby record store.

Instead of 21st-century favorites—Girl Named Nino, Northern State, Tacocat—she's thumbing through selections by Extreme and Candlebox, early 1990s commercial soft metal that was foreign to Darby just months ago. *Rachel's music*. Next thing, if she wasn't careful, Darby would be buying Tesla and Damn Yankees double-lives. Or worse yet, searching for hints of Rachel in the liner notes of a fucking Whitesnake album.

A store clerk walked by. "Need any help?"

"No thanks," Darby answered. "Say," she said to the clerk, "if you see me leave here with any of this Spandex music—please, push me in front of a bus."

The clerk shrugged. Funny or not, she wasn't kidding.

A day later, Darby remembered that she owed someone a visit. It was long overdue and yet might set her head straight. Martin was one of the only people who ever really understood her.

She stood outside Revolver Records, yet didn't miss owning it. Just like she didn't really miss the 21st century that much, nor the debates about Punk vs. Metal and The Clash versus Megadeth. She did miss Spacey; definitely her spark and insight, and the conversations they had about classic records, wish-list concerts, and the goodness of old, vintage everything. Wherever Spacey was in 1996, soon she'd be crawling, watching The Wiggles with the nanny, wearing a Green Day onesie over a first listen of *Nimrod,* before a diaper change and a nap.

As for Martin, he had lived a pretty long, good, full life. He loved music and selling it to other music lovers as much as he loved bucking the system and being an old rebel. Seeing him enjoying that life shouldn't be weird, she decided. Before stepping inside she tried to shake off her guilt for not visiting sooner.

She walked in, and the chime above the door cracked the store's silence. She was the first shopper to pass through Revolver's doors, just before noon.

"Ah, there you are, kiddo!" Martin said as he saw her face. "I was wondering when you'd stop in. Cut your hair, I see?"

"Yeah, I did. Hi, Uncle Martin."

"Too bad. Looked good on you. Guess we all gotta let it go some time."

Darby didn't see a time-pass watch on Martin's wrist but didn't necessarily expect to see one. She just wondered about the one in his old desk. *Who knows,* she thought.

"How are you, Uncle Martin?" Darby asked him.

Martin didn't answer that and got distracted in his typical funny way with another pressing thing. "I got something I set aside for you—hold on. Hold on, and I'll find it—hold on."

Uncle Martin was the same as always, talking a hundred miles a minute, pacing one way and back before completing one thought, to go to another. Seeing his bobbly Danny DeVito head just above the store counter made Darby savor the moment and smile just a little.

"Excuse me," Martin told her, "sometimes I just forget to stop and say hello."

"No worries," she said.

"I've been reading your column. Great stuff! So, I knew you didn't move."

"Nope." Right there, Darby felt the need to say something, even as Martin looked both happy and preoccupied. "Martin, I'm really sorry I didn't come by sooner. I'm sorry."

"Kiddo, forget it. You're busy doing good work! Life is a rolling train. Speaking of rolling trains—ah, here it is," Martin said. What he had for Darby wasn't time travel-related. "Here, you're gonna like this one. Just released by The Man In Black."

It was an album by Johnny Cash, not Cash doing Cash, but Cash doing covers. There were remakes of old country songs by Bobby George and Geoff Mack, and Cash covering Tom Petty, Beck, and other postmodern acts. Darby knew already that *Unchained* would go on to be a classic, and appreciated Martin's gesture and thinking of her.

"Thought you'd like his Soundgarden cover," he said. "It's real good, got a different feel to it. That's just Cash being Cash. I figured you'd be by eventually."

"Excellent. Thank you, Martin."

"Can't stay away from a good record store forever, can ya?"

"Nope."

When Darby first walked in she didn't know how it would go. But they had music in common—and that was something big. And instead of seeking advice on brushing away her sorrows, Darby got something to ease the pain. Seeing Martin was like a prescription for something—maybe anesthesia—that helped chase the aches away for a moment.

Heavy Rhyme
Experience

DECEMBER 14, 1996.

"Hey man, nice shirt," Darby said to Spiro. She was surprised to see—and finally find—her old Lollapalooza shirt on her friend's back, of all places. Now she knew where it ended up.

The music fest's inaugural lineup graced the back of it: seven bands, below a freaky, psychedelic pink lollipop logo.

Jane's Addiction
Siouxsie and the Banshees
Living Colour · Nine Inch Nails

Ice-T · Rollins Band
and the
Butthole Surfers

"Yeah," Spiro said. "I didn't even go to Lolla. Any o' them." He gave the brazen hint he'd been too high to remember half of the '90s, including concerts he had attended, or hadn't.

"It's funny," Darby said with a sarcastic hint, "I used to have one just like that."

"You did? No way! Found this in Europe. Someone left it at our hostel in Paris."

"Huh. No shit."

Spiro was intellectual through and through, but dense sometimes. Yet, finding that shirt on Spiro's back was the thing least driving Darby into the ground that day. The anesthesia from the days prior had worn off and she was aching for Rachel again, and maybe for Lina just a tad too. Maybe she was just down about being down.

On the way over to Spiro's, Darby rampaged inside her head over changing circumstances and things she couldn't control. Career moves and stupid surfer-named boyfriends. Her inability to make lovers feel valued enough not to wander off. Trivial things made her grumpy too. Traffic, Phil Collins' chart-topping album, the mere thought of more upcoming holidays. She'd become a crotchety alt-Andy Rooney, and fumed about fads that annoyed her:

1 — *Coffee Culture.*

Take the day's most peaceful moment and re-market it like fast food. Concoct fake-exotic, dumb menu items: frappe *this* and faux-chino *that*. Open cafes with insipid '90s TV sitcom-inspired names like *Lincoln Perk* and *Mad About Brew*. All so marketing execs can do for coffee what Chi-Chi's did for Mexican food. Even worse, people think it's awesome. *Ass-holes.*

2 — *Fancy ass beer, aka Microbrews.*

Alas, there's also *beer for snobs* too. Beer used to be just beer. Now people need something to separate *themselves* from *you*, the beer riffraff. Something quaint. Something from humbler places. Hailing from breweries run by pygmies and friars.

Marketed in inane concoctions like anise lemon grass lager or blueberry lamb's blood porter. After Y2K they'll call it "craft beer."

3— *Poetry slams.*
The whole thing about standing on stage, yelling anguished words for claps and cheers from a crowd of... other poets. What numb-nut thought of this?

</rant ended>

Spiro had once successfully dragged Darby along to the Green Mill, an old bar that was supposedly Al Capone's North Side hideout, and a spot that doubled on Sunday nights as poetry slam central. Tonight Spiro wanted to try out his poetic sea legs at the newly opened Hot House, which had its own weekly shindig for junior varsity poetry slammers. Darby agreed to tag along to support her friend's first stateside performance.

Spiro changed out of the Lollapolooza shirt and returned to the living room in slacks and a crisp button-down. "Michael-Leslie reads there sometimes, at Hot House," he said.

The apartment felt freer and more spacious without Spiro's idiot dude-bro roommate around. But Pete's trail markings were there. A spread of Bud Light cans took up half the sofa, and his Playboy playmates—Jenny McCarthy, Anna Nicole Smith, the whole crew—claimed the coffee table. On the wall, Pete's framed headshots of Ronald Reagan and Oliver North peered down on Darby as she waited for Spiro to start his rehearsal. With two hours before showtime, Darby, Ronny, Ollie, Jenny, and Anna Nicole would be Spiro's first tough crowd.

Spiro stood up on a plastic milk crate, cleared his throat, and smiled.

"So, I got this one I wrote in Paris. It's about *the man*."

"What man?" Darby asked.

"You know. *The Man*. Like IBM. McDonald's. Exxon. Burger King. Chuck E. Cheese."

"The mouse?"

"I mean the Business-Industrial Complex. Brands and profiteers. The symbolic white-collar monolith usurping all creativity and freedom in the world!"

Oh, *that* guy. Darby said: "OK, shoot."

Spiro then laid down his lyrics with firebrand finesse:

> *Corporate oppression. Bland brand expression.*
> *Strip mall maven, who the hell you savin'?*

Spiro stopped and looked up from his pages. "So?"

"Is that it?"

"Well, no, no. There's more. A lot more, but how do I sound?"

"You project well," Darby said. But she wasn't so certain that Spiro really wanted her thoughts on his poetry. "Do you need to go all deep and militant? With, you know, the whole 'fight the power' thing? This is your first time."

But Spiro had it planned like a bank heist. "Hard times call for dope rhymes. Besides, who wants to hear poems about rainbows and babbling brooks?"

He had a point. She didn't.

Later they arrived at the rustic, swanky Hot House. Its shimmery, red-painted walls encased its high windows, draped with black velvet curtains. A slow-growing crowd filled the room, enough to create a buzz. Another small group crowded the back bar area, but they looked to be there for the wine and not the wordplay. There was no stage, just a square in the middle, surrounded by a few rows of folding chairs and some tables with flickering votives. A spotlight shined down over the center, and there was a dramatic, boxing ring feel about the place. Maybe it was a ring for wordsmiths to do battle.

Spiro put his name on the sign-up sheet, and the two of them grabbed seats at the near side of the bar. There was no Michael-Leslie, only a familiar-looking coven of apparent impersonators, also in chopped bangs and dour facial expressions. Once the overhead music was turned down, a man in a trilby hat introduced himself to the crowd as Fernando. The host stepped to the spotlight and microphone.

"Welcome, poets! The time for rhyme is upon us," he declared.

Spiro cracked his knuckles nervously, before looking at his pages to re-rehearse.

Fernando then picked up a guitar and called up his five-year-old daughter, and a little girl ran up. Together they sang a song in Spanish about Cuba and *liberación*. The song was good enough and the little girl singing with her dad was cute as hell, and after the song concluded with a round of applause, the little girl ran back to her mother, just in time for Fernando to ruin it all with a heavy poem about Fidel Castro.

The host criticized Castro as a monster and a *matón*. Then began the rhymes.

> *Detention! Repression!*
> *Oppression! Forced confession!*

Darby looked over at Spiro, who tensely scribbled notes onto his stack of papers.

"Don't want to be a copycat," he whispered, nervously.

"Don't sweat it," she said to him. "Sounds like oppression is a *very* popular topic."

However it might shake out, Darby wasn't worried. Spiro had easily 20 poems ready.

After Fernando came two women. One read poems about nature without much inflection, in the way a teacher might read to kindergartners. Her three poems were about flowers and babbling brooks. The next poet to the mic came with a strong feminist angle and her poetry sounded more like a Rage Against The Machine jam.

When women lead
Men don't bleed.
Sylvia Plath,
wrought no wrath.
Read, learn and be kind to your brothers and sisters.

Darby knew that she was just politely observing, and realized that she really had no concept of what made good poetry, and decided not to judge but to listen and digest. Before Spiro's turn, there was an odd-looking old man, whom Fernando introduced as Muscatine Joe.

Muscatine Joe, possibly named after the Iowa town, looked more like a vagabond than a poet, in a tattered coat and with a mess of grey hair peeking out a traffic-cone orange knit winter hat. He came to the mic with ruffled papers, saying inaudible things and laughing like a mental institution escapee. This prompted an uncomfortable quiet among the guests. Joe mumbled about working on construction sites.

Tore that building down.
I fired my boss.
He tried to fire me.
Fuckin' jerk.

Muscatine Joe stopped just four lines into his ramble, then broke the fourth wall to make conversation with the audience. He would do this a bunch of times.

"Ever have a real bad job? I did. Hate that!"

Joe then scolded out another crazy old man's laugh and repeated that he'd worked in construction. The louder he spoke, the stronger his tooth-gap lisp became.

> *Killed my bossth.*
> *I was the bossth, not him.*
> [Something incomprehensible.]
> *I th-showed that guy.*
> *I killed that th-tupid guy!*
> *He'sth dead! Ha ha!*
> *Fucker!*
> [Silence.]

Joe's verse concluded upon that final spoken word—*fucker*. People clapped, confused, delighted, and yet unsure if they had just heard a murder confession. Luckily, Fernando reasserted himself as host to introduce Alex Spiro, who now was less jittery.

Both Fernando and the second female poet had peddled enough sociopolitical rage for an evening. And if Spiro was to begin with a zany salvo, he'd just got shown up by Crazy Joe. Instead, Spiro approached his audience with thoughtful humor and context.

"I know he's not here among us tonight. So, this first poem," Spiro said to the audience, "is about my very strange roommate."

The audience laughed, a good start. Even though Pete would never be somewhere cultured like a poetry reading, Darby looked around to be sure he wasn't lurking nearby with a *Penthouse* and a Schlitz in his hands.

Spiro's first poem was a humorous one about Petey's girlie magazine habits and grown men's immaturities, and his verse lampooned some of men's ideas of what women represent, what constitutes a man versus a grown-up boy. Mid-poem, Spiro described and depicted a fictional "hero" character out of Super Pete the Ladies Man.

Spiro's second poem struck more personal chords. It was about growing up in the suburbs of the American Midwest, about boredom, regret, and the triumph of changing your life.

Darby had to hand it to Spiro. She didn't know what to expect, but she was proud of her friend for being honest and in touch with his feelings enough to brave them in a public forum. Seeing the other poets applaud and approve of Spiro brought Darby's spirits up a little.

For certain, Darby had no plans herself of ever moon-lighting as a slam poet but took something home. If only she had Spiro's knack for introspection and expression, maybe Rachel would have stayed. Maybe Lina would have too. And Darby never would have left town in the first place.

Become What
You Are

DECEMBER 15, 1996

Deighv stood there in the loft's big living room in a spiffy tuxedo, upright and head high. His girlfriend Jenna was pulling and primping to see how well it fit, hopefully perfect. She tugged at his lapel, repositioned his collar, and stood back to look.

"What's the occasion?" Darby asked.

Jenna said, "New threads for another wedding."

"Just my new look," Deighv joked.

Jenna and Deighv were around a lot more. They had become much more social, sprouting personalities that Darby never knew they had. Also, their 1950s stylistics weren't just a play for Halloween. Jenna's hair was rolled up in the front and waved in the back, and it was probably the tenth time that Darby had seen them in their vintage style. Neither of them ever made the announcement that they were going retro for good.

Next to Deighv was a pair of shiny wingtips, total zoot suit riot stuff. Darby regarded weddings as mostly boring, sometimes worse than funerals. But they were going all in.

"Whose wedding—this time?" Darby asked them.

"Remember Nancy?" Jenna said.

Nancy, my secret lover? Sure, I remember. "The one with the skyline view?"

"Yes, that's her!" Jenna beamed. "But no more lakeshore condo. Nancy moved to L.A. Got a big promotion, so she's not technically my boss anymore, but we're still close. Anyhow, she's getting hitched next Friday. Small wedding, but should be fun."

"Huh. She didn't seem like the marrying type," Darby oddly said out loud.

"Maybe, maybe not." Jenna looked confused. Like, why would Darby say that?

"I mean—I remember this conversation we had," Darby explained. "At Memorial Day, about her, she said, being happily free and single. She seems like a free spirit."

"Total free spirit," Jenna said enthusiastically while motioning for Deighv to sit down and try on his shoes. "I don't know the guy. We'll meet him at the wedding."

So, Nancy *was* getting married—again? To Mike, Moe, Milton, whatever his name was.

"Well, tell her congrats. And, hello," Darby added, "if she remembers me."

"I think she'd remember you. Wish she still lived here. Sometimes I think it's too bad she's not our age," she said curiously.

"Why's that?" Darby asked.

"I don't know. I wish we could hang out more. And, it's funny—I thought once you and her might have got along, as good friends or something. Random thought, I know."

"No kidding." *Totally random.*

Deighv stood up again, fully dressed now, and looking the part. Jenna stopped fiddling with his bowtie and everything seemed set. Deighv then left the room and reentered, changed into his now-normal Fonzie get up: jeans, black duds, plus a plain white T-shirt, even though it was cold out. Deighv also now had much more ink on his arms, with another hot rod tattoo. His biceps, formerly twigs, were reinforced with greater muscle tone that suggested he'd been hitting the gym an awful lot.

"We're going dancing," Jenna said to Darby. "Rockabilly at The Rain-Bo. Wanna come?"

"You guys dance? Had no idea." Really, up until now, Darby couldn't see them doing much besides watching TV. But now, given every other style adjustment Deighv and Jenna had made, a night of swing dancing completed the picture. "Fun stuff. Thanks, but, no, I'm tired," Darby said, admitting that staying in was a little lame.

"Suit yourself," Deighv said. "Next time, we'll teach you to swing."

After they left, Darby peered out the front window to see them laughing just like the obtrusive winos who regularly traversed the block. Jenna yelled, "Woo!" as the two of them got into a shiny El Camino. Fuzzy dice bobbled near the windshield, and it signaled that she'd graduated from her mousy Cabriolet lifestyle.

"Kinda fits," Darby said. After all, the 1990s were all about that *be yourself* zeitgeist, and Deighv and Jenna were transformed by it more than anyone she knew. From couch potatoes to swing dancers. From boring next-to-get-married friends to greasers with a hot rod fetish. From future suburbanites to people Darby wanted to hang with more. You had to give them credit for finding their spark.

Back in the 21st century, Darby could have bumped into her friend Deighv—the *new* Deighv—all buff, bigger arms covered in ink, on the street without recognizing him. Instead, now, she looked forward to seeing her friends grow. She'd missed that in New York.

FIRE ESCAPE

After Deighv and Jenna went out swing dancing, Darby moped at home alone when the phone rang. She picked up, blandly saying hello, but knew the voice from the first word.

"Hello, Darby. Good to hear from you," Lina said, even though *she* had rung Darby up. "What are you up to these days, Darby Derrex?"

She was at a loss for sensible words. "You know, the usual. Things and stuff."

"Oh yeah? Hmm. Sounds very, very exciting."

Darby expected that Lina would call someday eventually. But the reason for calling would not be casual or comforting.

Lina would dispatch a showstopper announcement. That she'd gotten engaged or was already married. Or she was moving away—to Texas, Tasmania, Tibet, wherever. Darby would never see her again. Lina was at least courteous that way. Adept at tying up loose ends.

"SO! *Anyway,* I'm not calling to talk about the weather," Lina said. "I sorta need a date."

"A date? For what?"

"Oh, a little thing. An event." The library foundation had a gala, Lina told Darby. "You know, the donors love being wined and dined, and I have to be there, so I'd like someone I know to join me, next Friday, December 20th. Sorry, for the very late notice. You don't have another party, do you?"

"What about Tanya? Was that her name?"

"Oh, her? We only went out a short while, but we broke up."

Huh.

"She was sweet but very, very boring. Anyway, she's out, so can you come along?"

Darby had nothing planned for the next two decades. "Sure," she told Lina.

"Great!" Lina sounded overjoyed. "You'll need to dress up."

Darby remembered the first time she saw Lina dressed up for a different foundation shindig. How ravishing she looked, what fun they had. That evening, after a series of dates and friends' parties, was the first time she and Lina were intimate together.

Darby snapped out of it and asked: "Why, what are you wearing?"

"Something classy." Lina said that Books Bash '96 was going to be at the old Hilton, with a ballroom that was pretty impressive. Lina said they might meet the Mayor. "So, please, wear something nice. Think you can pull that off?"

"Yes, I think so," Darby said passively.

Lina kept at it. "I know jeans and a concert tee is all dressed up *for you.* But this is an important event. Classy people, but good people, so don't make fun of them. Besides, you don't have to be all punk rock all the time. You're not in a band."

True, Darby was no musician. But instead, she would be Lina's date. And if Lina wanted her to tease her hair, wear an ascot, or put on a Green Bay Packers helmet, she would.

"It's been a while," Lina admitted, finally.

"It has." Darby started to say *I'm sorry*, but Lina stopped her.

"It's OK," Lina said. "Past is the past. No hard feelings. We can be friendly now, right?"

Darby thought it comforting how cool Lina was about it all, treating her like a person and not an asshole ex, and someone she wanted to see again. She loved the idea of being in Lina's life, even minimally so, even if just as a prop for an evening out. Even if they were just "friendly."

Old words collided that evening, both Nancy and Lina coming up within the span of an hour. And Darby thought about what people say about fantasies—that they "don't deliver"—and how whoever said that was totally wrong.

Darby knew from her time with Nancy that that assertion was bullshit, not true. With Nancy, the fantasy *did* deliver, more than she'd ever imagined. And that was part of the problem. She knew that neither of three of her guy roommates could boast about a hot summer fling with an alluring, seductive older woman. She'd overheard guys talk about stuff like that—that mythical 40-something mistress, the hot moms, and divorcees. Darby had been there.

Yet Darby's Nancy fling didn't deliver in one way, and that was as a meaningful relationship. The fantasy was never meant to be such, and she knew that. The fantasy delivered as a fantasy, that's all. Yet, the fantasy was enough of a milestone in Darby's life to distract from something real. Something real with Lina.

Even though Darby's heart was always with Lina, that whirlwind *Summer of Nancy* blinded her of it and how to show it or truly deal with it. Now she wondered to herself if she'd used Nancy as an excuse to avoid the hard work. It was an open hatch, a fire escape.

When Friday the 20th rolled around, Darby knew she wanted to look good for Lina. She always loved the 'girl in a suit' look ever since she saw Annie Lennox doing it in Eurythmics' videos on MTV, in the 1980s. It was a look Darby had perfected in her Wall Street days, long before Kristen Stewart and Scarlett Johansson nailed it. So why not bring it back a decade early?

The evening of the bash, Darby appeared from her room in a nice dark suit and a white blouse, looking sharp. Simon, watching TV with Spiro and Rod, had something to say about it.

"Darby in a tuxedo!" Simon said jokily.

Rod had to correct him. "That's not a tux, Simon."

"Whatever it is, you're dressed like a penguin."

"Haha, Simon," Darby said. "Least I'm not shaped like a penguin. Anyway, Lina and I are getting along again, and she needed a date, so I need to dress up. Almost black tie."

"Too bad it's not *black tee*," Spiro cracked. "You could wear a concert shirt."

"You're right," Darby said. "Too bad I never got my Lolla shirt back."

Spiro then sat up, feeling bad. "Hey, I wasn't sure. I'm sorry. I'll give it back."

"Forget it. Lollapalooza's so 1991," she said. Plus, that shirt probably had holes in it by now. Ones that Spiro put there, but still. "You can have it, Spiro. Yours."

Before Darby left, Deighv gave an honest compliment. "You look beautiful, D. Almost gentlemanly." She took that as praise. Rod claimed that Darby had achieved peak James Bond style. Simon said again, "Well, to me, my friend, you look like a penguin."

Lina had told Darby to meet her out front of the Hilton, and on time, 6:15 P.M. sharp. Darby jumped into the first cab she could flag down, and once in, she started to make conversation with the driver. But the driver spoke first.

"Wedding, or wake?"

"Party, actually," she said. "A gala type of thing."

"Kind of late in the day for a funeral, ain't it?" the cab driver said.

"You're probably right."

The cabbie had a Chicago Cubs ornament swinging from his rearview mirror. Darby mentioned she was a Cubs fan and they talked about how bad the Cubs were.

"Sox fan numero uno, the Mayor, is gonna be at this thing tonight, so I'm told."

"Give him my regards," the cab driver said. "And tell him: White Sox suck."

Twenty-eight blocks later, the cab pulled up to the Old Hilton, sliding right under its bright plaza lights. A cold mist whipped the winter air around in a glittery way that made the people out front dazzle. A dark-haired, beautiful woman right in front stood out from the rest.

"Wow, look at her," the cabbie said, marveling at Lina. Darby's date stood there, bundled in a fluffy winter coat, clutch purse in hand, with her trademark symmetrical hair.

"Yeah she's mine," Darby said. "My date, just for tonight."

"*Oh.* Have a blast."

Darby paid and tipped the guy ten bucks. She felt lucky just to be there.

1997, AN EPILOGUE OF SORTS

NOT TOO SOON

JANUARY 6, 1997

Darby hadn't trifled with any New Year's Eve social festivities and she was motivated to get back to work, and start anew, right after the New Year settled down.

The Monday after New Year's Day, everything felt normal. She wrote about Daft Punk's debut, plus great second albums by the Dandy Warhols and Silverchair. Other new releases from Kenny G, Celine Dion, and Enrique Iglesias she was happy to pass over. The year 1997 already had something for everyone.

At about 11 A.M. Darby's desk phone rang.

"Someone's here to see you, Darby."

"Thanks," she told Sandy, from the front desk. "I need a minute. Tell him—"

"*Her*. It's a she."

"OK—tell *her* I'll be there in five. Front conference room's fine."

An exec from one of the local labels called Fright Wire Records was supposed to stop in, but Darby thought it way too early for anyone in the record biz to have rolled out of bed just yet. Darby didn't know Taylor Black, with whom she'd only communicated by email, and Darby never thought to ask, *Are you a he or she?* There were so many damn Taylors now— Taylor Hanson, Taylor Hawkins, Taylor Dayne, that Taylor character from Melrose Place—too many Taylors of all genders, so it was hard to guess either way.

Fright Wire's repertoire was loud industrial/dance music. Ry-Guy's type of shit. She chuckled, wondering what Taylor the goth record company exec looked like. *Would she have a vinyl suit, dark eye makeup? Dreads and a whip? Would her briefcase have spikes on it?*

When Darby got up and approached the conference room, she saw through the glass no suit or spiked briefcase. Instead, a familiar head of blond hair with a purple-blue streak. She went in, shut the door behind her, and looked up, dumb-founded.

"Hi, Darby!"

She had no words.

"Just wondering if you were OK. Thought I'd check on you."

Spacey sat up in the chair, smirking, enjoying the evident rise she got out of Darby. She looked exactly the same, in her jean jacket and combat boots. Today she had on a Stray Cats T-shirt, and as usual, was chewing gum and twirling her hair with that signature smart-ass expression intact. This wasn't a dream.

"OK, well. Seems you're good," Spacey said. "You're quiet today. *Weirdo.*"

"Hi, Spacey. How did you... get here? How are you—here?"

"Same way as you," she said. "Ya know, you're not the only one who knows about the Grey Line, Darby."

Around her wrist was a red, glowing time-pass watch like the one Darby had brought. It didn't explain how she could be here and still look all like 21st-century Spacey.

Befuddled, Darby asked about it. "How is it you're still—"

"Still the same me? And not, like, an embryo?"

"Yeah. That."

"You didn't read the instructions, did you?"

"Instructions?"

"Yeah, for your time-pass! C'mon. About the paradox button."

"That button thing?"

"Yup, that button thing," Spacey said. She then held up her wrist to show her, pushing the button in and out. "On and off. See: On, off. Paradox control on and off. You need to hit 'on' before you travel, in case you wanna stay as-is. Like, *21st century you*."

Darby flicked that button off before departing. It was why she was sailing through 1996—and now 1997—as an energetic twenty-something with no backaches.

"You look the same, kinda," Spacey continued. "Maybe less senior citizen-like. More attractive I guess, you know, *for you* that is."

"Well, thanks."

"You know, if I hadn't clicked 'on' on this thing, I'd be sitting on that 1990s train," Spacey said, "probably sucking my thumb, pooping my pants. I'd be fucked."

Darby eased up just enough to take a seat, finally.

"My god, it's good to see you. Welcome to the '90s. So, what are you doing here?"

"Like I said, checking in. So—how are you, Darby? Bet you've seen a lot of cool bands. *Seriously*, what up, boss?"

"Spacey, how did you find me here?"

"You said you worked at City Scene." Spacey looked around at the digs. "Cool office. Looks a little crunchier than I thought. Wasn't hard to find this place."

"How's the record store?"

"It's fine, Darby. Mark and Conrad haven't killed each

other yet, unfortunately."

"It's January, ya know. Don't you kids wear winter coats?"

"Yes!" Spacey, annoyed by the question, hunched over into the knapsack she brought along. "I got a heavy fleece in my bag, OK, grandma? Brought you some things too."

She pulled out another time pass and slid it across the table. It was illuminated brightly, fully charged, with its display showing ninety days.

"I knew you'd long run yours out by now," Spacey told her. "Wanted to make sure you didn't get stuck. Or miss any shows."

"How'd you get this?" Darby picked it up. "How'd you get two of these?"

"I told you I collected two things: concert posters and weird jewelry. Took me a while, but there were more than a few laying around town," she said. "Seems the charm of an Apple Watch that's not an Apple Watch wears off. They don't tell time and people sell 'em. Pawnshops were full of 'em. I found seven or eight, easy. I just might have bought them all."

Then Spacey pulled other junk out of her bag. First was a folded-over paper thing.

"You also left this on the printer. Your Grey Line map," she said.

"Shit, no wonder you found me," she said.

"Um, *yeah,* dude. After the fact. Who'd you think put your time-pass in the desk? You were sounding pretty nostalgic. All *mid-life crisis-y,* and I thought you needed a vacation or something," Spacey said. "I sold one of them and left one for you. Kept the rest."

Darby was touched that Spacey thought to look out for her. Twice, no less. She was the agent provocateur of Darby's little back-in-time journey. She also brought the Rock Log along.

"I've basically got this memorized," she told Darby, passing the book across the table. Darby said *thanks* and passed it back. She already had her crumpled yellow-pad list with only one or two more concert dates. That was all she needed.

"Keep it, Spacey. That's a final edition. Who better to keep it safe than you?"

Spacey was a child of streaming, Spotify, and Apple Music, but she had a better appreciation for good old tunes and legendary concerts than anyone Darby had ever known, even other people her age and from her generation. Musically speaking, Darby's favorite member of Generation Z traveled freely between the decades in a way that Darby couldn't do without a literal time machine.

Spacey then stood up and said she needed to go soon. "I'm hanging out in 1997 for a few days, then hopping back on, back to '96." There was an important show on the 10th. "Dreaded Letters! Lounge Ax. I'm going, dude! Should be awesome," Spacey beamed.

"Excellent. I'd go with you," she said, "but I've already seen it."

"Not the second show, you didn't," Spacey reminded her. "I'll give you a review."

Then Spacey sat back down, and she and Darby kept talking music for a while. Darby asked if she had yet discovered any other under-the-radar shows the Rock Log missed.

TOGETHER ALONE

JANUARY 24, 1997

Darby walked in and mindlessly said hello to the crew of sports bobbleheads on her swank mahogany desk. She wasn't in the mood to talk to humans and had a lot to accomplish early.

Twitt Coin was back—really back—and its stock was up too—back up where it goddamn should have been all along. She could trade up, and earn back some of the big amounts she'd lost. She wanted to prove her mettle and reestablish her worth. Also, her net worth.

Unfazed by the Manhattan panorama from her 46th-floor office, she settled in quickly and popped on her screens. Darby's office walls had the marks of career accomplishments, framed in real wood and glass. Acknowledgments from city clubs next to the framed picture of her, arms folded, proud and uncomfortable, on the cover of *BusinessWeek*. It tipped her the "Queen of Wall Street."

Then graphs started moving, changing, freaking out. Her screens went red. Stock tickers blinked and graphs nose-dived. Apps froze and beeped. Stocks were crashing. The market was going bust, maybe to zero this time. Alarms clanged and the ceiling sprinklers went off. Darby heard people outside her office door rushing, knocking over furniture, running out, as she froze.

"I woke up in a cold sweat," Darby told Tam. "Thought it was just a saying."

Tam snickered and laughed more *at* Darby than *with* her. "Well, you were due for a wake-up call," she said, semi-philosophically. "Made it back fine, I see." Tam threw her Skee-Ball down hard enough to shatter Darby's eardrums and the banality of her nightmare. "So, you're still going through *that thing.*"

"Thing?" Darby asked. "What *thing?*"

"The mid-life crisis thing. You're having a mid-life crisis. Still."

"No. No, I'm not," Darby insisted. "Just a bad dream."

Today, they had been forced off their computers because someone in the office opened a bad email. City Scene's servers had contracted something called the Cornholio-97 Virus. Ash and the techies were working to dispatch it. The time off provided a welcome furlough.

"How long does it take to fix a virus?" Darby asked.

"Don't know. Remember the Ebola virus?"

"That was a real virus, not a computer one, Tam."

"Oh, yeah, right." Tam was dim on some things, insightful on others. "Still better than that coronavirus bullshit. That's one good reason right there to come back in time."

It was Casual Friday again, but this time Darby was not at a bar. No one except Hammond dressed up most days anyway, so it seemed a lost cause to have Casual Friday at a place like City Scene. But for Tam, it provided a chance to test questionable outfits, ones even a stretch for Casual Day. Today it was a beat-up purple Northwestern hoodie with paint stains all over it. Tam's hair was harangued back in a makeshift ponytail under a White Sox cap. Heightening the clash of her garments, she had on her girlfriend's maroon and mustard yellow Iowa State sweatpants, which buckled atop Tam's red cowboy boots. In her über-casual spiritual state, she poked more fun at Darby's bad dream and its meaning.

"Guess, as bad dreams go, yours wasn't so bad."

"But it felt cold, hopeless. That fucking office, penned up like a little animal."

"Nice cage for an animal. Skyline view, mahogany desk? Even in bad dreams, Wall Street's white privilege reigns supreme. Even for you."

Tam rolled up a 100-pointer, taking yet another game out of reach.

"You *could* go back, you know," Tam joked. "Like, if your boss at work is an asshole."

Then Darby asked Tam, "Do you even miss *anything*—about the 21st century?"

"Well, I'm a little ashamed to say it but I miss some of the conveniences of... the future, our old life, our past in the future, or whatever you wanna call it. I loved Instacart, Amazon. Buying stuff without leaving my place—ever. E-commerce, what a great invention.*"

Maybe the mid-'90s' lack of robust internet options was the excuse for Tam's outfit. Then again, Casual Friday was made for people like Tam to abuse it. Someday Silicon Valley might set up a hoodie/sweatpants/western boots storefront, a CasualFriday.com.

And so far, Darby avoided deeper conversations with Tam. But she couldn't anymore.

"I'm glad this isn't what I thought," Darby said. "You know, like *Back To The Future*. That there's not two Darby Derrexes running around. Just me here, not another one that moved to New York to be a Wall Street hotshot who hated her life."

"Guess you're right. I can't imagine another Debra Tamczak wearing my clothes."

Darby looked at her get-up. "Wouldn't that be a catastrophe?"

"No, but for real," she insisted. "Imagine seeing some other chick who looks like me, playing first base on my softball team, partying with my friends, kissing my girlfriend."

"You mean... girl-*friends*."

"Well, not anymore," Tam insisted. "Or think about bumping into yourself hammered at a bar, dancing on a table. Then your friends notice *the other you*, back-in-time you, crashing a party where you're already acting a fool. That would be weird."

But there was something else besides the bad dream and time travel weighing on Darby's mind. As she picked up her ball to start another game, she just said it.

"I realized that I failed to say goodbye before New York, Tam." Darby let on that she didn't handle things well. "After all, you were a good friend. Then and now. And, I'm sorry."

"Aw, Darby. You don't have to apologize. You came back, didn't you? Maybe I should apologize too. I went 'off-grid' and didn't even think to invite you along for the ride. Where'd you get your time-pass, by the way?" Tam asked.

"Strange thing. Found it in a secret place. Where'd you get yours?" Darby asked Tam.

"Well, I'm not supposed to tell either, but—a friend of a friend of a friend," she said. Tam added that after sniffing out rumors, the same ones Darby had heard, she located a seller. "Someone I kinda knew through my old pot dealer had one."

"Huh."

"Offered her five hundred bucks." Tam took a second to describe the time-pass watch dealer. "Cute girl. Blond hair, blue dye in the front—maybe purple—I don't know. She was kinda punky, in a way. She looked like that singer, Billie Eilish."

"Interesting." Darby left it at that.

CRYPTIC WRITINGS

JANUARY 30, 1997

Tam never acted upon her threat to make Darby write about Billy Ray Cyrus, but she did dispatch her to chase up the newly popular country-rock outfit, Hill Billy & The Podunks. Their album was getting a lot of attention and they were in town for two shows that sold out quickly.

Darby sat at the bar at The Unholy Nun on a Thursday afternoon, with the band's singer killing time over a whiskey, an hour before soundcheck. Darby tried to keep it conversational.

"So, your band is from Texas?" she said a bit nervously. Unfortunately, she couldn't search their backstory on Wikipedia.

"I am," the bearded singer replied, peppering it with a head shake of sorts. "Technically, yes, by birth and other ways, I *am* from Texas."

"Everything... is bigger in Texas, right?"

"Ah, I hate that tagline."

"Sorry." Darby felt embarrassed.

"It's not you. No offense taken," Hill Billy said back to her.

"Damn marketeers, tourism board people. Slogans, like the whole 'Don't mess with Texas' things all over T-shirts and bumper stickers. Now they got everyone sayin' it. Kinda played out, that's all."

Up to that point, the band had gained a reputation for crazy-fun live shows and mayhem. Hill Billy & The Podunks' tunes were about down-home country life with a fun spin and anecdotes about booze, strong women, and crazy inbred uncles. Other songs involved tales of cowboys and preachers, like something out of a spaghetti western done in slapstick. The band first gained a following on the college circuit, and to Darby, their jumpy chainsaw guitars and tragic, hilarious lyrics made the band sound like a caffeinated Lynyrd Skynyrd or a dustbowl Dash Rip Rock. Given their rep and style, of course, Texas would come up. Otherwise, it would be like talking to Ted Nugent without mentioning guns and conspiracy theories. But after Darby's initial Texas inquiry, Hill Billy, whose real name was Tyler, had more.

"So, truth be told. I am just originally from Texas. I was born in Texas and lived there 'til I was twelve." His twangy tone validated better than any birth certificate ever could. "But southern Illinois, Champaign to be exact, that's where I grew up after that." He explained that his parents were both professors, but that that fact didn't make his own studies a priority.

Darby jotted that and a few other things down, and remarked, "Cool."

"Don't print that," he said. Then, he changed his mind, "Never mind, go ahead."

Tyler didn't seem to mind where the interview was going. So Darby asked more: "Some call you guys Southern Rock. Does that describe your sound?"

"Is that what we are? I dunno. We're just great music, I think."

"Grunge and Punk are dominant now. Where does your music fit?"

"Guitars and rockin' vibes. And we write good songs. That always fits somewhere."

"New album is grabbing new fans. What's next for the Podunks?"

"Whatever comes. Whatever we feel, we'll express in music."

Darby's Q&A was typical magazine stuff. And Tyler wasn't being evasive or playing the elusive rockstar. Instead, he was as transparent as the stale beer stench in the air. But Darby wanted to toss the rest of her prepared questions aside just to listen, so she did.

Tyler shared stories about opening for ZZ Top and playing the Oklahoma State Fair. He mentioned gigs in dusty towns with tumbleweeds rolling in streets. "Actual tumbleweeds!" Tyler said. During a show in Lubbock, Texas, Tyler said a giant bar brawl broke out, and they kept playing while punches and plastic cups were thrown. During the next show, two days later in another panhandle town called Turkey, Texas, a rooster appeared out of nowhere and jumped up on stage.

"So, of course, we played the Chicken Dance," he said.

Dropping her pen to hear Tyler's stories turned out to be the best thing Darby could do. They talked for an hour—two beers' worth of time—before a roadie stepped in, saying, "Soundcheck, ten minutes." Darby excused herself, prompting Tyler's "I won't go nowhere."

One thing about The Unholy Nun—besides all the great bands the place reeled in—was its epic graffiti. Graffiti was scratched both into the wooden bar, and written in marker, pen, and Bic Wite-Out all over the walls of the place. It was the bar's signature feature.

Scratched into the spot in front of Darby's barstool were a few declarative scrawls. Cryptic things like "Ozzy 8-5-'87" and "Tommy and Nikki were here" were dug into the bar, though it was doubtful either the Crüe or Prince of Darkness had truly visited.

The one-person washroom had the same spirit going. Going in, Darby locked the door behind her and looked up at more random wall screeds that climbed up to the ceiling. Two marks written with Sharpies and pens appeared to be authored by lost baseball fans:

~~Cubs SUCK~~
best thing about STL is I-55 North. Cards suck!

Someone from The Podunks' crew must have been by to use the washroom, as there was a Texas-shaped sticker with the band's logo on the wall. Other stickers hawked bands with catchy names—Pegboy, Dummy, Martha Rudy, Frisbie, Shelter, Local H, and The New Duncan Imperials. A random Misfits drooling skull sticker flanked the toilet, and above that, more smartassery. Darby loved graffiti, and read what the bathroom bards had to say:

Nirvana > Beatles
This is not Fugazi graffiti
Wesley Willis was here
Elvis was here too!

There were also dialectics about whether or not Rush and New Order suck, whether or not Kurt Cobain and John Lennon are rock gods, and what phone numbers to call for a good time. And right in silver marker was another barbed opinion. Darby didn't dislike the Seattle sound or any of its bands, but one scrawl left there atop the toilet was a screamer.

Pearl Jam's greatest hits ↓ ↓ Take one! Free!

After getting her fill, she went to the half-broken sink to wash her hands. Above it on the mirror was one last opinion-ated graffiti mark. This pronouncement courted no debate:

D'arby Derrix ♥s shitty bands ~ City Scene SUX!!

Her name was spelled wrong, but it was clear that she, not someone else, was being dragged here. Sure, music critics getting slagged off by music fans wasn't a new phenomenon, but seeing her name on a bathroom wall marked a new era. Social media didn't yet exist, so how else would the world's most miserable music dorks troll her?

"Welcome back, music critic," Tyler said, as Darby re-approached the bar. "What were you doing in there? I thought you got flushed down!"

Darby said, "Oh, nothing. Just reading all the funny stuff on the wall."

"Tough wash, being a music writer, huh?" Tyler said in an apparent bathroom-related pun. He continued, in an interro-gative TV news show voice. "So, Darby the music writer... DO *YOU* LIKE SHITTY BANDS?"

"So you heard?" Darby answered. "Guilty as charged."

They laughed and clinked their empty glasses. It was time for soundcheck.

PUSH THE BUTTON

SEPTEMBER 5-8, 1996

Four days after Darby returned to Chicago and 1996 last fall—and the same night Darby went to Lina's author presentation only to get brushed off—she went home and saw a message Rod put on the dry erase board in the kitchen. It said, "Darby, he's back," whatever that meant.

She had also gotten a piece of mail she hadn't looked at yet. It was postmarked the month prior and instead of a white envelope or some tourist postcard depicting the Eiffel Tower, this thing looked like part of an advertisement made of flexible poster board. The makeshift mailer pictured a happy Ronald McDonald with beautiful Euro-people, all of whom smiled, holding cheeseburgers. Alas, America's marketing had perverted the Old Country. The front of it read, in two languages:

> *Verdopple das Essen. Verdopple den Geschmack!*
> *Double the food, double the taste!*

The flip side was white, and clever Spiro fashioned it into his own postcard. Stealing it from a local McDonald's made it free. Right below the Bundesrepublik Deutschland stamp dated **18 Aug 1996** were scrawled words in Spiro's typical, nerdy bogus hip-hop lingo:

Yo, D-Smooth:

Ich bin kickin' it ins East Berlin mit mein German homeys. Great beer, excellent coffee. Had a date with a German babe last week! Off to Vienna, then Prague (poetry slam). Might date a pretty girl in each country!

~Spiro

PS: Never trust a McClown.

Darby then checked the answering machine. Two messages. The machine displayed a (513) phone number. *Ohio.* Darby hit play and out came a Germanic impersonation:

"Ah, yes hello. Zis is Doctor Henry Kissinger, I vill soon be in town for zih' Democratic Convention. I seek your assistance to prevent President Clinton from ratifying The Macarena. Vee hope you can attend Tupac Shakur's duet with the First Lady."
(Click.)

Also on the whiteboard, Simon had also scrawled that, "Margaret Thatcher called," and left a message. Simon also wrote: "Tell her FUCK RIGHT OFF!"

Darby pushed "play" to check the other message, also from the (513) area code. No strange voices or impersonations were in this one. Just Spiro being Spiro.

"Hey Darby, I'm back from Europe. For good. Call me..." Spiro's message also explained he was home in boring Dayton and had been back for two weeks.

After poking around for a few days in 1996, parts were still missing. Hearing her old best friend's voice already helped liven Darby's floundering reboot.

Alex Spiro was a good friend, probably the best kind. But he excelled at one other thing: pushing Darby's buttons. Her feeling about that aspect of their friendship was fresh and alive again, right at that moment. She hadn't dealt with it, but as she picked up the phone, she admitted that, *yes*, she had been angry—at least that one day, flying back to Chicago alone—when Spiro had dispensed of her on the Europe trip. Especially when she needed his ear. Especially when she needed a friend to listen, to understand.

The phone rang a few times and Darby heard an answering machine on the other side. She was about to hang up but the machine stopped, cut off by Spiro's voice.

"Hola, muthafucka!"

"Spiro?"

"Yeah! Hey, man, how's it goooooooin'?" Spiro said, in a stoner way.

"You answer your dad's phone like that? Isn't he in the military?"

"Yeah. He's not home. But—oh yeah—he's got caller ID. It's pretty cool. You can ignore telemarketers and stuff. His ex-wife—not my mom, but the other one—she's been calling here all day. So I've been ignoring her calls all day! Six times."

"*Wow*. That's *so* cool." Darby said. "Very cutting-edge technology you have there."

"So, how's Chi-Town?"

More like, How were the last 25 years since you saw me? Darby mused.

"Well... good," she answered. "Way less loud since you left." Darby then asked Spiro what his deal was. "Are you living in Ohio? Coming back? Bet you're bored out of your mind." That might explain Spiro's wacky messages.

"Bored, yes and no. Dayton sucks as usual. I saw City Scene's website—nice!"

"What? Really?"

"I read the classifieds to call up to get this sublet I think is gonna be excellent!" Spiro said that he'd found a new apartment and roommate, had already re-registered for school and wanted to come back pronto. Sunday he'd be driving back in his piece of junk 1982 Honda.

"So, can you help me out on Sunday, like, move boxes 'n' shit?"

"Sure."

Sunday night Darby went to the street where Spiro was moving. His new place at 1805 West Lejuene was on an east-west street, in a less derelict part of Bucktown. The rustic old neighborhood had morphed into an artist's abode, with a new Starbucks aground that began making things pricey. But characteristically so, Spiro lucked into a cheap place.

She sat against a big ornamental boulder in front of the grey-stone walkup. If the address was correct, it looked like Spiro was moving into a mini-mansion. She looked up at the trees swaying, waiting for Spiro to arrive in his time capsule originally at 6:30 P.M., now closer to 7.

Just before the top of the hour struck, Darby could hear Spiro's clunker before seeing it. The car turned the corner and zoomed slowly, sounding more like a vacuum cleaner than a car. Through a dirty windshield, she could see Spiro's huge smile as the Honda came closer and then clanked to a full stop right in front of the building. He had the windows rolled down.

"Hey! How's it hangin'?" Spiro excitedly yelled to her. "Snip snip!"

"Snip snip?" she replied. "What's *that* mean?"

"You got a haircut! Looks nice. Also, sorry, I'm late."

"No sweat," Darby said, feigning a look at her wrist.

Spiro got out and laughed for no reason, and the two friends gave each other hugs. She looked inside the car and could tell that wired Spiro had stopped several times for coffee, since The Coffee Beanery, Seattle's Best, and Boston Stoker all had their cup delegations represented in the front seat. Spiro popped open his hatchback, then walked straight to his new residence and rang the doorbell. There were no lights on in the place.

"Hopefully my roommate's home," Spiro said.

A minute later, a guy stuck his head out of a window. "Hiya. You Alex?"

"That's me!" Spiro said. "Hello there."

Pete introduced himself as "Peter" and said he'd be down momentarily. "Let me put some pants on," he said in a thick Chicago accent. "Just hang *ahhn*."

Darby stood on the walk in front of the stoop. She and Spiro looked at each other.

"I'm sure he has some sort of pants on," Spiro said.

"Be real weird if not."

Pete appeared a minute later at the door below, unshaven and sweaty, with messed up hair, wearing a stained white tank top, perched atop a pair of baggy Chicago Bulls shorts.

"Hey there. I'm Peter or Pete, whichever you wanna call me."

Pete wiped his hand on his shorts before shaking Spiro's hand. Darby, a good ten feet away, nodded *hello* comfortably far enough away and introduced herself as a friend.

"You look different than you sound on the phone," Pete said to Spiro.

"I guess I'm a chameleon."

Chameleon was a good way to describe Spiro after his alter egos phoned all week.

"You can say that again," Darby said.

Pete propped the doors open so that they could move in Spiro's boxes. An outpouring bouquet of smells implied the place was kept clean. Pete mentioned that a retired couple owned the building. "They're very nice. Probably won't ever see 'em, though. They're always in Florida," Pete said loudly. "They're rich, I think."

"Score," Spiro said back.

Except for the roommate part, Spiro had hit the jackpot. His building was like a majestic castle in front of a garden of lush, ornamental grasses and potted flowers that sat before a stretch of healthy grass, thick as carpet. Darby wanted to roll around on the lawn.

Once Spiro filled his huge new room in the back, Pete tossed him a set of keys, and then went back to watching TV. Spiro seemed satisfied as they walked out.

"Great place. My roommate seems interesting."

"He seems weird to me. Harmless but weird. You've got furniture though."

"Cable TV, too. And a big, phat room!"

They stood outside for a moment by the big rock next to the driveway. Spiro asked Darby if she wanted to grab a beer. Darby was ready to offer bar suggestions, but before she could finish Spiro spoke again.

"Hey, I didn't mean to ditch you in France. That wasn't my grand plan or anything."

"It's OK," Darby told him. "I don't know if you really ditched me."

"I did, in a way," he insisted. Spiro explained he was overcome with "*wanderlust,* as the Germans call it," and that he couldn't come back because a sense of joy had overtaken him. "I pretty much fell in love with Europe right away. Hope you weren't too mad."

She was and wasn't. "I know what it's like to want to get lost, believe me."

Darby had been back in 1996 barely a week, and little did she know that if she'd stayed just a few more days the first time, and never left, things would have fallen into place, as now they had. Spiro was glad he came back too.

"Only thing," Darby said, "I *was* annoyed with your 'shrooming episode with Cecily."

"Oh, yeah. Fried brains in Amsterdam. That was fun, kinda. I might still be high now."

"Fuckin' hell."

"Should've known she'd do that," Spiro said. "Cecily's always been a little out of control."

Darby wanted Spiro to know she held nothing against him, and Spiro had no idea about Darby's last decades in the 21st century, now erased. And it wasn't until days later, after Spiro had settled in, that the two would catch up at Urbanite. For now, he started joking as usual.

"Did you go to the convention?"

Darby was puzzled. "What convention?"

"The Democratic Convention!"

"No. Why would I?"

Darby never knew Spiro to care about politics, any other than fake socialist politics.

"Because! Tupac was in town, baby!"

"Oh, right," Darby said. "To do The Macarena with Hillary Clinton. With Henry Kissinger and Nixon's corpse shaking maracas."

She told Spiro that he was a bad impersonator, and Spiro laughed in his usual ha-ha-handclap of old. He yukked either because Darby's snarks and sarcasm were funny, or because he knew his prank calls were not.

"I had enough going on," Darby added. "I'm just happy you're back. You're probably the only person I can talk to about random things."

Darby did tell Spiro that she had thought about moving

away to New York, maybe business school and Wall Street while he was gone. But nothing more. Nothing about selling out, or that she began to date guys again for a while. And nothing about her handsome ex-fiancée, or about making big bank on bullshit crypto stocks and then losing it all. Nothing about moving back for a record store, nothing about the Grey Line. None of that mattered anymore.

The only thing that mattered for Darby was talking about more meaningless, stupid things with her best friend again. And that meant everything.

BEING THERE

MARCH 15-16, 1997

St Patrick's Day '97 was on a Monday, but the annual affair couldn't come soon enough for some. Years earlier, Chicago invented another reason to dress in green and drink beer.

The festivity known as Chi-Rish—a clever *very* portmanteau of "Chicago" and "Irish"—had been established so people could celebrate St. Patrick's Day early or twice perhaps. The all-day Saturday affair known for its drink specials and classic Gaelic fare like buffalo wings, cheeseburgers, and bar popcorn, kept young North Siders placated until the real thing. Each year, Chi-Rish partygoers from all over Lakeview, Lincoln Park, and Wrigleyville hit participating bars in their emerald sweats and green pajamas. By 1997, it had become a mega pub crawl that spilled over into the streets, like a big, drunken sleepover. Darby wasn't pleased about it.

But that day she had something more important to do than drink green beer. Dreaded Letters was set to do their first show since the release of *Velvet Mourning*, this time at Double Door. She'd finagled a spot on the evening's guest list, and the band's manager had told her in an email that if she got there "at the right time" perhaps he could squeeze her in for an interview. It was a big fucking deal.

Soundcheck was at five, and Darby was dressed and ready in her best '90s cool chick rock outfit: a black silk button-down and black jeans, her leather jacket, and a new pair of Doc Martens that she'd bought because she always wanted a pair. Looking in the mirror before she left the loft, she decided that she looked almost like a young Johnny Cash, or a punk version of Springsteen. Packed in her pockets were a pen and small pad, but also a Dictaphone that City Scene let her expense. She was more prepared than a rock 'n' roll boy scout. Rolling Stone wasn't getting an interview but she possibly was. Again, this was big deal.

Barely two o'clock in the afternoon, Darby still had plenty of time to kill but started walking. Nearby the venue and not too far from the loft was another old Chicago drinking establishment that would later be killed away by time. Riptide Lounge was the best combination of an old dive bar and swanky martini lounge. She hadn't been there since she'd come back, and when she walked in, she saw a face she faintly remembered. Denny the bartender also seemed to remember Darby, or at least her face.

"Hey, what's the story, bud?" Denny said, with the tagline he used with everyone.

Darby replied, giving Denny a handshake, "Same story, no story."

"Same here, my friend. You get a haircut?" Denny asked her.

"Yup, a while ago. But thanks for noticing."

The bar was half full, not bad for a dreary, cool Saturday. Everybody in the bar wore normal clothes, with no inebriated Lincoln Park idiots in green pajamas falling off barstools, at least yet. Riptide had their own special for anyone who did want to celebrate early.

"A Jamo shot and Guinness pint, three bucks," Denny said. "And, happy St. Pat's!—We don't say Chi-Rish here."

The neighborhood and Riptide's block had a sort of junkyard look. Darby wondered why someone would live out here in this stretch of town, next to the Expressway.

"Denny, you live on the block?"

"Nope. Bridgeport."

"South Sider, huh?" she said. "And it's worth your while to come *here*?"

"Riptide's an institution. Quick drive, not bad. Gets me out for the day. Why would I wanna live on the North Side?"

Darby paused, then answered before the South Sider could.

"Because... we have... great minor league baseball?"

Denny laughed. "You can say that again."

Darby finished her pint and told the bartender, "Nice to see ya. Go Cubs."

Nearby Riptide and halfway over to Double Door was the house that Lina bought, just two blocks away. Maybe it was more like four blocks, Darby wasn't sure. But she helped Lina move that day before their fight, into the small semi-Victorian two-flat Lina had bought. As Darby walked out of Riptide, she wondered if Lina still lived there alone.

If so, she might be home on a midday Saturday, because, as Lina always used to say, she wasn't a partier. And she definitely wasn't Irish.

Darby's blood-alcohol level wasn't a factor to influence her next split-second decision: to stop by to see if Lina was home. She hadn't seen Lina since the Books Bash, but she wanted right now to see her. Besides, Darby had an alibi. She was, after all, in her neck of the woods to see an important band, the one band they both liked.

Darby walked up to Lina's place and rang the doorbell before she decided to stand back from the stoop to see if Lina would look out the window. She hoped there wasn't someone else in the picture who might open the door. *Hopefully, Lina will be home. Just her.*

Then Lina did appear, and she opened a window.

"Hi, Darby. What are you doing here?"

"I was... in the neighborhood."

"Oh, were you? Really? Why?"

Seeing her face, she forgot all about the band and the big show.

"Stopped in to see your lovely neighbors at Riptide."

"Oh, I love that place."

"Me too." Darby made small talk. "Charming dive, ain't it?"

"Are you drunk, Darby?"

"No." At least she didn't think she was. "Happy Chi-Rish!"

"Happy what?" Lina said back to her.

"Chi-Rish. You know. The fake version of St. Patrick's Day. It's like a pre-party."

"You *are* drunk, Darby."

"No, I have to report, very unfortunately, I am not. Would you like me better if I was?"

Lina laughed. "Who said I liked you in the first place?"

Darby asked Lina if she was going out for an early St. Pat's drink, and she told Darby that, no, she was staying in and being lame. Lina's birthday was the next day and she said she was saving her mettle for the next night out with old friends. But then Darby had an idea.

"This is a nice conversation we were having," she said, "but I'm a little cold now." Darby reiterated that she was not drunk.

"OK, I believe you."

"Let me get you coffee or dessert for your birthday."

Lina really loved desserts, and there was an Italian pastry shop down the block. Darby looked over her shoulder and saw some green pajama partiers tumbling out of a cab. Another batch of kids wearing shamrock-shaped sunglasses and green beads walked by.

"C'mon. I'm cold," Darby said to Lina. "Besides, your neighbors are scaring me."

Faustino's was an eccentric Italian bakery with great lunches and coffee, and an "off-the-beaten-path" allure, like the kind you'd read about in *National Geographic*. Lina said she couldn't make out how the little place stayed in business, but it was a perfect spot for an unplanned date. Faustino's mustachioed owner seated them.

"I had fun with you, you know," Lina said. "At the Books Bash."

"Me too," Darby said. She noted how cool it was the Guest of Honor sat at their table.

"Mayor Daley seemed impressed with your baseball knowledge. What's that team that he likes?" Lina asked.

"He's a Sox fan."

"Should've chatted him up more," Lina half-joked. "You could be best friends by now."

"I think he was being polite," Darby said. "Besides, I doubt we like the same bands."

Lina sipped her huge milky cup of latte and wanted to know about Darby's recent life. Though a lot had happened—some concerts, Rachel, and plenty of things—Darby brightened up and gave her the run-down.

"Spiro's the same. Still a fake socialist and a poet. Simon still sings and makes jokes, and Rod is still short, needlessly overdressed, and dating supermodels." Deighv and Jenna were still a pair, yet more interesting, she said. "Dave and Jenna have a whole new look. They're greasers now."

"What? No way."

Lina also asked about Tam, "that nice girl we double-dated with that time."

"She's great, and she's my boss now." Darby said that Tam and her girl were back together and very happy. "In a nutshell, they sort of figured it out, I guess."

"That sounds nice. Some people are meant to be together," Lina said. "What are you doing, work-wise? Any music I've actually heard of?" she joked.

"I've interviewed a few bands, a few artists."

"What about Liz Phair?" Lina asked. "She's *so hot.*"

"Yeah, I keep hearing that from all the straight women I know too."

Their server then came over with an extremely decadent slice of chocolate cake, with a candle on it. Along with a Sicilian-looking barista and the place's owner, Darby and the Foustino's camp began in singing Happy Birthday to Lina, who then blew out the candle.

"Looks like I picked the right time for cake," Darby said.

"And the right time to come by. I wasn't expecting to see you again." Then Lina asked, randomly: "What was that nickname you used to call me?"

It seemed provocative that Lina would bring this up. Definitely not a "let's just be friends" move, if that was still her position.

"Hmm, you can't remember?" Darby said.

Darby's nickname for Lina didn't have a pop culture reference behind it. But Lina loved having a nickname, even if it had no meaning other than that it was hers.

"Just say it," Lina said.

"Moon Star," Darby said to her.

"I loved that name. Now... let's eat some cake."

They quieted and devoured the cake together. But Darby found it somewhat hard just to enjoy the moment silently. She had to explain something.

"I'm sorry I screwed up," Darby said, breaking out to tell Lina about it. "And I am sorry that I screwed us up—"

Lina touched Darby's hand. "It's OK, forget it."

In the morning Darby woke up confused again, wondering where she was. Just like Lounge Ax's morning after, she was relaxed but a little out of it. This time there was no bump on her head, and the bed wasn't a stiff futon. Instead, she was in the warmest, most comfortable bed ever, ending the best sleep she'd had in a while. The windows let in a subtle light that mingled amidst sounds of *Meet The Press* on the TV upfront, and the smells of good coffee.

Darby sat up quick, less confused now. She looked to the curtain and out the window, conjuring up yesterday and now. Green pajamas. A drink at Riptide. Lina at the upstairs window. Coffee, songs, birthday cake, and the touch of her hand. A kiss.

Darby also remembered holding Lina, touching her bare shoulders and looking over that darkened skyline, and feeling Lina's fingernails scrape the back of her neck. "Come to bed with me. Like you used to," she had said. Hopefully, it wasn't just a pleasant dream.

Lina yelled over the TV: "Darby, you up?"

Lina was up and probably had been for a while, fairly early

on this Sunday. *That's how she is*, Darby remembered. Darby yelled *yes*, loud enough to be heard a hallway away.

After washing up and brushing teeth with a spare tooth-brush Lina left out, Darby came out to the living room, her cool haircut visibly messed up. But she was refreshed and awake.

"Good morning, long sleeper," Lina said to her.

"What time is it?"

"Nine twenty-seven."

"That's hardly sleeping in."

"But we went to bed pretty early," Lina pointed out.

Darby hadn't kept close track of time, only moments. "How early?" she asked.

"Oh, probably nine."

"We didn't just sleep, right?"

"Well, *that's true*." Lina gave Darby a suspect smile, and then cozied up in the fluffy love seat, to face the TV with her hot mug. She pulled up a fuzzy blanket that hung slightly over her bare legs and red-painted toenails, peeking out to say hello from below.

"Nice threads," Darby said. Her old maroon University of Chicago sweatshirt looked nice on Lina. "Not bad for someone who went to Northwestern." Like the Lolla shirt on Spiro's back, Darby had found her other old favorite, right where it most belonged.

"Yeah. I love it, It's very comfy. As you can tell, I like to keep things," Lina said. "I like what you've done with your hair, by the way," she poked, making fun of Darby's dishevel-ment. Lina then motioned to *come closer*. Darby did and she sat down. Lina threw her arms around Darby, adding a kiss and one more thing. "Don't know where you've been for so long."

"Nowhere good," she said. "Make you a deal. Shirt's yours if we can hang out more."

"Deal."

Darby spent the rest of that Sunday morning with Lina, doing nothing, wearing the same clothes from the day before. Just being there was the best thing ever.

In the afternoon Darby left so that Lina's work friends could take her out for her second birthday celebration. She knew she'd see Moon Star a lot after that; every day if she wanted.

Walking home from Lina's place, Darby thought about the fact that she had no idea she'd left so many parts of herself behind. She crossed a bridge over the North Branch of the Chicago River and pulled out from her leather jacket pocket the time-pass watch that Spacey brought back for her. Its display was still illuminated, and read DAYS LEFT: 49.

Darby stopped at the middle of the bridge and looked at the greenish waters below. And she figured that she'd seen just about every past 1990s rock concert or small club show she needed to see. Then she realized that she'd totally forgotten about Dreaded Letters the night before.

Who needs to discover the biggest band in the world? she thought. Right then she knew she had everything she wanted. *And who needs a fake Apple Watch—in 1997, no less?*

Darby tossed the time-pass into the river and walked on home.

UNTITLED

PRESENT DAY

Lina's parents were in town for the entire month of August and they were staying with them. This all worked out, since little Marty was off at least another month from school. He loved watching and re-watching the same Marvel movies again and again with G-Mom and 'Buelo. For Darby and Lina, it was also free babysitting. Tonight they were heading out to a dinner thing, and to celebrate Darby getting an award.

"Nervous?" Lina asked Darby. "You seem a little amped up."

"Not really. Maybe a little," she said. Whenever Darby rushed around to get ready or to look nice for any occasion, she usually got amped up. The first time Lina had ever seen her in that sleek Annie Lennox suit, they weren't together, just "friendly," Darby *was* amped up.

"Am I always like that?" she asked, and this made Lina laugh.

"Yeah, kinda. It's one of the things I like about you, I think."

"Who said—you liked me anyway?"

"Yeah, lemme think about that."

Their recurring jokes like that one were dorky but symbolic. And important to them.

Dressed up, and ready for the big night, Darby looked over her shoulder to catch a glimpse of Lina, who was dressed and ready way too early, but looking around for shoes to match her outfit. She wanted to poke more at Darby's nervous fiddling and adjusting, and Darby noticed Lina looked perfect as always. Lina kept looking at Darby.

"I'm proud of you, music dork," Lina said.

"Well, thanks, library dork."

Lina was more excited than Darby was that Darby was getting an award from the Weigel Center for Media Excellence. Getting a Weigel was a big deal in Chicago journalism, and Darby was a little surprised that the weekly radio show she'd signed onto a few years ago was a big enough deal for it. Darby early on suggested the show be named "Untitled" and with Tam as co-host and producer, and they had sort of become the Siskel & Ebert of local music, but a Siskel & Ebert Gen-Z kids had heard of. The weekend show gave Darby yet another reason to talk music on local public radio. It also gave music nerds something to do on a Saturday night, especially the ones who had followed Darby since the start of *Latecomers' Reviews*. And, it took some effort, but Darby got Tam to let go of her New Country fetish, at least for the sake of listeners.

"So—what are you going to say?" Lina asked. "You did prepare a speech, didn't you?"

"I got some notes on a card. Was just gonna wing it."

"Right. Because you're so good at winging things."

Good point.

Lina liked to give Darby a hard time, and she was used to it. And their levity seemed to be one key ingredient to a good relationship; one that was well onto its third decade. Lina was thoughtful too, and she had something to mark tonight's little celebration, even if Darby thought getting an award was no big deal.

"You got me a card?"

"Well, there's something in it, doofus," Lina told her. "I think you'll like it, and besides, I didn't know what to get you, since you own every album and mixtape known to human-kind."

Darby opened the dark blue envelope and inspected its contents. Inside was a smaller, shimmery, silver envelope that held something hard inside, probably a gift card. Instead of opening the smaller envelope, she read the card first. Out loud, in her best Lester Holt voice:

"To Darby, my best friend, and partner in crime..."

"You don't need to be corny, you know." Though Lina loved Darby being corny.

"—and a great wife, too. Congratulations on your great achievement, yada yada."

Lina said: "Hey, I came up with that myself!"

"Thanks, babe, I appreciate you."

Darby gave Lina a kiss. But she hadn't opened the envelope.

"Go ahead, open it," Lina said to her. "All the way."

Two things were inside. The first thing was a photo booth strip, the same one from January 1996, that night the two of them saw Dreaded Letters' first ever show. Darby was floored.

"I know you loved that show," Lina said. "And even though we broke up for a while, I kept them." Lina said, "We still don't have enough pictures of us."

"I'll work on that," Darby said to her.

The second item in the birthday envelope was that plastic thing, that gift card, covered in blue sparkles, with a very retro logo that rang familiar of an old friend's style. The card read:

Spacey's Sounds
(formerly Revolver Records)
Vinyl & New Music ＊ Mixtapes ＊
Weird Jewelry ＊ Cool vintage shit

"Wow, thanks," Darby said semi-sardonically. "You know, I love music!"

"See, I do know what you like," Lina shot back. "Let's go."

They both missed Uncle Martin but knew the right person had taken his legacy into the next century. Darby thought she would pay the establishment a visit very soon, possibly tomorrow. Even better, she knew that the new owner might even have some tips on the next new, cutting-edge bands that Darby could help the world discover.

ABOUT ATMOSPHERE PRESS

Atmosphere Press is an independent, full-service publisher for excellent books in all genres and for all audiences. Learn more about what we do at atmospherepress.com.

We encourage you to check out some of Atmosphere's latest releases, which are available at Amazon.com and via order from your local bookstore:

Dancing with David, a novel by Siegfried Johnson

The Friendship Quilts, a novel by June Calender

My Significant Nobody, a novel by Stevie D. Parker

Nine Days, a novel by Judy Lannon

Shining New Testament: The Cloning of Jay Christ, a novel by Cliff Williamson

Shadows of Robyst, a novel by K. E. Maroudas

Home Within a Landscape, a novel by Alexey L. Kovalev

Motherhood, a novel by Siamak Vakili

Death, The Pharmacist, a novel by D. Ike Horst

Mystery of the Lost Years, a novel by Bobby J. Bixler

Bone Deep Bonds, a novel by B. G. Arnold

Terriers in the Jungle, a novel by Georja Umano

Into the Emerald Dream, a novel by Autumn Allen

His Name Was Ellis, a novel by Joseph Libonati

The Cup, a novel by D. P. Hardwick

The Empathy Academy, a novel by Dustin Grinnell

Tholocco's Wake, a novel by W. W. VanOverbeke

Dying to Live, a novel by Barbara Macpherson Reyelts

Looking for Lawson, a novel by Mark Kirby

ABOUT THE AUTHOR

ANDY FRYE has written for *Rolling Stone*, ESPN and other publications. Currently, he writes about sports business for *Forbes*. Over his career, Andy has interviewed hundreds of athletes, rock stars, and TV celebrities.

Some recording artists he's interviewed include Smashing Pumpkins, Oasis, Morrissey, Jimmy Eat World, Rage Against the Machine, and Alice in Chains.